"Both doors are locked on the inside," I said.

Sellers looked at me. His eyes were eloquent. Then his big hand gave me a shove. "Out of my way," he said.

He went back a half a dozen steps, lowered his shoulder, braced his elbow, ran forward and hit the door like a football player hitting a line of opposing players.

The seat of the knob pulled out with an explosive, splintering crash.

The crumpled figure of a woman lay on the tiled floor. She was dressed for the street, but sprawled now in unconsciousness, the skirts up almost to the hips; the legs, neatly stockinged, bent at the knees; the garters showing a V against the pink flesh. Her head lay face-down and her hair was in complete disarray. One arm was stretched straight out, her fingers extended as though they had been trying to get a fingerhold on the smooth, white octagon tiles.

I stepped around to feel of her wrist.

There was no pulse...

Fools Die
ON FRIDAY

by **Erle Stanley Gardner**

WRITING UNDER THE NAME 'A. A. FAIR'

A HARD CASE CRIME NOVEL

A HARD CASE CRIME BOOK
(HCC-157)
First Hard Case Crime edition: February 2023

Published by

Titan Books
A division of Titan Publishing Group Ltd
144 Southwark Street
London SE1 0UP

in collaboration with Winterfall LLC

Print edition ISBN 978-1-80336-012-6
E-book ISBN 978-1-80336-013-3

Design direction by Max Phillips
www.maxphillips.net

Typeset by Swordsmith Productions

The name "Hard Case Crime" and the Hard Case Crime logo are trademarks of Winterfall LLC. Hard Case Crime books are selected and edited by Charles Ardai.

Printed by CPI Group (UK) Ltd, Croydon CR0 4YY

Visit us on the web at www.HardCaseCrime.com

Author's Note

There are many people who do not know that from time immemorial Society has decreed there shall be thirteen steps to the gallows. There may be, therefore, readers who miss the significance of the title of this story. In California, as in many other states, executions invariably take place on Friday.

FOOLS DIE ON FRIDAY

Chapter One
Pattern for Poison

I nodded to the receptionist, crossed over to the door of my private office, opened it, scaled my hat onto the shelf of the coat closet, and said to Elsie Brand, "What's new?"

She looked up from the typing. "Donald, is that a new suit?"

"Uh huh."

"You look—"

"Well?" I asked.

"Swell," she said.

"Thanks," I told her. "What's cooking?"

"Bertha wants to see you."

"Client?"

She nodded.

"Okay," I said. "I'll go in."

I walked out to the reception room, gave a perfunctory tap on the door that was marked *B. Cool—Private*, and walked in.

The girl who sat across the desk from Bertha was just opening her purse. Bertha's greedy little eyes were glittering. She turned away from the purse to frown at my interruption and then said to the girl, "This is Donald Lam, my partner." To me she said, "Miss Beatrice Ballwin. She's a client."

I bowed and smiled and said the four-word formula of pleasure. And, somehow, Miss Ballwin seemed relieved and reassured. She said, "How do you do, Mr. Lam," and then added, "I've heard a lot about you."

Bertha's chair creaked as she twisted her hundred and sixty-five pounds of hard muscle impatiently. Her eyes were back on the purse in the girl's lap.

"I hope we can be of some assistance," I said.

Bertha said impatiently, "I'll tell you about it afterward, Donald. I have all the data. We won't take time to go over it now. My notes cover everything."

Her diamonds glittered as she moved her hand in a sweeping gesture over some scribbled notes on her desk.

I looked over Bertha's shoulder and saw that the notes consisted of half a dozen names and the figure $500 written out half a dozen times all over the yellow sheet of legal foolscap.

Bertha liked to doodle with figures.

The girl's hand hovered over the half-open purse, but didn't make any effort to bring out a checkbook.

Bertha's office chair squeaked again in high-pitched protest. She said, "Well, dearie, I guess that's all," and then added, "I'll make you a receipt. Let's see, two hundred and fifty dollars now and two fifty more tomorrow."

The girl's hand went down inside the purse, came out with some bills neatly folded together.

Bertha's chair gave a quick, impatient squeak as she reached forward for the money. Then she started scrawling a receipt.

While she was writing, the girl looked up at me and smiled; then she took a cigarette case from her purse, raised her eyebrows in silent invitation.

I shook my head. "Not now, thanks."

She took out a cigarette, tapped it on the edge of the cigarette case. The cigarette case was silver with gold initials brazed onto the silver.

The initials were *C.H.*

She saw me looking at the cigarette case and her hand slid over to cover the initials.

Bertha Cool handed her the receipt. The girl dropped it in her purse, took a cigarette lighter, and lit the cigarette.

Her hand was shaking a little.

She dropped the lighter back into the purse, folded the receipt, said, "Well—thank you so much. You can start work immediately?"

"Immediately," Bertha said, unlocking a cash drawer in the desk and dropping in the money.

"It'll have to be fast," the girl said, "because I think—well, I think there's some danger right now. You'll have to find some way to frighten her."

"Don't worry, dearie."

Bertha beamed.

"And you'll protect me?"

"Of course."

"I'm your client?"

"Naturally."

"So you'll always have my interests in mind?"

"Certainly."

"Even if—well, even if someone should try to buy you off?"

"We can't be bought off."

"How long," I asked, "will you want us on the job?"

"For a week. I think that's the period of greatest danger."

"Starting when?"

"Starting right now."

"Our rates were for a week," Bertha said.

"I understand, Mrs. Cool."

The girl got up, took a deep drag at her freshly lit cigarette, then ground it out and dropped it into the ashtray.

"Thank you," she said to Bertha. Her eyes turned to mine. They looked at me for a long two seconds; then she was moving forward and I was holding the door open for her.

She was a nice number, brunette, trim, with nice curves and I liked the fit of her skirt in the back. I watched her cross the reception room.

"Well," Bertha said, "don't stand there gawking all morning. I—"

"Just a minute," I told her.

I slipped quickly into my office, grabbed the back of Elsie Brand's stenographic chair, and jerked her away from the typewriter.

"What in the world!" she said, protestingly.

I said, "A cute little trick in a grayish skirt and jacket, with a fluffy green blouse collar, a brown handbag, tan shoes and stockings, twenty-four or twenty-five, about a hundred and twelve. She's just at the elevator now. She hasn't seen you. If she takes a taxicab, get the number of it. If she doesn't, try to tail her but don't let her know she's being tailed."

"Oh, Donald, I can't do that sort of thing. I'm no good at—"

I pushed her out through the door.

"Get started."

She walked across the office and out through the door to the corridor. I went back to Bertha Cool's office.

"For God's sake," Bertha said, looking me over.

"What's the matter?"

"Another new suit."

"What's wrong with it?"

"What's wrong with it! Are you going to spend all of your money on clothes?"

"Not all of it."

"Well, I should hope not. There's an income tax, you know."

I opened my eyes wide with surprise. "The deuce there is! You mean the government's finally passed one?"

Bertha's face got red and then almost purple. "Sometimes I could kill you."

I sat down in the client's chair and lit a cigarette. The chair was still warm from Miss Ballwin's occupancy.

"Well, what's it all about?"

"Her name's Beatrice Ballwin."

"You told me that before."

"Her uncle is Gerald Ballwin. He's in some sort of a real estate business. His wife Daphne is going to poison him. He doesn't suspect anything. We're to stall for time and scare the wife."

I blew smoke out through my nostrils, "She live in the same house with her uncle?"

"No. She has an apartment of her own. She does some sort of research work, but she says we aren't, under any circumstances, to call her at her apartment because she has a roommate who is very curious and very suspicious."

"How *do* we get in touch with her?"

"We aren't supposed to. She's going to call us. But if anything should happen, if there should be any emergency, she says that we can call Gerald Ballwin's house and ask that Mrs. Ballwin's secretary come in at once for another fitting on her suit. She says she'll get that message and understand what it means."

"Just how are we going to go about keeping this Ballwin guy from getting cramps?" I asked.

"How the hell should I know? That's in your department, Donald."

"Okay. I'll do some thinking," I said, and went back to my own office and opened the morning newspaper to the sporting section.

Chapter Two
Low-Pressure Salesman

Elsie Brand was back in about five minutes, her face beaming. "I had a lucky break, Donald."

"Good! What was it?"

"There was a cab just pulling in to the curb as I came out. She was in a hurry to catch that cab as it discharged its passengers, so I was able to follow closely and get the cab's number."

"You didn't hear the address she gave?"

Elsie shook her head. "Gosh, was I supposed to do that?"

"Not one chance in a hundred," I told her. "I thought perhaps you might have. Okay, give me the number of the cab."

She passed a piece of paper across to me. "I wrote it down so there wouldn't be any chance of forgetting it," she said.

I took a look at the number, said, "I think we're in luck, Elsie. That cab hangs out at the hotel down at the next corner. I'll go down after a while and see if I can find out anything."

I picked up the paper, turned to the classified ads, and chased down through the real estate opportunities. I found an ad of the Ballwin Real Estate Company, listing about a dozen choice buys. Running through the ads, I detected a couple more with a street address that was the same as the Ballwin Realty Company —225 West Terrace Drive.

I told Elsie I probably wouldn't be in until after lunch, and went down and got the agency car out of the parking lot.

I went out to 225 West Terrace Drive. It was up in the hill country on the edge of a subdivision. Apparently Gerald Ballwin had played papa and mamma to this new tract.

The office was one of those screwy little houses with a freak peaked roof, curved gables, and a colonial arched doorway, that are so typical of California real estate subdivision offices. Probably they are built on the theory that the subdivision promoter wants an office the customer can't possibly mistake for a residence. Anyone who has seen California architecture realizes a man has to build something pretty bizarre to get something that can't be taken for a house.

I would have said offhand that the style of this was Chinese–Mission–Colonial. The only thing it lacked to be complete was a minaret.

I opened the door and walked in.

A girl was seated at a desk, pounding away at a typewriter, making out some contracts. She looked up at me, then turned back to the typewriter and kept on pounding.

I walked over to stand at a counter that ran the full length of the office.

The girl at the desk kept on typing.

I coughed significantly.

The girl stopped copying long enough to call out, "Miss Worley."

Nothing happened.

The girl got up, walked to a desk, and pressed a button. Almost instantly a door marked *Private* at the far end of the room popped open and a young woman came out.

She was smiling as she came out of the office, and she kept a smile as she walked directly toward me. She had left the door open behind her, and looking past her over her shoulder I could see a man of about thirty-five seated at a desk. He kept his profile toward me. If he noticed that the door had been left open, he didn't do anything about it. Perhaps it was all part of the act.

He had nice, wavy dark hair and a straight nose. He'd put on too much weight and his double chin detracted from the nice features. He was picking up papers, studying them, and putting them down. His eyes were unblinking in concentration.

I decided it was an act.

Miss Worley, I gathered, was his secretary and also the contact girl who received customers. The girl at the typewriter looked thoroughly competent, but they evidently felt it took a little sex appeal mixed in with real estate statistics to sell lots in West Terrace Heights.

Miss Worley wore a sweater.

"Good morning," Miss Worley said. "I'm Mr. Ballwin's secretary and assistant. Is there something I can do for you this morning?"

"I wanted to find out the prices of lots," I told her. "I'd like to look around a bit, if you don't mind."

She had nice teeth and kept showing them. "Unfortunately all of our salesmen are out at the moment," she said, "but I expect one of them will be back very shortly."

"Could you," I asked, "give me a map of the subdivision with the various lots that haven't been sold, and the prices—"

She interrupted me, smiling so sweetly that I wouldn't have noticed my mind was being changed for me if I hadn't been concentrating more on the man in the private office than on Miss Worley's personality.

"Oh, no," she said, "we *couldn't* do that."

"Why not?"

Her eyes were smiling, and she waited until mine shifted from the figure at the desk to meet hers. Then she said, "You'll pardon me, but we do so much of this we perhaps know a little more about— Well, let me put it this way. Suppose you went into a shoe store to buy a pair of shoes. You wouldn't like it if the owner of the store simply turned you loose to walk among the shelves and pick out the pair of shoes that you wanted."

"Why not?"

"Because the function of a clerk in a shoe store is not to *sell* you a pair of shoes, but to help you find the shoes that you want. He selects from a large stock the proper size and style to fit your needs.

"Now it's the same way in selecting a lot in a subdivision. We'd want to know what sort of a lot you wanted, whether you wanted it for residential purposes, whether you expected to put up a twenty-thousand-dollar house or a ten-thousand-dollar house, whether you were perhaps buying the property for speculation, or just what you *did* have in mind."

The man at the desk, apparently moved by some telepathic warning, got up from his swivel chair, walked across and closed the door.

I said, "I'm not intending to build right away. I hope to build sometime in the future a house that will cost around twelve or fifteen thousand dollars. I thought that I'd buy the lot now and —well, I felt that it wouldn't go *down* in value."

She nodded brightly.

"If it goes up high enough," I said, "I might be tempted to sell, but the primary purpose in buying is not for speculation."

She walked around to the end of the counter, pressed a concealed catch, raised up a section of the counter, pushed out a gate, and came around to join me.

She said, "I think that's very, very wise, Mr.—er—er—"

"Lam."

"Oh, thank you, Mr. Lam. I didn't mean to be inquisitive. Many people don't like to give their names to a realtor, but you seemed so different, so sort of friendly. Did you want your wife to look at the property with you?"

"I haven't got a wife. I have hopes—that's why I want the lot."

"Yes, indeed, I think you're *very* wise, Mr. Lam. You're making a *very* wise decision. Now let's see—there should be someone I can send you out with. One of our men is off today and one of the others is out showing some business property at the other end of town. You see, Mr. Ballwin has a great many interests....Now let me *see*."

She walked to the door and I walked along with her.

The girl at the typewriter looked up, giving me one mildly curious glance in which I thought for a moment I detected a flash of sympathy. Then her eyes were back on the document she was copying, pounding away at her typewriter.

Miss Worley ran along in a conversational stream, evidently trying to keep my attention distracted much in the manner of a stage magician keeping up a line of patter.

"I didn't give you my name, Mr. Lam. It's Ethel Worley. I'm secretary to Mr. Ballwin, and when he's busy I try to take as much detail as I can off his shoulders. You caught us at something of a disadvantage this morning. But there should be a salesman along just any minute—just any minute. I wonder if this car is one of the salesmen. No, it isn't."

"Perhaps another customer," I suggested, hopefully.

"No," she said, shortly, and I could see that the approach of this car that was coming up the grade was simply an added complication.

The car came to a stop. A tall, thin man with gray, dejected-looking eyes pushed the door open, languidly slid out, and said, "Hello, Beautiful!"

"Good morning."

"Why the formality, Precious? Aha, I see. A customer. The boss in?"

"He's in, but he's terribly busy."

"Never too busy to see Carl Keetley."

She turned to me with a note of desperation in her voice. "Would you mind waiting here for a moment? Please don't go away. I *must* go to see Mr. Ballwin for a moment."

I nodded my head in a silent promise.

She said to Keetley, "Wait just a minute. I'll tell Mr. Ballwin that you're here. I know he'll see you if it's possible, but I'm afraid he's just too busy."

"Don't get yourself all worked up, Wiggle-Hips," Keetley said. "I'll go in and tell him myself."

"That's just what I don't want you to do. Excuse me a moment."

She flounced into the office and took the precaution of slamming the door shut behind her.

Keetley looked at me and grinned. "Nice weather."

I nodded.

"Warm."

"Isn't it."

"Not unusual for this time of year, however. We have a nice climate here. Particularly nice in this section."

"Meaning the West Terrace Heights?"

"Sure. Best climate in the whole damn city right here. What are you doing, buying a lot?"

I nodded.

"That's fine, my boy. You can't do anything better. Old Gerald will sell you the best lot in the whole damn subdivision, wrap it up in cellophane and put your deed in a nice little envelope with flowered decorations on it. Gives you a feeling of substantial security, eh what?"

I nodded.

"Beautiful view from up here," he went on. "Look out over

the city and—let's see if I can quote my distinguished brother-in-law. The entire city spreads before you in a beautiful panorama, looking like a collection of doll houses by day, a sea of stars by night. Here the blue sky reaches down to the horizon, while fleecy clouds drifting—"

The door opened. Ethel Worley said, "He's too busy to see you, but I'll take a message to him."

"Tut, tut, what a rebuff. Tell Gerald that my business with him is personal, Bright Eyes."

"I'll take the message to him."

"It's personal."

She pushed her chin up. "How much?" she asked.

"I need two hundred. You see, I—"

The door slammed.

Keetley grinned at me. "Had a little bad luck with the ponies yesterday. Gerald doesn't approve of playing the races. Not even when I win."

I said, "You can't always pick winners."

"How right *that* is," Keetley agreed.

"You said he was your brother-in-law. You're his wife's brother?"

"His *former* wife's brother," Keetley said.

"Divorced?"

"She died."

I said, "I'm sorry. I didn't mean to be personal."

Keetley's eyes were no longer listless. They were looking me over with calm insolence. "The hell you didn't!" he said.

The door opened. Ethel Worley came out and handed Keetley a twenty-dollar bill. Her manner was that of a woman giving charity to a beggar.

Keetley took it without a word, folded it, pushed it down into his pocket.

Ethel Worley's eyes looked beseechingly at me. "Please wait just a few moments, Mr. Lam. I'm certain one of the salesmen will show up."

"Hell," Keetley said, "climb in the car. I'll show you around. What's your name? Lam?"

Ethel Worley said, coldly, "That's not at all necessary, Mr. Keetley. One of the salesmen will be here any minute—"

"How do you know?" Keetley asked. "What school of telepathy did you graduate from? Do you take the Morse Code, or does the stuff just come to you in flashes?"

She glared at him.

Keetley said, "Don't run up your blood pressure. I think you're getting fat, Grapefruit. Your girdle looks a little tight this morning. Gerald likes curves, and your sweater looks great, but— Well, come on, Lam, get in the car. I've got a map of the place here somewhere with a key to all the prices and—"

"You don't know what lots have been sold," Ethel Worley said. "You don't know a thing about it. You haven't kept up with—"

"Now don't get yourself in an uproar," Keetley said. "It's bad for you. Didn't dear Gerald brief me on my duties as a real estate salesman? Didn't he suggest I come up here and go to work?"

"And didn't he also suggest that you quit?" Ethel Worley flared.

"Sure he did. That was because my heart wasn't in it. I didn't have the enthusiasm. In other words, I told clients the truth. Come on, Lam, do you want to see this place, or don't you?"

I looked at my watch and said, "Well, I can't wait much longer."

"Come on, come on. Get in. It isn't going to cost anything. I'll drive you around the place and show you the best buys. I hope you're not looking for anything cheap because dear old Gerald doesn't give the boys that much of a break. But it's good. Oh, yes, definitely good."

I said to Ethel Worley, "I'm sorry, but I can't wait any longer," and walked over and got into Keetley's car.

Ethel Worley turned on her heel and went back into the crazy little real estate office. She slammed the door so hard she must have cracked the plaster.

Keetley walked around the car, opened the door on the other side, and jackknifed himself in behind the wheel.

"What kind of a lot you want, buddy?"

"Something that I can build on later. A lot around two thousand."

"How much later for the building?"

"I don't know."

"How big a house?"

"Maybe fifteen thousand."

Keetley started the motor. "Okay, let's look around."

He swung the car around one of the contour drives. "Now here on the left we've got some very choice lots at three thousand bucks," he said. "Do you like them?"

"They look pretty good."

"The trouble with them," Keetley said, disgustedly, "is that they're on the wrong side of the street. When these other lots are sold off and people build on them, they'll shut off your view. In place of the panorama of the city by day and the sea of stars at night, you'll be looking into your neighbor's front bedroom. If his wife is pretty, you'll still have a desirable view. If she's a crabby old bitch, you'll lose your enthusiasm for women every time you look out of your window. I wouldn't advise one of these."

"How about the lots on the other side, then?"

"Thirty-five hundred. They're pretty much on a sidehill. Your house will be four stories high on the low side and one story on the street side. If you want to know the truth, my opinion is that this whole damn hillside will start settling when a lot of houses are put on it and the rainy season comes along. There'll be a lot of excavation for foundations and stuff, and by the time the place is built up there's going to be a lot of extra weight put on this hill. The way these lots run, you'll have your entrance and front rooms on the street. Only the back part of the house will get any sort of a view. If you want a view in your living room, you'll have to put it under your bedroom or vice versa. You'll have to put your kitchen and your backyard on the part of the house that opens on the street, or else you'll have to put it way downstairs and run back and forth upstairs with dirty dishes and food for the dining room. That's the worst of these steep sidehill lots."

"They don't sound very desirable," I said.

"They aren't. And if you put your bedroom on front, the guys who will have built on the three-thousand-dollar lots will be watching *your* wife."

"What else do we have?" I asked.

"In the price range that you want to pay, not a damn thing."

"After all," I said, "a view isn't everything."

"That's right."

"Those lots up there on the rolling, hilly ground might be all right, particularly if one put up a two-story house and could look across the roofs of the houses on the other side of the street. As you so neatly point out, those houses must necessarily be limited to one story on the street and three stories on the side of the hill."

"That's right. You're a better salesman that I am. Want to sign a contract?"

"Let's look some over."

"Of course," Keetley went on, "you have to assume the assessments."

"What are those?"

"You pay them just like you pay taxes. You'll hardly notice them."

"What do they amount to?"

"Oh, forget it. It's just like taxes."

"Tell me more about the assessments."

"You'll have to ask at the main office about those. The subdivision has washed its hands of them."

"I'm afraid I don't get it."

"It's okay. Nothing to worry about on assessments now. Of course, there was a time when Gerald did what everyone else did."

"What was that?"

"Used the assessments to pay for the property. They all worked that stunt. Well, let's say most of them did."

"I don't get it."

"Know anything about law?" Keetley asked.

"I was a lawyer once."

He looked at me in surprise. "The hell you were!"

I nodded.

"What happened?"

"I got disbarred."

"For what?"

"For telling a man how to commit a murder and get away with it."

"Would it work?"

"It would if the courts maintained a consistent position. It's already been decided in the California courts. Of course, they might change their minds."

"They do that once in a while. I must remind you to tell me how to commit a good murder some day."

"Do that," I said.

"I will. Well, we were talking about assessments. If you know law, I can short cut things. You look under your general laws and you'll find any quantity of different improvement acts. A couple of them are dillies that the boys slipped across in the days of legislative credulity and rapidly increasing real estate values. A company gets property. They engage a contractor to pave the streets, to put in sewers, electric conduits, and all that stuff. Then they issue bonds to pay for the stuff and the city can approve the subdivision and underwrite the bonds. After that they become a lien on the property and are collected just like taxes."

"Well, what's wrong with that?"

"Nothing," Keetley said, "except the smart boys used to arrange with the contractors to pad their bids so that they not only included enough to pay for the improvements, but also enough to pay for the whole damn subdivision as well. The contractor would get his money, hold out his share of the take, and kick back to the owners of the subdivision. That would give them what they'd paid for the property in the first place, and everything after that would be velvet."

"That isn't done in this case?"

"I don't know," Keetley said. "Heavens, I hope not—for your sake."

"They're nice lots."

"Aren't they?"

"A beautiful view."

"Fine."

"The air must be nice and bracing up here, well away from the grime and soot."

"Marvelous."

"Plenty of sunlight."

"You said it."

"A nice breeze."

"Sure is. You want a lot?"

"No."

"I didn't think you did. Let's go back."

We drove back to the crazy-looking real estate office. Keetley brought the car to a stop. "What's your game?" he asked.

I grinned at him.

"Okay by me," he said. "Dear old Gerald is getting too smug lately. He's becoming positively legitimate. You don't have anything in the third race this afternoon, do you?"

"Not a thing."

"Oh, well, I can make a killing on the second. I've got a sure thing there. Want to go back inside the office and meet the beautiful Miss Worley again?"

"I don't see any reason why I should."

"Okay. Sorry you wouldn't buy."

We shook hands. I walked over to the agency car, and out of the corner of my eye saw Keetley take a pencil and notebook from his pocket. I turned and walked back to his car.

"The heap over there," I said, "is registered in the name of B. Cool. Look her up in the business directory and you'll find the name of Cool and Lam. We're partners."

"What's your line?" Keetley asked.

"We call ourselves private investigators."

"Why the interest in dear old Gerald?"

I grinned and said, "You can't tell. It might be Ethel Worley."

"Oh, oh!" Keetley said.

"And then again," I told him, "it might be you."

Keetley said, "Get the hell out of here. I've got some thinking to do. You're just the sort who would tell the truth, make it sound like a lie, and go away smiling. Or you might tell a lie and make it sound like the truth. I suppose you noticed Miss Worley's sweater?"

"Not particularly."

He shook his head sadly. "That lie doesn't sound the least bit like the truth. Get the hell out of here. I have to think."

I got in the agency car and watched him in the rearview mirror for a minute. He took the crumpled twenty-dollar bill Miss Worley had handed him from his pocket, smoothed it out, took a roll of bills that would choke a horse from his hip pocket, slipped the twenty on the outside of the roll, and snapped a rubber band around the roll.

I started the motor and drove away.

I went down to the hotel and hunted up the taxi driver who had picked up our client. He remembered the ride. It was out to the twenty-three hundred block on Atwell Avenue. "A big house," he said, "sort of a Colonial type." He remembered there were round, white pillars and an arch over the doorway.

I slipped him a buck and went back to the office. Bertha Cool was just getting ready to go out for lunch, standing up in front of the mirror putting on her hat. A hard-boiled steam roller of a middle-aged woman, whose personality would have dominated anything she could have put on her head, she was getting a dinky little hat adjusted to just the right angle. Perhaps she was trying to look coy.

She said, "Hello, Donald, darling. You've been working, haven't you?"

"Uh huh."

"Bertha likes that in you, Donald. You're energetic, and when we get a case you don't let any grass grow under your feet. What have you found out, lover?"

I said, "Did you notice the initials on the cigarette case?"

"What about them?"

"C.H.," I said.

"Well, what does that mean?"

I said, "The name she gave us was Beatrice Ballwin. This cigarette case says her initials are C.H. I don't like it."

"Don't like what, darling?" Bertha asked ominously.

"The setup."

"Why not?"

I said, "Look, someone comes to us and tells us that Gerald Ballwin's wife is getting ready to slip poison in his coffee. We're supposed to protect him. How are you going to protect a man from having his wife give him a teaspoonful of arsenic over the intimacy of the morning breakfast table? You certainly aren't going to do it standing around watching the front of the house."

"Well?" Bertha asked.

I said, "You'd have to be inside sitting at the table. You'd have to grab the wife's arm when she started to put the sugar in the coffee, and slap her wrist and say, 'Naughty, naughty.' You can't do that."

"What are you getting at, Donald? Tell Bertha."

I said, "In the first place, you can't get in the house. In the second place, you can't be sitting at the breakfast table, and in the third place, you can't tell until after the man begins to get cramps whether that's arsenic in the sugar, or just sugar."

"Go ahead," Bertha said.

"But," I told her, "suppose somebody intends to slip ground glass in Gerald Ballwin's coffee. He sends someone up to tell us that Gerald's wife wants to ease him out of the picture. While we're running around in circles, Gerald gets a tummy ache and joins his ancestors, as the Chinese so nicely put it. We tell our story. The agency was on the job trying to protect him. We've accomplished two things: We've directed suspicion on the wife, and we've shown ourselves up as bunglers."

"So what, lover?" Bertha asked, cooingly.

"So," I said, "I don't like it. The initials on the cigarette case show the girl is a phony."

Bertha strode angrily over to the desk, took a key from her purse, unlocked the cash drawer, jerked it open, pulled out the neat package of ten-dollar bills, and said, "And *that* dough says she's a client."

She slammed the money back in the drawer, closed the drawer, locked it, and went out to lunch.

Chapter Three
Anchovy Paste and Soft Soap

I rang up a couple of operatives who work around for different agencies and arranged to have a shadow put on Mrs. Ballwin, one of the men to work days and the other to work nights until midnight. Not that I had any idea she'd walk into a drugstore and buy poison "to take care of those bothersome rats in the basement," but one never could tell, and I didn't intend to overlook any bets.

I had lunch and stopped in at a delicatessen store afterward.

I looked the place over pretty thoroughly. There was a full carton, which had just been opened, containing two dozen tubes of anchovy paste. It was a brand I'd never heard of before, and I bought the whole carton.

I drove out to the Ballwin residence on 2319 Atwell Avenue, parked the car, walked up the front steps, and rang the bell.

A butler answered the door.

He was a young chap about twenty-six or -seven and good-looking in a weak-mouthed sort of way. His livery looked out of place on him and he was as self-conscious in it as a man is in his first full dress.

"You're the butler?" I asked just to watch his expression.

"The butler *and* the chauffeur. Whom did you wish to see?"

I gave him my best smile and said, "I'm representing the Zesty-Paste people, and we're looking for women who are prominent socially, the sort of woman who represents the average, high-class American housewife. We're going to do some advertising—"

"Mrs. Ballwin is definitely not interested," he said, and started to slam the door.

I said, "You don't get the idea. I'm not selling anything. All I want is to get Mrs. Ballwin to pose for a picture that will be used in all of the big national magazines under the caption, 'Society Woman Uses Zesty-Paste for Hors D'Oeuvres.' My name's Lam and I'm head of the advertising department."

The butler hesitated, said dubiously, "I don't think…"

I interrupted, "If you pass up an opportunity for Mrs. Ballwin to get a made-to-order social status and have it advertised in all of the national magazines, you'll be back waiting tables in a beanery. Get my message to her and see what she says."

He flushed, started to say something, caught himself, turned his back, said, "Wait there," and closed the door in my face.

Five minutes later he was back. "Mrs. Ballwin will see you," he said with frigid dignity, and a manner that said more plainly than words that he very much disapproved of the entire business. He'd been hoping he could tell me to go jump in the lake and slam the door in my face. Now he had to invite me in.

He ushered me through a reception hallway into a living room. Mrs. Ballwin made a regal entrance. She wasn't a bit hard on the eyes. I suppose she was thirty-one, or thirty-two, but she managed to look quite a bit younger until one made a pretty careful appraisal.

"You're Mr. Lam," she said. "Won't you be seated? I'm Mrs. Ballwin. Now, perhaps you can tell me just what it was you had in mind."

She was cordial without committing herself. She was all fixed either to be polite and gracious, or cold and haughty, depending on which way the cat jumped.

She sat down in a chair with her knees together, her skirt down over the kneecaps, her face having just the right polite smile, and her eyes cautious and wary.

I opened the package of anchovy paste. I said, "Our people are preparing a national advertising campaign. It will be four or five weeks before we're ready to shoot with it, but when we do, we're going to broadcast the entire nation.

"Zesty-Paste is the best, most tasty paste prepared from fine high-grade imported anchovies. Once you taste it, you'll recognize its superiority over all other brands. I'm going to leave you this trial carton. I'd like to have you try it and if you like it and start using it regularly, then you will perhaps consent to pose for a picture."

"What will be done with that picture?"

I said, "It'll be displayed prominently in all of the national magazines. There will be a caption 'Popular Leader of the Younger Set Uses Zesty-Paste.'"

I sat quietly then, waiting for it to soak in. I could see that the 'younger set' had registered.

She eased her position in the chair, crossed her knees, and the smile grew more cordial.

The crossing of the knees hadn't been accidental. She wanted me to see what she had to photograph.

It was nice.

"Of course," I went on, smoothly, "there's no obligation on your part. You simply take this sample of Zesty-Paste, you try it out, and see how you like it. If you think it's good and would like to use it, that's fine. Some of these concerns that use photographs of prominent people go in for snob appeal," I went on. "We don't intend to do that. We want to get people who are outstanding, not so much because of wealth or social position, but because of personality and popularity."

"How did you happen to call on me?"

I smiled. "Don't ask me that. That's the main office. They have been preparing this campaign for some little time and making some pretty careful investigations. The main office tells me that they want women who stand right out in a photograph. They want women who have sufficient personality to punch the reader right between the eyes. We don't want a lot of blue bloods that look as though they had adenoids. We want life. We want zest. We want snap. We want punch."

She moved her leg a little bit. "And you think I have it?" she asked.

I lowered my eyes, then raised them rapidly.

"I know you have it. What's more, so does the home office."

"Well," she said, "I'd want to discuss the matter with my husband, but I see no reason why—if, of course, I like the paste. I wouldn't want to recommend anything that wasn't—"

"Of course not," I said. "That's why I'm leaving this carton of Zesty-Paste. You can try it at your leisure."

She leaned forward and pressed a button. "If you don't mind," she said, "I'd like to have my secretary here. I want to be quite certain there isn't any misunderstanding."

"There won't be."

She settled back in the chair. Her eyes were half closed, the long lashes veiling them with an air of seductive mystery.

"I think," she said, "that this is *your* idea."

"How do you mean?"

"I think you thought this up. It's a very clever, a very ingenious and a very nice way of advertising the product, and somehow it seems to have a certain dynamic touch that—well, it seems to fit in with your character."

I said, modestly, "I made a few suggestions at the home office. That's all."

"The idea of having people who have sufficient personality to—what was it you said—punch the reader right between the eyes—"

She laughed throatily.

The door opened and the girl who had been in Bertha Cool's office that morning came in.

"Miss Carlotta Hanford, my secretary," Mrs. Ballwin said, "and this is Mr. Lam."

The girl froze for a moment, then recovered her self-possession as I came up out of the chair, bowed, and said, "I'm very pleased to meet you."

"How do you do, Mr. Lam?" she said, quite coolly.

Mrs. Ballwin was beaming. She said, "Mr. Lam is representing a very high-grade anchovy paste. It is known as the Zesty-Paste. He is leaving a sample with us that he wants us to use. Then, if we find that it is something I can recommend, he wants to take my picture. At a cocktail party, or something of that sort, I assume, Mr. Lam?" she asked, turning to me.

"That would be very fine," I said, "serving hors d'oeuvres to some of your close friends."

She nodded. "I think that might be arranged."

She glanced at her secretary, then frowned slightly and elevated her eyes as though wishing to shut us out of her vision while she concentrated.

"How soon would these pictures be taken, Mr. Lam?" she asked.

"Well, of course, it would depend on whether you liked the paste; how long would it take you to try it and realize that you like it?"

She nodded to her secretary. Carlotta Hanford pressed a button. The chauffeur–butler stood in the doorway. "Yes, Mrs. Ballwin? You rang?"

She looked him over with half-amused, languid appraisal. "Yes, Wilmont. Take this tube of anchovy paste. Spread some of the paste on those little round crackers we had last night, and serve cocktails. What do you prefer, Mr. Lam?"

"Old fashioned."

"Mine will be a Martini, Wilmont," Mrs. Ballwin said, "and Carlotta isn't drinking."

"Very well, Mrs. Ballwin."

His back was straight as he marched from the room.

"Wilmont his last name?" I asked. "Seems to me I've seen him somewhere before."

"Wilmont Mariville. He's both butler and chauffeur. As a butler, he is very decidedly inexperienced," she went on, smiling archly. "But as chauffeur, he is exceedingly skillful. And city traffic is getting so congested these days that it's a strain on one's nerves to try to do even the simplest errand in a car."

I nodded.

"And then, of course," Mrs. Ballwin went on, "I'm trying to help the boys out. So many of these boys are having trouble getting themselves positions that are at all satisfactory. Wilmont is improving as butler all the time. Another two or three months and he'll be perfect. I don't think he likes it. He's crazy about driving. A very, very perfect chauffeur."

Again I nodded.

Abruptly Mrs. Ballwin said, "Excuse me for a moment, will you please, Mr. Lam?"

I got to my feet as she left the room,

Carlotta Hanford said, in an angry half-whisper, "What's the idea of a stunt like this?"

"What's the idea of lying to us about your identity?" I asked.

She glared at me.

I grinned and said, "Don't worry, Carlotta, I'm putting psychological handcuffs on her."

"The name is Miss Hanford," she said angrily.

"Okay. Okay. Wilmont have any other capacity than chauffeur and butler?"

She tilted her chin and tried to act the part of haughty anger.

I said, "If you don't want the job done, why, it's okay by me."

"Of course I want it done. Why do you suppose I spent my good money? But don't you realize how dangerous this is?"

"No."

"Well—"

She was trying to find words with which to finish the sentence when Mrs. Ballwin came back and said, "The cocktails will be here in just a minute, Mr. Lam."

I said, "Your husband's in the real estate business?"

"Yes."

"Handles a subdivision, I believe."

"You seem to know my background."

I said, "Background is an important part of any picture. But it's *you* the company is interested in. We will, of course, want to show your husband as part of the background."

She laughed and said, "That's expressed rather tactfully, isn't it, Mr. Lam?"

"I hope so."

"Now it's definitely understood there's to be no obligation on my part, and the pictures aren't to be used unless I give the word. Is that correct?"

"Generally, that's correct."

"What part of it isn't correct?"

I said, "The pictures won't be taken unless you give your consent. After you give your consent, and the pictures have been taken, they will become the property of the company."

"Well, I suppose that's all right."

Wilmont brought in the cocktails and the hors d'oeuvres. Mrs. Ballwin took one of the crackers and bit into it tentatively. Then she made little tasting motions with her mouth as she appraised the flavor of the anchovy paste. She couldn't have gone through any more agony if she'd been the highest-priced anchovy taster in the world.

"Good," she said.

I beamed at her.

She raised her glass, saluted me with her eyes over the brim. They were smoky, inviting eyes that held an expression of languid amusement, the same glance with which I'd seen her looking at Wilmont Mariville. I wondered if it was a glance she reserved for men who interested her.

Wilmont stood stiff-backed and ill at ease.

Carlotta Hanford was angry.

Mrs. Ballwin and I drank our cocktails, had a dividend, ate four or five of the crackers and anchovy paste.

"You like the paste?" I said.

"Definitely," she said. "I think it's a very superior anchovy paste. I will want to consult my husband, of course, before I make any final acceptance of the plan you have in mind."

"Oh, certainly."

"But I don't anticipate any difficulty."

She smiled at me.

I smiled back, trying to convey the impression that a woman of her charm would never have any difficulty with anything masculine.

"And if my husband makes no objection," she said, "how soon would you be ready to go ahead?"

"Almost immediately."

"Would it take long?"

"No, it could be done quite quickly."

"It wouldn't take long to take the pictures?"

"No. Say sometime within the next five or six days? I'd have to get in touch with the Eastern office and then I'd have to dig up a photographer."

"The pictures would be published several months later?"

"Just a few weeks."

"I see," she said, musingly, and then added with a laugh that was meant to be light. "Of course, in these days one never knows what might happen. I might move away from this city, or—"

"Once we have the pictures and your permission," I said, smiling, "that's about all we'd need. If you'll pardon me for saying so, you're quite decorative and I think you would have quite an impact on the magazine reader. That's exactly what my people are looking for."

"Well, I'm quite satisfied it can be arranged. I'll talk with my husband. Where can I communicate with you?"

I said, "I'm in and out. I'd better call you—perhaps tomorrow morning?"

"Very well. Give me a ring about ten-thirty. If I'm not up by that time, Carlotta, my secretary, will have a message for you."

Her tone indicated that the interview was over, and I arose and started for the door.

The butler–chauffeur handed me my hat. I waited for him to open the outer door.

I could feel hostility radiating from him like heat vibrations from a hot stove.

"Good afternoon," I said.

"Good afternoon, sir."

I waited for the slam of the front door. He closed it as gently as though he'd been a burglar.

Chapter Four
Psychological Handcuffs

I climbed in the agency heap and drove slowly down Atwell. At the first boulevard stop I pulled my car in to the curb and sat there waiting, watching the road behind in the rear-view mirror.

I saw a car coming down Atwell Avenue fast, and slid my car out into the right-hand lane, driving along slowly.

The car behind started to pass; then I heard the squeal of tires on pavement and an impatient blasting on the horn.

I turned around, putting as much surprise as I could on my face.

Carlotta Hanford was at the wheel of the Chevrolet. She was still mad. She parked her car just ahead of mine, then got out and came marching back, heels beating a rapid *click-click — click-click* on the sidewalk.

"Hello," I said. "What are you doing driving—"

She said, "You make me sick! Of all the fool ideas! What do you expect to gain by this absurd masquerade?"

"You hired us to keep Gerald Ballwin from getting poisoned, didn't you?" I asked.

"Of course I did. That's what I wanted, and the only thing I wanted. The idea of you coming to the house with all of this song and dance about representing anchovy paste and wanting pictures. What are you going to do when—"

"I'm going to take pictures," I said.

"You had to go snooping into things and find out who I was, and now the fat's in the fire."

"Why is the fat in the fire because we found out who you are?"

"Because I wanted to keep out of it."

I took a package of cigarettes from my pocket and pushed it across to her. "Want one?"

"No. I'm too mad to smoke."

I said, "Don't stand there on the sidewalk. Folks will think you're propositioning me. Get in the car; then you can tell me the rest of it."

I opened the door. She hesitated a minute, then flounced into the seat beside me.

"Nice legs," I said.

She glared.

I said, "As far as knowing who you were, Carlotta, I knew your name wasn't Beatrice Ballwin the minute I saw the initials on your cigarette case."

"Miss Hanford, to you," she said.

"And as far as keeping Gerald Ballwin from getting poisoned, I think I've done a smart thing."

"I'm glad *you* think so."

I said, "The trouble with you, Carlotta, is that—"

"Miss Hanford," she snapped.

"—you tried to slip something over on us. You thought you could be really smart by saying you were Beatrice Ballwin and that you wanted this, that, and the other, and that we'd never suspect your real identity. You must have thought we were pretty dumb."

"Thought!" she exclaimed. "I *think*—I *know* you're dumb."

I said, "Let's look at it this way. We'll suppose that Daphne Ballwin has made up her mind she's going to slip a little powdered glass into her husband's cereal. You come to us and ask us to stop it. How are we going to stop it—stand by the side of the table with a sieve, or hide in the closet and wait until Gerald puts his spoon in the breakfast food and then dash forward, false mustache and all, and say, 'Hold it a minute, Gerald, my lad. I think part of the windowpane is in there'?"

"Don't be facetious."

"I'm just trying to paint a picture so you can see it."

She said, "I don't care *how* you do it. If I knew how to do it I wouldn't have paid you my hard-earned money in the first place."

"What *is* your salary?"

"None of your business."

"You're certain that was *your* hard-earned money? It couldn't have originally been earned by someone else?"

"What do you mean?"

"I'm just asking questions."

"Well, try minding your own business for a change!"

"I guess it is hard-earned at that," I went on. "You probably don't have an easy life working for Daphne Ballwin. I imagine she can be rather exacting at times."

"She's—"

"Yes, go on."

"Nothing."

"And," I said, "it was quite a lot of money for a working girl to dig up by way of retainer. How much *do* they pay you, Carlotta?"

"I could slap you!"

"Don't do it. It wouldn't get you anywhere. How much do they pay you?"

"None of your business."

I said, "Two hundred and fifty smackers is quite a chunk of dough for a working girl to dig up just to see that her boss's husband isn't given metallic indigestion."

"What are you insinuating?"

"I'm not insinuating anything, Carlotta; I'm just making comments."

"Well, keep your comments to yourself."

I said, "Any time you want to come down to earth and listen, I'm ready to talk."

"I'm listening."

"You're not down to earth."

"As far as you're concerned, I don't ever intend to come down to earth."

I puffed at the cigarette.

"Well, go on," she said.

"Look, Carlotta, let's be reasonable. You wanted me to accomplish something that was virtually impossible. You wanted me to keep Daphne Ballwin from poisoning her husband's food. It simply can't be done. You can't stand there behind Gerald Ballwin's chair and taste every bit of food he puts in his mouth. You can't follow his wife around into the kitchen to see that she doesn't dust a little cyanide onto his grapefruit. We'll have to think of some other way."

"Well, why didn't you do it then?"

"I did."

"Like fun, you did."

"Yes, I did, Carlotta. A woman of Daphne's type is vain and exceedingly proud of her appearance, her position, her sex appeal, and—"

"You're not telling *me* anything I don't know," she interrupted savagely.

I said, "I go to her and give her an opportunity to get her picture in a flock of national magazines. I don't even tell her how big the picture is going to be or how much space we're going to buy. Her eyes light up and she immediately visualizes herself on a full-page ad in *The Saturday Evening Post,* squeezing a tube of Zesty-Paste onto a soda cracker. And, in case you want to know it, the thing that really got her sold was the crack I made about getting some of the leaders of the *younger* set."

"My goodness," she said, with mock surprise and her voice etched with sarcasm. "How *smart* you are, Mr. Lam!"

"She fell for it," I went on, "and, having fallen for it, there are certain new factors which enter into the situation. You could see her thinking those new factors over all the time I was talking."

"What factors?"

"Well, for one thing, she was very anxious to have me go through with the idea I had outlined. She wanted to have her picture in the national magazines and wanted to be acclaimed as a leader of the younger set."

"Well, why not? It didn't take any great amount of salesmanship to put an idea like that across."

I grinned at her and said, "No, Carlotta. The brain work came in thinking the thing up in the first place."

"What's so clever about it?"

"A woman who is about to get some gratuitous advertising in a flock of high-class magazines doesn't let anything happen to her husband."

"Why not?"

"Because, darling, if her husband dies while this idea is cooking, she'll be in mourning. She couldn't go out and pose in a magazine as a leader of the younger set serving hors d'oeuvres at a cocktail party."

She was silent for a while, thinking.

I turned half around and glanced in the rear-view mirror. A car was coming up behind. I noticed casually that it was moving pretty fast.

I said to Carlotta, "I had to do it, Carlotta. I had to think up some scheme—"

"Shut up. I'm thinking."

I kept quiet and let her think.

She turned to look at me just as the car that was coming up from behind slid on past, and I heard her gasp.

Daphne Ballwin was sitting in the rear of the big Packard that purred smoothly on past us. Wilmont Mariville was doing the driving.

"My God," Carlotta said in dismay, "do you suppose they saw us?"

"She was looking right at us," I said, "but there was no sign of recognition."

"There wouldn't have been," she said. "She's clever. Oh, why didn't I realize this probably would have happened! I was a fool to stop and talk with you right here on Atwell Avenue not over a dozen blocks from the house."

The operative whom I had hired to shadow Mrs. Ballwin went unobtrusively by us in an old Ford. If he saw me, he gave no sign.

I sat there watching the two cars out of sight. There wasn't much traffic on Atwell Avenue and that made it pretty difficult for my operative to do the shadow job and not be spotted, but he was doing the best he could.

Carlotta Hanford watched both cars, then got the idea. "Are you having her shadowed?" she asked.

"Sure. Why not?"

"What for? What do you hope to gain?"

"I want to find out who her boyfriend is."

"She hasn't any."

I said, "Don't be silly. A woman doesn't put arsenic in the lemon pie unless there's a boyfriend."

"I tell you she hasn't any."

"I tell you she has."

"I know her better than you do."

"What's the idea of the poison party? Does she want the insurance?"

"I—I don't know."

"Been any friction between her and Gerald?"

"Oh, not exactly friction. Just the usual thing. They're getting on each other's nerves and they'll have little sharp quarrels, and then each one will make an elaborate attempt at self-restraint; but there's always that feeling of tension in the house. You feel that Gerald is glad to get away."

"Who's *his* girlfriend?"

"He hasn't any."

I said, "That's quite a picture you paint. Daphne wants to poison her husband. It's a household of hate and of friction. She's willing to take a chance on first-degree murder in order to get him out of the way. There isn't any particular reason for it except that she doesn't like him. She doesn't care for anyone else.

"And then there's Gerald, a good-looking chap with nice wavy hair, Hollywood sideburns down from the ears, a secretary who wears a short skirt and a sweater and—"

"Heavens!" she exclaimed. "Do you suppose there's anything there? That could be. Do you suppose Ethel Worley is—"

I just sat there looking at her.

"Well?" she asked.

I said, "Personally, I think you overdid it."

"Overdid what?"

"The shocked surprise business, and then the sudden realization. It was good acting—just a little too good acting."

She met my eyes indignantly and then suddenly her eyes softened and she laughed.

"Well?" I said.

"You win, Donald," she said. "I thought I'd keep you from finding out. It's Ethel Worley. And I simply don't know whether Daphne Ballwin knows about it or not."

I said, "That's a lot better. Save your acting until you get your Hollywood screen test."

"I'll have the cigarette now," she said.

I gave her a cigarette and held a match for her. She sucked in a deep inhalation, then shifted her position in the seat of the automobile with a quick, lithe motion, swinging her knees up onto the seat.

"Nice legs," I said again.

She said, "Can't you get them off your mind?" and made a show of pulling her skirt down over her knees.

"Go ahead," I told her. "You were going to tell me about Ethel Worley."

She said, "I don't like to be catty. After all, I don't *know* a thing. I just surmise."

"All right. What do you surmise?"

She said, "Mr. Ballwin is fascinated by Ethel Worley. I think it's just a fascination. I think he plays around. Daphne acts as though she didn't have the faintest idea of what's going on. She never throws Ethel Worley up to him at all."

I said, "That sounds like a very sensible way to take things."

"What?"

"Sit in the background, wait until she can get the proof, and then squeeze the last dime out of him that she can get by way of settlement. Smart women are doing that every day. The poison idea doesn't sound so logical. Daphne Ballwin looks smart to me."

"I'll say she's smart. She's smart and ruthless."

"How much property?"

"I don't know. Quite a bit. I do know that two or three years ago when Mr. Ballwin was mixed up in a business deal that might pay off big or might fold up leaving him with a bunch of liabilities, he put nearly all of his property in Daphne Ballwin's name. I think there was some letter at the time stating that it was in her name purely for the purpose of convenience, so that he could get it back if he wanted it. But—"

"Does he want it back now?"

"I think he does."

"And she isn't having any?"

"She feels that she should have some protection."

"I still can't see the poison angle."

She said, "Well, I've told you all I know."

"I'm not so certain. What about Wilmont?"

"The chauffeur?"

"And butler."

"He's just a boy—a nice boy."

"Your friend?"

"Why, whatever makes you ask that?"

"Is he?"

"No."

"Had to stall for time on that one, didn't you?"

"No."

"Is he Daphne Ballwin's boyfriend?"

"Don't be silly!"

"Is he?"

"No."

"Think she'd like it if he were?"

"Yes."

"That's better."

"Understand, that's only a hunch, based on things—"

"Things Wilmont has told you?"

"Yes, in a way."

I said, "Okay. It's my hunch she's going to be a good girl until after these publicity pictures are taken. It's just a guess, of course, but it's the best I can do. I'll stall along on the picture-taking. That will give us a chance to get a little more data on what's going on."

"How long can you stall those pictures?"

"Depends on the circumstances and on her and on the breaks we get. One week anyway, perhaps two weeks, perhaps three or four."

"I—I guess I made a mistake about you. I guess you're clever."

"Don't be silly. That's just routine. I can't get in the house to watch her. I'll use this scheme to put psychological handcuffs on her poisoning ambitions. Now, I want to know about this brother-in-law, Keetley."

"Keetley!"

"Yes. Tell me about him."

"He was the brother of Anita Ballwin. That's Mr. Ballwin's first wife. She died about three years ago."

"And I suppose Gerald Ballwin waited the conventional year before remarrying?"

"About six months, I think."

"And what about Keetley?"

"I don't know much about him. He was very successful at one time, I understand, but he got to playing the horses—and I guess he is an intermittent drinker. He'll make money for a while and then skid to the bottom again. Then he'll go to Mr. Ballwin for a touch. He doesn't come to the house at all. Daphne hates him."

"Does he have something on Gerald?"

"I don't know. Sometimes I wonder!"

"Gerald always stakes him?"

"I guess so."

"Edith Worley hates him?"

"I guess so. I don't know."

"There's a lot you don't know."

"There's a lot you keep asking me about."

"How does Keetley feel toward Daphne?"

"He hates her."

"Why?"

She started to say something, then changed her mind.

I said, "You mean Daphne was in the picture before Anita died?"

"Yes."

"And how did Anita Ballwin die?"

"She just died."

"What caused her death?"

"I don't know, some sort of complication of very severe— I don't know."

"It was sudden?"

"Yes."

"You weren't working for Mrs. Ballwin at the time?"

"No. I've only been there six months."

"Was Anita Ballwin poisoned?"

"How dare you make accusations like that!"

"Accusations?" I asked. "I was simply asking a question."

"She died a natural death. There's a—she had a doctor. There's a death certificate on file."

"So Keetley hates Daphne?"

"I think he does. He— I think his sister knew about Daphne before— Well, I think Anita may have talked with Mr. Keetley."

I said, "If you had put your cards on the table right at the start, it would have saved complications all around."

"I was afraid you'd betray me in some way if—well, you can see what would happen if anyone knew *I'd* been to you."

"There really is a Beatrice Ballwin, a niece?"

"Yes."

"What sort?"

"Good enough. She's an artist."

"She knew you were coming to see me?"

"Yes. I told her that I was going to borrow her identity for a little while. She's a good scout."

"Suppose I'd gone down to see her?"

"You wouldn't have. She wouldn't have seen you. I had it all fixed so she could front for me."

I thought things over for a few seconds, then said, "Look, Carlotta, we can't sit on the lid forever. This stall about the advertising campaign will hold things for a while; but when that's finished, we're finished."

"I know. I only want—well, I think that the next few days will be the critical time."

"When you talked with us, you told us a week."

She nodded.

I said, "I can probably stretch that to ten days or two weeks, but that's going to be the limit."

Again she nodded.

"You understand that?"

"Yes."

"And you're looking for something to happen within a week?"

"I think—I think things will be worked out by then."

I said, "Okay. Get back in your car and let me go to work."

She said, "I'm sorry."

"About what?"

"About the way I acted. I thought you'd just thrown the fat into the fire. I had no idea how carefully you'd planned things."

"Everything's okay now?"

"Everything's okay, Donald. Thanks."

She gave my hand a squeeze, got out of the car, flashed me a smile, walked rapidly ahead, climbed into her car, and drove away.

Chapter Five
A Hellcat on Wheels

When I reached the office, Bertha was signing the mail on her desk.

"Hello, Donald dear," she said. "You've been working, haven't you?"

I nodded.

She handed the letters to her secretary, said, "Get these all folded. Be sure you get them in the right envelopes, and be sure each envelope is stamped with the proper amount of postage. I want them all to go in the afternoon mail. Do you understand?"

"Yes, Mrs. Cool."

Bertha nodded, gave a perfunctory smile, and turned to me as the secretary went out.

I said, "Don't you suppose she knows what to do with letters?"

"She does now," Bertha snapped.

"You tell her that every time you send out mail."

"You have to tell 'em over and over," Bertha said. "My God, I don't know what's happened to office help these days. The damn little trollops go about their work in a half-daze, thinking about their own affairs all the time, just making motions on a typewriter to get a little dough because they have to live. Say an unkind word to the little tramps and they flounce out of the office and leave you flat. The employment agency sends over someone else that's just as bad as the one that left, and the one that left goes to some place someone else has flounced out of.

Damn 'em. They're as independent as a politician the morning after election."

I said, "It's the old law of supply and demand."

"What the hell are you talking about, Donald? There's just a demand. There isn't any supply. What've you been working on, lover?"

"That Ballwin case."

"What have you found out?"

"Our client isn't Beatrice Ballwin. She's Carlotta Hanford, secretary to Daphne Ballwin."

"What did she lie to us for?"

"It could have been any one of half a dozen things."

"Well, name one."

"She doesn't like the woman she's working for."

"Who the hell does?" Bertha snapped. "Look at this secretary I've got. My God, I'm paying her twice what she's worth and I'll bet even money she hates my guts."

I didn't say anything.

"Well, what's this girl's hating Daphne Ballwin got to do with it?"

I said, "There's just a chance Gerald Ballwin's the one who's afraid he's going to get poisoned. He may have hired his wife's secretary to come here and retain us to protect him."

"Yes, I suppose so," Bertha said, "although I don't see why he didn't come himself."

"He might have been a good businessman."

"What do you mean?"

I said, "Apparently he's pretty well heeled. He's made some money in real estate."

"So what?"

"So we might have charged him a little more than—"

Bertha got the idea immediately. "Fry me for an oyster!" she exclaimed, her little greedy eyes glistening with avarice. "Why, damn his soul. Do you suppose he—"

"That's just *one* explanation."

Bertha said, "I think it's the one I'm going to like. What are some of the others?"

I said, "Perhaps someone else wants to poison Mr. Ballwin and wants to direct suspicion on Ballwin's wife. By hiring us to keep Gerald Ballwin's wife from poisoning her husband, he's already put two strikes against Daphne. In case anything happens, the police will find that we've been on the job, call on us to see what it was all about, learn that we were trying to protect Gerald from his wife, and immediately start giving the wife the works."

Bertha said, "That would mean that the money that had been invested wouldn't be of any use to the person who invested it unless Gerald Ballwin got poisoned."

"That's the idea I'm trying to convey."

Bertha teetered back and forth in her swivel chair, the chair creaking indignant protest. Then suddenly she snapped straight up to rigid attention.

"Donald, dear," she snapped, "do you know what?"

"What?"

"In both of those explanations it means that this girl who came to the office—you say her name is Carlotta Hanford?"

I nodded.

"Well, it means that babe is slipping one over on us. It isn't her money at all. It's money that someone else gave her."

I said, *"All* of the explanations that I have figure that way."

"Why?"

"Because I don't think it's her money. There was too much of it. Suppose you were working for some woman at a hundred and fifty or two hundred dollars a month and you thought she was getting ready to poison her husband, what would you do?"

"Probably nothing," Bertha said. "After it was all over I might tell the police. Or I might get mad and quit and tell the husband. Or I might go to the police."

"Exactly, but you wouldn't go to a private detective agency, pull out two hundred and fifty dollars from your savings account just to protect the husband of the woman for whom you were working."

"Not unless I loved him."

"And if you loved him, you'd go to *him*. You wouldn't go to a detective agency. Anyway, Carlotta says Ballwin is in love with Ethel Worley, his secretary."

"Fry me for an oyster!" Bertha repeated.

"Do you want to know what I've been doing?" I asked.

"Hell, no," Bertha said. "You run the investigating end of the business, and I'll run the financial end. Right now Bertha's trying to think of some way to get that two-faced little hypocrite in a position where she has to pungle up more money."

"That may not be easy," I said. "I don't think it will be; you've already made the financial arrangements."

"Easy?" Bertha snapped at me. "What the hell do you know about finances? You throw money around like a dog that's been out in the rain shakes raindrops all over the furniture. You couldn't get juice out of a watermelon. I've put in my whole life getting blood out of turnips. Get out of here and let Bertha think."

I went over to my office, told Elsie Brand a story, and sat around waiting for the report on Daphne Ballwin.

The operative who had been shadowing her didn't call up until five o'clock. He said that he thought he had something, that his relief had taken over, and did I want it over the phone?

I told him to come up.

He promised to be there in ten minutes.

He arrived on schedule and I gave him a chair. I could see he was pretty well pleased with himself.

"Okay," I said, "where did she go?"

"Her chauffeur stopped in front of the Pawkette Building. She got out and went in. I parked in front of a fire plug, thinking you'd figure it was worth the five. I managed to get in the same elevator with her. Her mind was occupied with something that crowded everything else into the background. You could see just from looking at her she was going some place that was important and she wanted to get there in a hurry."

"You don't think it was an act? Don't think she'd spotted you and was trying to—?"

He shook his head emphatically. "I've had them do that too," he said, "but they aren't good enough actors. They'll always look at you out of the corner of an eye, or something, and occasionally stop to make sure you're tagging along behind. People just can't act that good."

"Perhaps *this* woman can."

"Well," he said dubiously, "perhaps, but I don't think so."

"Okay, what did she do?"

"Went directly to her dentist."

"Her dentist?"

He nodded.

"Who?"

"Dr. George L. Quay."

"What's his address?"

"695 Pawkette Building."

"Okay, what happened?"

"Well, I have a tooth I knew needed a little attention. I thought I could bust on in and see the dentist myself."

"That was dangerous."

"I know it is ordinarily, but this woman was all wrapped up in what she was doing. She was like a sleepwalker."

"Go on," I said doubtfully.

"Well, she went up to Dr. Quay's office and I followed her in. As soon as the office nurse spotted her I could see there was antagonism—and Mrs. Ballwin didn't sit down and wait. She just stood there imperiously and nodded to the nurse. Well, there was a fellow sitting there in the office, looking pretty impatient, and he said to the nurse, 'Are you going to run anyone else in ahead of me?' or something of that sort, and the nurse smiled and said, 'This woman is having some very special treatment,' or something like that, and the patient blew up and said he'd had an appointment and already two people had been run in ahead of him, and so the nurse told Mrs. Ballwin to sit down, and she wouldn't sit down. She told the nurse to tell Dr. Quay she was there. You'd have thought she owned the joint. The nurse went back and we could hear words and then an argument, and then she came back and told Mrs. Ballwin to come in. Her lips were tight and her eyes were flashing."

"What happened to the other patient?"

"He got up and walked out."

"How long was Mrs. Ballwin in there?"

"About ten minutes."

"Did any other patient come out when Mrs. Ballwin went in?"

"How do you mean?"

I said, "There must have been someone in the chair. What happened to the patient who was already in there?"

"I don't know. I think Mrs. Ballwin went into his laboratory, I didn't wait in the office."

"What did you do?"

"While she was in there I went down and waited in my car,

keeping the motor running. When Mrs. Ballwin went out, I followed her."

"Get a ticket for the fire plug parking?"

"No. I was only in the building three or four minutes. Then I went down to the car and sat in it, waiting for her to come out. It was twenty minutes."

"And then what?"

"She went shopping. I lost her after a while. She'd have the chauffeur let her out at a store and tell him what time to be back. I'd tail the chauffeur and his car and then pick her up when he did. Finally he found a parking place. There wasn't one for me. I drove around the block. The third time around he'd gone. I cruised around and couldn't spot him, so I went back to the joint on Atwell Avenue. She came home about ten minutes after I got there. She had a bunch of packages. The chauffeur took them in. I think he was mad. He acted like it.

"I waited until my relief showed up at five o'clock and then phoned you. I thought you'd want to know about the dentist."

"Get the name of Quay's nurse?"

"Mrs. Ballwin called her Ruth."

"How about a description?"

"It's hard to make them stand out when they're in the uniform of an office nurse," the operative said, "but she's redheaded, about twenty-seven, and easy on the eyes. She has a freckle or two and you get the impression she could be an armful of fire or a hellcat on wheels, depending which way you took her."

"Or which way she took you," I said.

He nodded.

"How tall?"

"Sort of average weight and height. White stockings and white shoes, and I have an idea she has a pretty darn good figure."

"How about the tip of her nose? Turn up or down?"

"Straight."

I looked at my watch, said, "There's just a chance," and looked up the number of Dr. Quay's office and dialed it.

For a while I thought no one was going to answer. Then a feminine voice said, "Dr. Quay's office."

I said, "You don't know me—that is, I've never been in before, but could I get an appointment to have a tooth fixed?"

"You'll have to call sometime tomorrow," she said. "Dr. Quay isn't here now. He's gone home."

"You his nurse?"

"Yes."

"Well, can't you tell me about an appointment?"

"I will have to consult with Dr. Quay about that."

"Look here," I pleaded, "how long are you going to be there?"

"Not over ten minutes," she said, firmly. "And it wouldn't do you any good to talk with me. I—I have no authority to make appointments."

"Is Dr. Quay going to be back this evening?"

"Definitely not. Please call tomorrow. Goodbye."

She hung up.

I looked at the operative and said, "She's going to be there for ten minutes. It's after five-thirty. The Doctor isn't going to be there any more tonight. She won't make an appointment. Do you suppose she's quitting and cleaning out her desk?"

"Or perhaps she's been fired," the operative said.

"Okay," I told him. "Keep on Mrs. Ballwin until I tell you to stop. Telephone in reports whenever you get a chance. If I'm not here, dictate them to my secretary over the telephone, if it's something real important. Come in with your reports at the end of each day."

He went out and I followed along behind him, climbed in

the agency car, and rode to the Pawkette Building. I parked the car opposite the entrance and waited just on the off-chance.

At this hour there were virtually no people entering or leaving the building, just a few late stragglers, and nearly all of those were businessmen who had been forced to stay and work long after the help had gone home.

I parked in front of the fire plug and stayed in the driver's seat, leaving the motor running, watching the exit of the building. A girl with a bundle might accept a ride from a stranger if the stranger had a little different technique than the average. The chances were ten to one against it, but the only chips I was shoving in the pot consisted of ten minutes of time and a quart of gasoline.

She came out, a trim redheaded girl, carrying a little bag that was bulging so that it seemed ready to burst at the seams and a package wrapped in newspaper.

I opened the door of the car and gauged the distance. A quick sprint across the sidewalk, a shoulder knocking into the girl, the package spilled all over the sidewalk—contrition— helping her pick up odds and ends—an offer to drive her directly to her destination—would it work?

I looked her over and decided it wouldn't.

What's more, there was something in the way she was walking that made me think she wasn't headed for a streetcar. The package was too big and bulky—and the way she acted, the way she carried the stuff, the way she walked—

I sat tight.

She went into the parking lot next to the building.

I took a big chance and drove around the block, then slowed down as I got to where I could watch the entrance to the parking lot, and barely crawled along.

She came out driving a car that was still well ahead of the

junk heap, but wasn't anything the Blue Book would take into serious consideration.

She headed west, which was a break for me, and I was able to tag along behind without attracting any attention.

I didn't know how far we had to go, so I couldn't take too many chances. However, I felt pretty certain that if she lived in a nearby apartment she would find it easier to take the streetcar than to rent space by the month in the parking lot. Of course, if she had planned on quitting she might have—

I dismissed that thought as soon as it occurred to me. She hadn't planned on quitting; otherwise, she'd have had her things packed and would have been out of there by five o'clock.

I followed her car out to one of the through-boulevards. Traffic was pretty heavy, but one of the big busses finally gave me the opportunity I wanted. I knew that big bus was going to crowd out to the left. The girl was in the lane next to the bus. She didn't figure the bus soon enough. When she did, she gave an indignant blat at the horn and swung out to the left. I shot ahead and let her run into the rear end of the agency car.

I heard the sound of a crash, felt the jar of an impact, and a ripping of sheet steel as a fender came off.

The big bus, invincible in its weight and power, purred smoothly along. A couple of passengers pressed their faces against the back windows. Aside from that, no interest was shown.

I motioned for the girl to pull in to the curb, and swung over. And as I drove in close, I could hear the *scrape—scrape— scrape* of one of my fenders rubbing against the right rear tire. A glance in the rear-view mirror showed me that the left front wheel on the car behind me was wobbling. Traffic behind us simply blared horns and went tearing on past. There must have been two dozen witnesses to the accident, and every one of them got out of there as though he were trying to win a road race.

I got out of the car and walked back to the girl's car. Before she had a chance to say anything to me, I said, "Didn't you know that bus was going to swing over to the left?"

"Didn't you?" she retorted. "You came tearing along without giving me an inch, not an inch!"

I said, "You should have dropped back behind and let the bus come out."

"It should have waited. I had the right of way," she asserted angrily.

I grinned at her and said, "Well, let's look at it from the standpoint of the bus driver. If he waited until all the cars were out from behind him in order to turn back into traffic after discharging a passenger, he'd be all night going six blocks."

"I don't think I'm going to like you," the girl said.

"Well, let's look at the damage," I told her, smiling, "and see who has to like whom."

There was a crumpled fender on the rear of the agency car, which was about what I'd expected. I'd done the same trick before with the car when I had to scrape an acquaintance fast with someone who couldn't be contacted in the regular manner. It's surprising how a suspect may refuse to fall for even the most carefully laid plans, but will fall for the automobile accident approach.

The fender on the agency car had been split a couple of times and welded. Now it was split again.

I pulled it back from the tire and said, "It looks as though that's all the damage here except for the hub cap."

"Something has happened to my front wheel," the girl said. "It wobbles."

I pulled out my driving-license.

"I'm Ruth Otis," she said.

"Driving-license with you?"

She opened her purse, icily displayed her driving-license, said, "That isn't the correct address anymore. The correct address is 1627 Lexbrook."

I said, "That's quite a ways out."

"Well, what of it?"

"Nothing, except I don't think your car will make it."

She looked at me and suddenly started to cry.

I made the mistake of taking out my pencil and notebook and jotting down her license number. That made her mad.

She said, "You don't need to be so nasty-nice, self-righteous. As a matter of fact, if you could drive worth a damn you wouldn't have run into me, regardless of whose fault it was. And I don't think it was my fault, either. I don't think you even saw that bus until after you hit me, and I think you were going too fast, anyway."

I indicated the rear of the agency car and said, "I didn't run into you, sister. You ran into me."

"No, you ran into me."

"Just how could I do it with the rear end of my car?"

"I don't know how you did it. You sort of swung around."

I smiled a superior smile. She took a pencil and a small note-book out of her purse and tried to take down the number of the agency car. Her hand was shaking so she could hardly form the figures.

I said, "You'd better take a look at my driving-license. I'm Donald Lam."

She snatched the driving-license from my hand and steadied her notebook on the right front fender of her car. She carefully copied my name, my age, my address, my height, weight, color of my hair, and the color of my eyes.

"And, the car," I went on affably enough, "is in the name of Cool and Lam. That's a partnership."

"What's the address of that?"

"It's on the certificate of registration wrapped around the steering-post on the inside of the car," I said. "You'd better take it from that."

"Thank you. I will."

She walked over to the front of the car, twisted the certificate around so she could see it, and copied all of the data from that too.

I said affably, "Don't take it so hard. Let the insurance companies straighten it out."

"I'm not insured."

I let her see that I was shocked and surprised. "That makes it different."

"How does it make it different?"

I said, "I'm insured."

"I don't see how that makes any difference."

I said, "I'd hate to have my insurance company collect your wages."

"Don't worry. It won't. My lawyer will collect from your insurance company."

"After all, why not?" I told her affably. "When you come right down to it, perhaps there *is* a good deal to be said on your side. Regardless of who had the right of way, I should have realized that you were too close to that bus. Perhaps if I had only given you an inch or two, you might have made it."

"What are you trying to do?" she asked. "Fix it up so I can collect from your insurance company?"

"Perhaps."

"Well, don't do it. Whatever is right is right. I'm not going to start being crooked so I can save the price of a fender and a bent axle, or whatever it is."

"You think it was my fault, don't you?"

"Yes."

"Well, if I think so too, what's wrong with that? That isn't sticking the insurance company."

"Yes, it is. I should think it's your fault and you should think it's my fault. That's the normal way."

"Well, let's not argue about it. I'll give you a ride home."

"Thank you, I'll get home by myself."

"Okay by me," I said, cheerfully. "Want me to call a taxi?"

"I'll take care of that myself."

I said, "All right. Fine. You've got some things in your car, I see. Be sure you lock it up when you leave it. And, if you're going home in a taxi, you'd better take that stuff with you. In fact, there isn't a streetcar line within a mile of here. I suppose it's none of my business, but even if you telephone at this hour of the night, you'll have a hard time getting a cab to come out here. They're all busy in town around the rush hours."

She looked at the things in the automobile, looked at the agency car.

I raised my hat and said, "Well, if you don't want to go with me I'll be on my way. You can—"

"Which way are you going?"

"Straight down the boulevard."

"As far as Lexbrook?"

"I'm going right past there."

She said abruptly, "All right. I'll ride with you."

I hesitated a moment as though getting ready to tell her that my offer to take her had been outlawed by the statute of limitations. It was just enough hesitancy so she could see that I wasn't eager about it. Then I said, somewhat grumpily, "Well—all right. Get in."

I held the door open for her and she went back to her car and brought the bag and the bundle wrapped in newspaper.

She got in and we rode along in silence for a while. She blinked back tears for a minute, then kept her face a grim mask.

I said, "I think something's wrong with the rear of this car." I pulled in to the curb and got out and took a look around the back end, shaking it a few times.

"Well?" she asked when I got back in.

I said, "I can't see it and yet it doesn't feel exactly right. Would you mind getting out and watching the wheels as I drive forward? I want to make certain that the rear wheels are in direct line with the front wheels. I'll drive forward and you can stand and watch, and then I'll stop and back up."

She got out without a word and stood by the curb. I drove the car slowly ahead for about a hundred feet, then backed it up.

"It looks all right to me."

"You didn't notice any wobbling in the rear wheels?"

"No."

"And they were lined up all right?"

"Yes."

"That's a load off my mind," I told her. "I was afraid perhaps the frame had been sprung."

"I thought you were insured."

"I am, but I have to use this car to make a living. When a frame has been sprung it's a serious thing and it takes a little time to make repairs."

"What do you do?" she asked.

I said, "I'm a private investigator."

"You mean a private detective?" she exclaimed.

"That's right."

She was silent for four or five blocks. Then she said rather guardedly, "It must be exceedingly interesting."

"Yes, I suppose it is to someone who isn't in the business."

"And exciting."

"At times."

"It certainly is different from the drab, routine jobs most of us have to hold down."

"Oh, it has its drab moments too. We have a lot of routine in this business, shadowing people and things like that."

I looked at my watch, said suddenly, "Oh, my gosh!"

"What's the matter?"

"I was supposed to telephone the office. My partner is waiting there to give me a report on some stuff I have to have. That accident and all of that drove it out of my head. I was to have called her ten minutes ago."

"Her?"

"Right."

"You mean your partner is a woman?"

"That's right. B. Cool," I said. "That 'B' stands for Bertha. Middle-aged, a hundred and sixty-five pounds, hard-boiled as an Easter egg, and as difficult to handle as a coil of barbed wire. Wait here, will you, and I'll go telephone."

"Where are you going to telephone from?"

I pointed toward a restaurant. "They'll have a phone. It seems to be the only one around here."

I went inside the restaurant and looked the place over. It was a pretty fair little Chinese restaurant that had moved out into a district where there were cheaper rents.

I went back out and said, "I've missed her. She'll probably be back inside of ten or fifteen minutes, but Bertha's peculiar that way. She gets mad every time I'm a little late on a telephone call. I want to be where I can keep phoning. Look, would you mind coming in and waiting with me? We can lock up the car. That place is a Chinese restaurant where there's some pretty good food. I'll make you a bargain. If you'll wait with me until I get my phone call through, I'll buy you a dinner."

"And suppose I don't wait?"

"Then," I said, "you'll just have to stand here by the car and wait until a taxicab comes along, and flag it down. And," I added ruefully, "right out here that's going to be a long, long time. Hang it, I'm sorry about this thing, Miss Otis."

"You should be. I wanted to get home. I'm late now."

"Well, I'm sorry," I said, glancing impatiently at my wrist watch. "That's the way it is. If you want to come along, I'll lock up the car and your things will be safe here. If you don't want to come, I'll lock it up anyway and you can flag a taxi. After you get the taxi, come on into the restaurant and I'll unlock the car for you. I've probably got an evening of hard work ahead and I've got to take aboard some nourishment. In this business, you eat when and if you get it."

I was impatiently jingling the keys to the car while I was talking and she said, "Oh, all right, I'll come along."

I locked the car and we entered the restaurant. We took a booth by the telephone. I made a great show of dialing the office number and waiting. Then I regretfully hung up the receiver, got my nickel back, and slid over on the cushioned bench which ran around the small booth and circular table.

A waiter came and brought us tea and rice cakes. I asked her if she liked Chinese food and she said she liked the egg dishes. "The *foo yung ha*, I think it is," she said. I realized that her experience had been with the conventional Chinese dishes, so I made a show of dialing the office number again, waiting until there was no answer, and getting my nickel back. Then I went back to the table and gently took the bill of fare from her fingers. "If you don't mind," I said, "let me order. I'll get you some stuff that perhaps you haven't had before, stuff that will taste good."

I didn't add that I knew darn well it would be stuff that would take at least twenty minutes to get ready.

"All right," she said.

I ordered some Chinese appetizers, *sohn keau tau,* some chicken and pineapple, fried shrimp, and some of the pork spareribs with sweet and sour sauce, and another pot of tea.

The waiter went away and we sat there sipping tea.

"I think the only thing I ever ate in a Chinese restaurant," she told me, "was *chop suey* and egg *foo yung ha.*"

"That's about the limit of Chinese dishes most people order."

"How do you like having a woman for a partner?"

"It's all right."

"Did you organize the partnership together?"

"No. Bertha was running a detective agency. I was pretty much on my uppers. I came to her looking for a job."

"And gradually worked into the partnership?"

"Yes."

"How did you do it?"

"Oh, I don't know. Just a certain number of coincidences, I guess. We ran into some rather big cases and Bertha got to the point where she needed my help because they were new types of cases. Before I got into the partnership she'd been handling mostly routine work, getting addresses for collection agencies, doing a little shadowing in divorce cases, and getting specialized information for lawyers in personal injury cases."

"You don't like that type of work, do you?"

"No."

"What kind of work do you like?"

"The kind we're having now."

"What's that?"

"All sorts of cases," I said cautiously.

"What made the change?"

"I don't know. We just started getting in the big-money and somehow we just stayed there."

"I suppose one thing leads to another—one case gets you others. Is that right?"

"I suppose so."

"A certain amount of word-of-mouth advertising?"

"Yes."

She held out her cup for more tea, and then said abruptly out of a clear sky, "I just lost my job today."

"You mean you're quitting?"

"I mean," she said bitterly, "I was fired."

"That's too bad. What happened? Didn't you do the work?"

She laughed grimly and said, "I guess I did the work too well. I had the best interests of the boss at heart—more than he did."

"What was it?"

"A woman."

I said, "Oh, I see."

She didn't like the tone of my voice. "No, you don't see at all," she flared. "This woman was ruining my boss's business. She is arrogant. She's—she's a selfish woman, and she does everything that a selfish woman does."

"I see," I said owlishly. "And because you're in love with the boss and he's in love with her, it makes a peculiar triangle—"

"What are you talking about!" she blazed. "In love with the boss—I hate his guts!"

I let my eyes show surprise. "Then why quit?"

"I tell you I didn't quit. I was fired."

And then suddenly she started to cry.

I said, "Okay. Okay. Forget it."

"I can't forget it. It makes me so m-m-m-mad. She was b-b-b-busting up his business and when I t-t-t-t-told him—"

"He thought you were definitely assuming too much authority, is that it?"

"I don't know what he thought. He just fired me. I sometimes think she'd told him to fire me."

I said, "Well, don't tell me about it if you don't want to."

"I feel as though I'd like to have someone to talk to."

"I'm a stranger."

"That's why I'm talking to you. I don't think I'd ever tell one of my friends."

"Also, I'm a detective. I might be working on a case that involved the very thing you're talking about."

She threw back her head and laughed at that one, a nervous, tearful laugh. Then she opened her purse, took out a handkerchief, wiped away the tears, and said, "I cry when I get mad, and then when I realize I'm crying, that makes me all the madder."

"You're mad at your boss?"

"At my former boss. I guess I'm mad not so much at him as at the injustice of the whole business."

"What does your boss do?"

"He's a professional man."

"And the woman, I take it, is a client?"

"Definitely *not*. He's a dentist, not a lawyer."

"And the woman came to his office frequently?"

"I'll say she did. And when she came there it was like the Queen of Sheba dropping in for a royal visit. She wanted to go lording past everyone. You can't treat patients that way. Well, I guess there's no use in me talking about things now."

"Why not? Get them off your chest."

"No. I've said enough. I guess I've said too much. Let's talk about something else. Tell me something about your business. You say this Mrs. Cool is middle-aged?"

"Yes."

"And tough?"

"Tough."

"How do you get along with a woman like that?"

"Sometimes I don't."

"Isn't it trying on your nerves to have a close association with someone that—well, you know, that you don't get along with?"

"Not particularly. It's good exercise once in a while. It keeps me from getting too soft."

"You don't argue with her, do you?"

"No."

"What do you do?"

"I do what I want to and let her do the arguing."

She said, "You're a funny boy. There's something about you that—well, you're sort of quiet and—well, a person would almost think you could be pushed around. And then there's a streak in you that's just as hard as concrete."

"Oh, I don't think so."

"Well, I'll bet your Mrs. Cool thinks so. I'd like to talk with her and see what she says."

"After all, it isn't important, is it?"

"No."

I went over to the phone, dropped a nickel, and dialed the office, went through all of the procedure of waiting and frowning as I hung up the phone and got my nickel back.

"They still don't answer?"

"No."

"You think your Mrs. Cool is angry because you didn't call her at the time you were supposed to?"

"I know it."

The waiter started bringing food and we began to eat. Two or three times while we were eating, the girl looked at me appraisingly. I didn't try to pump her. I felt that if I did, she'd instantly become suspicious.

Abruptly she said, "How much do you suppose it's going to cost me to fix my car?"

"Twenty or twenty-five dollars."

"Any old time!" she said. "I'll bet it costs seventy-five or a hundred."

"It shouldn't cost too much....I'll tell you what I'll do. I'll pay for it myself."

"*You* will?"

"Yes."

"Why?"

"Because I'm beginning to think it was my fault."

She said, "I don't understand just how it happened. I was mad and driving along and thinking about Dr. Quay— Oh, I shouldn't have done that."

"What?"

"Told you his name."

"It doesn't make any difference," I said. "I've got to call the office again."

I went over and dropped a nickel, went through the motions of dialing the number, and, just to be on the safe side, waited until I heard the sound of ringing at the other end of the line. Then I started to hang up the phone and get my nickel back. I had the receiver halfway to the hook when I heard a rasping, metallic sound coming from it. I put the receiver back to my ear and said, "Hello."

I couldn't imagine what anyone would be doing at the office at that hour, but there certainly had been a squawk of sound come out of the receiver.

I'd no sooner said, "Hello," than Bertha Cool's angry, exasperated voice came roaring over the wire, "Well, where have *you* been?"

"Eating. What are you doing there?"

"What am I doing here?" Bertha screamed. "Well, isn't *that* nice! What am *I* doing here? I'm trying to run the damn agency and keep us from being the laughingstock of the whole town. You and your master-mind. You and your ideas of tying Mrs. Ballwin's hands with psychological handcuffs!"

"What are you talking about?" I asked.

"Talking about!" she screamed at me. "Talking about Gerald Ballwin getting poisoned."

"You mean—"

"Of course I do," Bertha yelled. "What the hell do you suppose I'm up here at the office for? And this Carlotta Hanford wants her money back and claims we're an incompetent bunch of boobs. Gerald Ballwin is poisoned, and there's hell to pay. Get up here."

"Right away," I told Bertha and hung up the telephone.

Ruth Otis was looking at me with a strange expression on her face. "What's the matter, Mr. Lam?"

"Just routine," I told her.

"You jumped as though someone had stuck a pin in you when you were talking on the phone. I could hear the voice on the other end of the line all over the room. It came in so plain. Was that Mrs. Cool at the other end of the line?"

"That very definitely was Mrs. Cool."

"She must have been screaming."

"She was."

"I couldn't help hearing some of it. She turned the telephone receiver into a loudspeaker."

I nodded.

The blue eyes of Ruth Otis kept searching mine. There was a peculiar, direct intensity in their regard that had me thinking back trying to remember just what Bertha Cool had said.

"Was it Gerald Ballwin that was poisoned?" she asked.

"Why?"

"The woman that I was talking about was Gerald Ballwin's wife."

"Indeed."

"Was it Gerald Ballwin that was poisoned?"

I said, "You can read the papers tomorrow. Right now I'm busy. I'm going to pay the check, bust a few speed records getting you out to your house, and then get up to the office as fast as possible."

"Gerald Ballwin poisoned," she said slowly, pushing back the chair and standing up, her hands on the table.

"Gerald Ballwin poisoned," she repeated again, and her face became a peculiar greenish color. She clutched at the tablecloth. Then she started to sag as her knees buckled.

By the time I got around the table, she was flat on the cushion, out like a light.

The waiter came up, took a look, and then ran back to the kitchen. Ten seconds later, a Chinese woman, a girl, an old man, and two young fellows were standing around, seemingly all talking at once in Chinese, their voices high-pitched with excitement.

I picked up a glass of water, poured some of it on a napkin, kept gently slapping the girl's face with the wet napkin until she came to. Then I tossed a five-dollar bill on the table and made Ruth Otis get to her feet. She was still in a daze as I piloted her out to the car.

Chapter Six
A Slight Case of Homicide

The old agency car really did its stuff as I went tearing down the street from the Chinese restaurant.

Ruth Otis, sitting over on my right, rolled down the window so that the fresh air could strike her face.

After a while, she said, "Can you imagine me doing a thing like that?"

I didn't say anything.

"Tell me, Mr. Lam, what is *your* interest in the Ballwin family?"

"Do you think you can hear names that well over the telephone when you're simply listening to the sound blast which comes through the receiver?"

"But she said he was poisoned."

"I can think of two dozen names that would have sounded like Ballwin under similar circumstances."

"But the poison—that—that all ties in."

"Ties in with what?"

She hesitated a moment, and then said, "Nothing."

I drove on in silence.

"Someone must have hired you to investigate some phase of the case."

I kept quiet.

"Are you—I mean, do you know anything about Dr. Quay?"

"Why should I?"

"About the fact that Mrs. Ballwin was at his office?"

"You keep talking about a Mrs. Ballwin," I said, my eyes busy with the road ahead.

"I wonder if you were trying to shadow me," she went on, "and then when that bus turned out you were caught in a trap just as you were trying to go ahead....Is this entirely a coincidence?"

I kept right on driving.

"You aren't saying anything," she charged.

I said, "Listen, sister, I'm trying to get you there in one piece. You're talking like a very foolish girl."

"A while back," she said, "you were anxious to talk. Your eyes were inviting me to keep right on with what I was saying. You were listening so your ears stuck out. Now you don't want me to say anything."

I said, "Driving at this rate of speed takes a certain amount of concentration. I'd hate to pile you up, and I'd hate to have to put you out on the sidewalk and let you wait until some wolf came along to pick you up. You might not like it as well as riding with me."

She was thinking that over when I came to Lexbrook Avenue. I spun the wheel so that the car screamed on the turn and before she could get her thoughts together was slamming on the brakes in front of 1627.

It was a little apartment house originally intended to house people who worked in the immediate neighborhood, but with the housing shortage it had become filled with people who worked in the business district.

I got Ruth Otis out of the car, grabbed the package wrapped in newspapers, and said, "I'll take this up for you. You'll have trouble getting your doors open carrying all of this stuff."

"No, no, I can get it up. You're in a hurry."

"It will only take a second."

She unlocked the outer door, led the way up a flight of stairs, down the corridor of the second floor to an apartment in the rear.

I said, "Apartment number ten—that must be the last number in the building."

"It is."

She fitted her latchkey, opened the door, and I followed her into the apartment, a small, somewhat cramped place, dingy with dark walls and furniture that had been stained in a color conventionally known as "oak." It had that peculiar stale smell which is indefinable, the aftermath of years of human occupancy—a drab little dwelling-place that had become a landlord's gold mine.

Ruth Otis went across and opened the window. I put her package down, took out my billfold, dropped two twenties and a ten on the table while her back was turned.

She said, "It was nice of you to take me home, Mr. Lam. I'm sorry—I'm sorry I made a fool of myself, but there was such a shock there that—well, I've had a pretty upsetting day," and she laughed nervously.

"That's all right. I understand."

"Would it be too much to ask you—you know, not to say anything about it?"

"About what?"

"You know, about my pulling that faint."

I hesitated.

She came toward me, then. Evidently she'd been thinking it over, rehearsing in her own mind just what she was to do. Her blue eyes were wistful. "You won't say anything about it, will you?"

I said, "It's okay. Take it easy and don't worry."

Her eyes caught sight of the money on the table. "What's this?"

I said, "Money for the accident. I'm going to admit it was my fault and put the bill on the expense account."

"You—you can't do that."

"It's done."

She started to cry then, and I said breezily, "Cheer up, Ruth. You're a big girl now, you know," opened the door and went out into the corridor.

I ran down the stairs, jumped into the agency heap, spun it in a U-turn, and headed back for the office.

Bertha Cool was rocking back and forth in her creaking swivel chair as I opened the door of her private office. She swept her jeweled hand to the cigarette in her mouth, whipped it out from her lips, and said sarcastically, "Well, well, well, the old master-mind himself."

"The same," I told her.

"My God," she said angrily, "I don't know why I always have to be on the firing line when your bright ideas backfire."

"What's the matter?"

"Matter!" she screamed at me. "Matter! A woman hires us to keep Gerald Ballwin's wife from poisoning him. She pays us two hundred and fifty bucks, and she's going to bring in another two hundred and fifty bucks tomorrow, and you go out and pull the old razzle-dazzle and tell her not to worry; that because you've given the buzzard a couple of dozen tubes of anchovy paste she won't do a damn thing. And then walk out and leave me holding the sack."

"What sack?"

"What sack! My God, be your age. *You* don't have *your* phone listed in the telephone book. You drift around from one apartment to another. Even *I* don't know where to catch you at times. And how you do it I don't know. God knows it's hard enough for decent people to get apartments, let alone some bachelor like you. But here I am, listed in the phone book—B. COOL, *residence*.

"I wouldn't have answered the phone at that, if I hadn't thought it was you calling about something. And it's our client. She's all worked up. I have to come to the office at once. Well, I humored the little trollop because she was going to give us another two hundred and fifty bucks tomorrow. Well, she got here, and what she told me was plenty."

"What was it?"

"She wanted to know what good we'd done, messing around and throwing monkey wrenches in the machinery. She said you were one hell of a detective, and I agreed with her. Going out and messing things up, snooping around. You might just as well have taken a sign saying *I'm a Private Detective hired to gumshoe around the place,* and picketed the damn house. Of all the bungling, incompetent, cockeyed ideas of how to play detective, you and your damned anchovy paste!"

"Come on down to earth and tell me what happened."

"What happened! Hell's bells, the thing happened that we were hired to prevent. You messing around in the thing just brought the whole business to a head. Mrs. Ballwin decided she wasn't going to have much time left. And then you very kindly came along and gave her the thing she'd been looking for."

"What?"

"A good safe opportunity to poison her husband. You and your anchovy paste."

"Any time you want to tell me what happened, I'll listen."

"What happened," Bertha said, and gave me a contemptuous little snort. "All right, *lover*," she spat at me, "I'll spell it out for you in words of one syllable. I should have realized that that master-mind of yours couldn't contemplate the ordinary ramifications of the English language. You need a diagram. Damn it, you need a nurse.

"Gerald Ballwin came home, and Daphne—in the presence

of witnesses, of course—cooed that the most wonderful thing had happened. Their pictures were to be in all of the national magazines endorsing some marvelous anchovy paste, and she'd made some hors d'oeuvres for her husband to try.

"And so she brought out a nice little plate of hors d'oeuvres, took one herself, handed one to her husband, and then proceeded to gush all over the place about how their pictures were going to be in the magazines, warming up that line of bunk that you'd handed her.

"It was a line that wouldn't fool a clever woman, but it was just enough to fool Gerald Ballwin, at least before he'd had an opportunity to think it over, and she played it up big, putting on a big song and dance about how she'd always claimed that it paid to entertain and to be a gracious hostess and now her personality had begun to pay dividends. The things she'd strived so hard to accomplish had actually been achieved. She had a reputation of being a leader among the *younger* set.

"And her fat-headed husband fell for it and smiled at her over the anchovy, and they had a cocktail, and he looked over the tubes of anchovy paste and did some critical tasting and said how nice it was, and then after a while turned green and got sick and thought the paste in the tube must have been spoiled. His wife promptly called a doctor and described the symptoms. The sawbones told him he had food poisoning and told him what to do and said to preserve the tube of anchovy paste for evidence, because it must have been spoiled and the taste of it would disguise the fact that it was spoiled and all that blah-blah-blah."

"Then what happened?"

"Then Carlotta Hanford who had been sitting there eating anchovy paste went out and called another doctor, told him that Gerald Ballwin had been poisoned, called for an ambulance, notified the police and raised hell generally, and the result of it was that Ballwin got to a hospital in time and they *may* save his life. They've been pumping out his stomach and all that."

"Carlotta Hanford notified the police?"

"That's right."

"And how about Mrs. Ballwin?"

"Skipped out," Bertha said, "Took a powder."

"When?"

"Apparently about the time Carlotta Hanford telephoned the police that Gerald Ballwin had been poisoned. She knew then the jig was up. She ducked out of the house."

"Police tried to pick her up?"

"That's what I understand. They'll probably find a ton of poison in one of her cold cream jars somewhere. But the point is that we were hired to keep this thing from happening and what we've done has made it happen. We even furnished the anchovy paste—and I suppose you put that on your expense account."

"Sure, I did."

Bertha groaned and said, "That's the trouble with you. Instead of buying one tube of anchovy paste and handing it to her, you have to go buy a carton of two dozen tubes. My God, when you start running up an expense account you act as though the whole world was made of money. You toss money to the birdies, you throw it in the gutter, you burn the stuff up."

"You don't know the half of it yet," I said. "I had an accident with the agency car."

"Well, thank God, it's insured."

I said, "The woman I ran into didn't want to make a claim, so I paid her fifty bucks out of expense money."

Bertha's chair gave one sharp, indignant squeak as she came to an erect position. "You *what?*"

"I gave her fifty dollars out of the expense account."

"What did you do that for?"

"Because I ran into her on purpose. I thought she might be connected with the case and I wanted to find some means of making a contact with her so she wouldn't be suspicious. I manipulated the car so that I ran into her and smashed the front end of her car so she couldn't drive it and—"

"My God," Bertha screamed, taking the cigarette stub from her lips and hurling it across the room. "Not only does he do things the most expensive way, but even when we are insured he pulls fifty bucks out of his pocket and throws it to the birdies too. So," she said with elaborate sarcasm, "you couldn't think of any way of getting acquainted with a girl except by running into her. God Almighty, walk out on the street and look around. There are seventeen million two hundred and eighty-six thousand four hundred and ninety-one pick-ups taking place every night. Go to any of the night spots, and if you don't have a girl with you, some baby doll will be draped all over you in ten seconds flat. Ride down the street and honk your auto horn at the babes and you can get a car full of them, even with all the murder and rape that's been going on. Just lift your hat and smile sweetly at a girl and ask her where Twenty-Fifth and Broadway is, and she'll give you the once over and say, 'I'm going in that direction myself. If you'll walk along with me, I'll tell you when we get there.'

"There are millions and millions of ways of picking up women, but you don't use any of them. You want to be original. Those brains of yours have to play horsie. You think up some way that's going to smash up a car and cost fifty bucks. How much other money have you spent?"

"I've had a couple of operatives shadowing Daphne Ballwin."

"Oh, you have, have you? And all that stuff costs money too. You have *two* men shadowing her."

"That's right. A day man and a night man."

"Well," Bertha said. "We're to be congratulated that, thanks to your efforts, the poisoning took place so soon. Otherwise you'd have had the firm bankrupt. If Mrs. Ballwin had only held off until tomorrow, you'd have managed to have eaten up all of the two hundred and fifty dollars in expenses and left Bertha to think out some way of paying the rent and the help."

"How about the butler, Wilmont Mariville?" I asked Bertha.

"What about him?"

"Did he serve the hors d'oeuvres?"

"Hell, I don't know. I guess so. Isn't that what a butler's for?"

"How does Carlotta feel?" I asked.

"How does she feel? It's lucky for you that you weren't here to find out how she felt. You should have heard some of the things she said about you. Sitting in the automobile, pretending to be a big shot, talking to her about how nice her legs were, handing her a cheap line of hooey, telling her how you'd tied Mrs. Ballwin's hands with psychological handcuffs, so she couldn't do anything rash until after the picture-taking was all over, and all that sort of tommyrot. All you really did was to hurry up the poisoning and charge the stuff that did it on the expense account. Well, you sure played hell. You— Oh, for God's sake! Now who's this?"

There was a heavy banging on the outer door.

"I suppose that's Carlotta Hanford coming back," Bertha went on. "And I'm going to open the door and let you get a load of it. I'm good and sick of trying to front for you and trying to tell Carlotta that there must have been some factor in the situation that we didn't know about, because she hadn't told us the whole story."

"You did that, did you?" I asked. The banging was resumed on the outer door.

"Of course, I did," Bertha said. "I'll give you hell, but I wasn't going to let that little trollop push the agency around. I gave her the devil. I told her that I knew damn well you wouldn't have failed in anything that you set out to accomplish if it hadn't been for the fact that there were some factors in the situation that she had concealed from us. I put her on the defensive and—lover, open that door and see who's making the racket."

I said, "It sounds very much like the police to me."

"Well, I don't care if it's the king of England," Bertha said. "We're paying rent on the office and whoever it is, is wrecking the door."

I crossed over the office and opened the door a crack. "What's the commotion about?" I asked.

Detective-Sergeant Frank Sellers pushed his weight against the door and said, "Well, well, well, if it isn't my friend Donald. How're you, Donald?"

I braced my hand against his crushing grip.

"Where's Bertha?"

"In there."

"Well, ain't that swell! It's been a while since I've seen you. How've you been?"

"Okay. Come on in. I take it this is an official visit?"

Sellers tilted his hat over on the back of his head, looked at me quizzically. "Now is that any way to greet an old friend? I come on in to see you and have a talk, and you start making cracks like that."

"Who is it, Donald?" Bertha yelled at me from behind the closed door of her private office.

I said to Sellers, "Suppose you tell her."

Sellers walked across the room and opened the door. "Hello, Bertha."

"For the love of Mike!" Bertha exclaimed, grinning.

"Well, how's everything?" Sellers asked. He walked across to the client's chair, sat down, put his feet up on the desk, and fished a cigar from his pocket.

Bertha said, "Haven't you learned any manners since the last time I saw you?"

"Oh, yes," Sellers grinned, "that hat! I'd almost forgotten about that."

He took his hat off, ran his fingers through thick, unruly hair, winked at me and scraped a match on the sole of his big police shoe. "How're you coming, Bertha?"

"I could have been dead for six weeks as far as you're concerned," Bertha said. "Why the sudden interest in my health?"

Sellers said, "The question was primarily related to business. Knowing you as I do, I know that the mazuma comes first and everything else second."

"You go to hell," Bertha snapped, but there was a twinkle in her eyes.

Sellers looked her over approvingly. "God, Bertha, any time you want to quit this business and come down to go to work for the City, you certainly could get a job as matron. You'd really make a swell matron. You know your way around and you could give them a little advice now and then, and if they ever started to get tough, you sure as hell could handle them."

"I sure could!" Bertha admitted.

"Well," Sellers said, "I've been intending to drop around to see you folks for a week or so—but you know how it is. We're busy as the devil and it seems as though the faster we catch crooks and put 'em away, the quicker the new crop comes up. Getting so it's just like pouring water down a rat hole and we've got the prison so full that whenever we stick ten new men in, they've just about got to let ten old men out."

"Odd hour to be paying social calls at an office," Bertha said.

"Now don't get impatient, Bertha. I was just saying I've been trying to get around here for a week, and then this Ballwin case came up and it looks as though you folks are sitting on that and the Captain sez to me, 'Frank,' he says, 'you know those folks up there and get along with 'em swell. Why don't you run up and see what it's all about. No rough stuff, you understand. No threats. Just be courteous and ask 'em questions. We know they'll cooperate.'"

Bertha looked at me and said nothing.

I lit a cigarette.

Sellers evidently didn't like that silence. He took the cigar out of his mouth, clasped his hands behind the back of his head, looked at the ceiling, and said musingly, "If you want my opinion I think that was damn white of Cap. You know how it is. With most agencies we'd have got tough. Private agencies are supposed to cooperate with the police when there's any phase of the case that the police are interested in. With most agencies, we'd have given them hell for not hunting us up and putting the cards on the table as soon as they knew there was something wrong, but the Cap says to be nice with you folks, nice and gentle."

Neither one of us said anything.

"So," Sellers went on, bringing his eyes back from the ceiling to look at Bertha, "what's the lowdown on the Ballwin case?"

Bertha nodded toward me. "Donald's the big shot in that case. I just rake in the dough."

Sellers shifted cold eyes to me. Under his dark eyebrows, those eyes had suddenly turned professional.

"Okay, Donald."

I laughed and said, "Save the gimlet eye for the crooks, Sergeant."

He took the cigar out of his mouth, blew out smoke, and said, "Oh, that's okay, Donald, I'm just practicing on you, because you may be in a cell yet. Give me the lowdown. Begin at the beginning and don't leave out anything."

I said, "Some woman came to the office. She wanted the lowdown on what was going on at the Ballwin residence. I took two hundred and fifty bucks, or rather Bertha did, and tried to find out."

"What did you do?"

"Oh," I said. "I put a tail on Mrs. Ballwin, just to see if she was playing around any, and then I tried to think up some scheme for getting in the house."

"That's the reason you bought— Well, never mind. *You* tell *me*."

I said, "That's the reason I bought the anchovy paste. I thought this business of taking photographs for an advertising campaign and giving Mrs. Ballwin a fancy build-up would pay off in dividends."

"So you bought the anchovy paste."

"That's right."

"Where?"

"At a delicatessen on Fifth Street."

"Know the name of the place?"

"I don't. I think I could find it again. It wasn't too big a place."

"Why anchovy paste?"

"To tell you the truth, I was just looking for something that I could use that she couldn't check up on. I thought at first of going into a drugstore and buying some facial creams. The trouble is that those manufacturers are too accessible and I was afraid she might check up on me; but no one ever heard of advertising anchovy paste that way and as soon as I got to prowling around in the delicatessen store and saw the anchovy paste, I thought it was a natural."

"You aren't kidding me?"

"No."

"You didn't get something that could be put on soda crackers and doped up with arsenic, deliberately?"

I said, "Do you think I'm mixed up in the poisoning?"

"Well, I just wanted to know," Sellers said.

"Well, I've told you."

"Any chance this anchovy paste could have been planted?"

"How do you mean?"

"Any chance someone knew you were going to get anchovy paste—"

I interrupted him by shaking my head.

"Any chance someone put the idea in your mind? Think carefully on that one," Sellers said. "It's pretty easy for someone to come along and tell you a story about how someone got an entree to a house by pulling an idea of this sort and mentioning anchovy paste. It might have been a week or so ago that this happened but the idea was left in your mind and—"

"Not a chance," I said.

"No, I don't suppose there is," Sellers admitted.

"Hell," Bertha said, "it's a typical Donald Lam scheme. No one else ever thought of it. It's got 'Donald Lam' stamped all over it."

"It has, for a fact," Sellers admitted. "So you went out there this afternoon and left the carton of anchovy paste and had a big build-up powwow with Mrs. Ballwin."

"That's right."

"Think you sold her?"

"I thought so at the time."

"I think she was a little smart for you," Sellers said. "Who was the dame who gave you the two hundred and fifty bucks?"

I shook my head. "We can't divulge the names of our clients."

"You'd better cooperate with the police," Sellers said. "This isn't playing guessing games. This is a murder case."

"Murder?"

"Well, he isn't dead yet, but—well, hell, you can't tell about poisoning."

"You sure it was poisoning?"

Sellers nodded and said, "Sure, it was poisoning. The guy was heaving up soda cracker, anchovy paste, and arsenic. The police laboratories saved the stuff and ran a quick test."

"Of course," I said, "it could have been in something else."

"Of course," Sellers said sarcastically. "Hell, how do we know? The guy may have been a chap who bit his fingernails and when the manicurist gave him the works this afternoon, she dusted a little arsenic under his fingernails so that when he started nibbling on them he had cramps—and then again, someone could have filled up a tube of anchovy paste with arsenic and let it go at that."

"You're testing the anchovy paste?"

Sellers looked at me pityingly.

"Okay," I said, "I just wanted to know."

"You say you had a tail on Mrs. Ballwin this afternoon?"

"That's right."

"Where did she go?"

"Just to a dentist and shopping. That's all."

"Didn't stop at any drugstore?"

"She may have. We can talk with my operative who was shadowing her. He said she did some shopping."

Sellers said, "I'll take the name of your operative and have a talk with him."

"Glad to have you do it," I said. "He's Sam Dawson. You know him?"

"Don't seem to place him. I'll talk with him later. Who's the dentist?"

"Chap by the name of Dr. George L. Quay in the Pawkette Building."

Sellers pulled out his notebook, made a notation of the name and address. "What time did this operative of yours go off duty?"

"Five o'clock today. He reported to me about five-thirty."

"Think she might have gone out after five o'clock?"

"I had a night man on the job."

Sellers said, "Oh, it was that important?"

"Well, I only thought it was a matter of a day or two. I wanted to find out if perhaps she was interested in someone."

"Uh huh, I know. So you had a night man."

"That's right."

"Going to take on from five o'clock until when?"

"Five o'clock until midnight tonight," I said. "It was a short day, because this is the first day. Tomorrow the day man goes on at eight o'clock in the morning, works until four in the afternoon; the night man goes on at four and works until midnight."

"And from midnight to eight you were going to have no one?"

"I figured her husband could probably be depended on during those hours."

Sellers yawned, said to Bertha, "Donald always makes the case sound simple. He'll pitch you a curved ball, tell you it's straight over the plate, and then if you catch him at it, he'll explain that there must have been a wind blowing because he threw it just as straight as he could aim."

I said, "If you're trying to be funny, that isn't it."

"I don't think so either," Sellers said. "Well, there's going to be some explaining to do. Mrs. Ballwin slipped the arsenic in the anchovy paste right under your nose."

I said, "Have a heart. I wasn't supposed to be standing out there making chemical tests of everything that Gerald Ballwin put into his mouth. I was doing the best I could."

"Sure, sure," Sellers said soothingly. "You couldn't tell what was going to happen. I can see it from your standpoint, Donald, but the Captain is funny that way. He wonders how it happens that you managed to dig up the anchovy paste. The way you explain it now, it's clear to me, but I don't know whether I can make it so it's clear to him. You see, she needed something that would get the poison to him on a fairly empty stomach. The way I understand it, arsenic works a lot faster and a lot more certain if you give it on an empty stomach. Now if she put it in the soup, or something, and then the dinner came right afterward, it would have taken a lot more arsenic to do the job, and then there wouldn't have been anything certain about it because when he got sick, he might have heaved it all up; but giving it to him before dinner that way, when his stomach was empty, and giving it to him in a concentrated dose, really enabled it to take effect. And that anchovy paste was a positive inspiration. It had just enough strong, sharp flavor so she could have really loaded it with arsenic."

"I thought the stuff was supposed to be tasteless."

"The way I understand it," Sellers said, "is that the stuff varies. Sometimes people have complained of a burning taste when they've eaten stuff that has arsenic in it, but if you really wanted to poison someone and take no chances, the slickest way would be to get a fresh, crisp soda cracker, mix your arsenic in anchovy paste, and there you have an unbeatable combination."

I said, "Oh, well, there's no need to argue about it."

"Sure not, sure not," Sellers said soothingly. "That man you had working on Mrs. Ballwin tonight was pretty much asleep at the switch."

"How do you mean?"

"She took a powder and—"

"Say, wait a minute," I interrupted. "Don't be too sure. He may be on her, but hasn't had a chance to report."

Sellers jerked his hands from behind his head, shifted his position in the chair, and said, "And *now,* sweetheart, you've got something! If you folks have a tail on Mrs. Ballwin and he's on her right now, the Captain is going to kiss you on the forehead. Hell's bells, even if she gives him the slip, he can tell what she's doing, how she's getting away, whether she's headed for the airport, whether she's driving a car, whether she's taking a bus or going down to the depot. Cripes, just a little of that stuff would be a big help."

"Well, stick around," I said. "We should be getting a report."

"Of course," Sellers said, "if he was staked out there at the house and saw ambulances and cops come messing around the place, he might have just gone on home and called it a day."

"Not this chap," I said. "He's good. He's an old timer at the business. You hire him to shadow someone and he'll stay on the job. When he quits, he'll make a report. How much activity was there out there at the house, Sellers?"

"Not too much," Sellers said. "Carlotta Hanford, secretary to Daphne Ballwin, was the one who telephoned the police. Apparently Mrs. Ballwin phoned a doctor. She described the symptoms, and the doctor said it was food poisoning. He prescribed a treatment over the telephone, something that would work with food poisoning. But Carlotta Hanford knew what it was. She phoned another doctor, and told him to get out there quick, that it was arsenic poisoning. Then she called for an ambulance, and then she called the police. Boy, I mean that girl covered a lot of ground and covered it fast. If Ballwin recovers he'll owe it to her quickness of thought and determination.

She didn't beat around the bush a bit. She went right to the bat."

"She said it was *arsenic* poisoning?"

"That's right."

"And that's what it was?"

"Yes."

"Sort of a coincidence, isn't it?"

"I'd say so. Don't worry about us, Donald. We aren't dumb."

"How about the butler?"

"He served the hors d'oeuvres, but apparently Mrs. Ballwin made 'em up. Ballwin was mixing cocktails. He had the shaker in both hands. His wife took one of the crackers, had him open his mouth, and popped it in. Then she took one herself. The butler put the plate down and went back to see about the dinner."

"Was Carlotta there?" I asked him.

"Yeah, she was there. If Ballwin pulls through, it'll be because she was there and because she went right to town."

"Carlotta eat any of the hors d'oeuvres?"

"Uh huh."

"Get sick?"

"No. Don't forget Mrs. Ballwin picked out the one she wanted and fed it to hubby."

"What do you make of the butler, Sergeant?"

"Hates his job—may be playing around and thinking he could get a nest full of feathers. Don't worry so much about us, Donald. We aren't *that* dumb."

"And what happened after Carlotta telephoned?"

"She got action, but while she was telephoning, Daphne Ballwin saw the handwriting on the wall and skipped out."

I said, "Well, she—"

The telephone rang sharply and insistently.

Bertha simply pushed the instrument to one side.

"Better answer it," Sellers said. "In the first place, they know I'm here, and in the second place, it may be your shadow reporting on Daphne Ballwin. Boy, oh, boy, if that happens, that'll *really* be something!"

Bertha picked up the receiver, said, "Hello," then said, "Okay, hold the line a minute, he's here."

She motioned to Sergeant Sellers. "It's for you, Frank."

Sellers scooped up the telephone with his big hand, said, "Okay, what's the pitch?"

He listened for a minute, frowned at me and said, "Donald, one of my detectives out there on the job says he's spotted a chap watching the house. He shook him down, and the fellow has credentials as an operative and says he's working for you on a shadow job."

I said, "That means he's still there then."

"And that Mrs. Ballwin has slipped through his fingers. What'll I do? Tell him to go home?"

I grinned and said, "He wouldn't go home on a bet unless either Bertha or I told him to. That business of telling a man he's dismissed is old stuff. He's a veteran, I tell you. He'll stay on the job."

"Well, he let her slip through his fingers."

"She probably went out the back way. But, even so, this chap is pretty smart. Let's go out and have a talk with him, Frank."

"Okay by me," Sellers said. "And then we'll go down and pick up this operative that tailed Mrs. Ballwin on her shopping trip. I want to talk with him. Damn it, Donald, you folks may have been a help. If she went to a drugstore, your shadow will know which one. Well, let's go out and have a talk with your man."

"I'll follow you in my car," I said. "I want to get back."

"Hell, I'll take you back," Sellers said. "I don't want to be slowed down waiting for you to get through traffic. I've got a siren and we'll go places. Come on, let's go."

Bertha said, somewhat mollified, "I'll wait here, Donald. Give me a ring as soon as you get things cleaned up."

"Okay," I said. "Come on, Frank."

Chapter Seven
The Invisible Room

Jim Fordney, the operative I had hired to work nights, was a leather-faced veteran. Nothing ever took him by surprise; nothing ever ruffled the even tenor of his calm.

It was reported one time that Fordney and another man had been shadowing a woman along a somewhat crowded sidewalk, keeping just a few steps behind her, one on each side. All of a sudden the woman had disappeared, vanished into thin air. The other man had gone completely nuts. Fordney had gone back to about the place where the woman must have disappeared and kept looking around. Finally, he stepped on a loose coal chute cover.

It turned out the woman had stepped on this cover, shot down the coal chute, and was lying in the coal bunkers with a broken ankle, unconscious.

Fordney got the manager of the building, an ambulance, took the woman to a hospital, then calmly took up his station in front of the hospital despite the fact that the woman had a broken ankle.

The story may or may not have been true, but it could easily have been true. It was typical of Fordney.

Fordney looked up as Sellers and I approached the automobile. His wrinkled face twisted into a grin. "Thought maybe you'd be showing up," he said to me. "I wanted to get away and report, but I was afraid she might come out if I did."

"She's out," Sellers said.

"What's happened?" I asked Fordney.

"I've got it all down here, the time the ambulance came, then the time the police cars came. One of the boys is over there now. He came out and tried to chase me but I wouldn't chase."

I said, "Well, it looks as though she gave you the slip at that, Fordney."

Fordney shook his head.

"I guess so," I told him. "She must have gone out the back way."

"Then she climbed over a seven-foot board fence," Fordney said.

"Perhaps she went through a gate."

"Not without my knowing it," Fordney said. "I'm sitting right here where I can watch the only gate in that back fence."

"You must have taken your eyes off of it for a minute or two."

Fordney slowly shook his head. "My eyes are trained so that when there's any motion anywhere, they see it."

I looked at Sellers. "Are you sure she's gone?"

"Hell, yes," Sellers said. "We got the keys from Gerald Ballwin. My men are in there now."

"You searched the place good?" Fordney asked.

Frank Sellers looked at him speculatively. He started to say something, then stopped.

I said, "Let's take a look, Sellers, just for the fun of the thing."

"We'll check up with the boys," Sellers said. "Come on."

Fordney settled back in the automobile. "You want me to wait?" he asked.

"Wait," I told him.

"Hell," Sellers snorted, "what's that for?"

I didn't say anything.

We crossed the street and climbed the steps to the house.

A plainclothes man was stationed at the door. He opened it

when Sellers knocked, said, "Oh, hello, Sergeant. Come on in."

"How're you boys doing?" Sellers asked.

"Haven't found anything yet. There's only the two of us."

Sellers said, "Okay, we'll take a look around."

We walked through the living room where I had talked with Mrs. Ballwin earlier in the day, through a dining room, a serving-pantry, and into a kitchen.

The other officer who was searching the place was in the pantry rummaging around.

"Find anything?" Sellers asked.

"Not a thing, Sergeant. But I'm prowling around, looking things over."

"See if you don't find an extra sugar bowl or something of that sort," Sellers said. "Sometimes they don't hide the stuff, but put it in an obvious place."

"I'm looking everything over," the man said, "even shaking out a little of the stuff from each of the cans. Pepper, paprika, nutmeg, and all that stuff."

"That's fine. You've been upstairs?"

"Yes, we cased the joint, and then I came back to start a detailed search."

"Nobody in the house?"

"Not a soul. No."

Sellers looked at me.

"Did you look in the basement?" I asked.

The officer turned to regard me with an appraisal that lacked cordiality, with an undertone of insolence in it.

"Yeah," he said shortly.

"Let's take a look, just in case," I told Sellers.

"Oh, sure, I'm going to look around."

The officer looked at me coldly, quite obviously disliking the idea I was conveying that his search hadn't been good enough.

"How about servants?" I asked Sellers.

"Well, there were several. A cook and a housekeeper and a butler. We bundled them out and have them up to headquarters, questioning them. I don't think they know a damn thing, but we didn't want them hanging around the house while we were looking for poison. You know how it is. A servant sometimes, through a feeling of loyalty, will mess up the evidence for you."

"Let's take a look upstairs."

We went upstairs and walked around through bedrooms and bathrooms.

The front bedroom, containing masculine clothes, quite evidently was used by Gerald Ballwin. It had two large closets and a bath. The door, which evidently led to a connecting bedroom, was locked.

We found Mrs. Ballwin's bedroom directly behind this room. Here were a closet, a dressing room, then a bathroom which in turn communicated with another bedroom directly behind Mrs. Ballwin's bedroom and toward the rear of the house.

I tried the doors, looked in the various closets. When I came to the locked door, Sellers said, "That's the door that communicated with the other bedroom. Funny they'd have it locked."

"Let's open it," I said.

"Okay, why not?"

I twisted the knob back and forth a couple of times, said, "Apparently it's not locked from this side; it's locked from the other side. Frank, do you suppose this *isn't* the door to his bedroom?"

"Sure, it has to be," Sellers said. "His bedroom's on the front of the house, directly ahead of this one—"

"But look at the way these closets are made," I said, "and

there were closets on the other side. I don't think the rooms adjoin. Let's take a look."

I memorized the location of the closets and the dimensions of the house. I paced the distance back along the corridor, entered Ballwin's room once more, paced the distance back to the locked door, tried it, and also tried the knob.

"Same story," I said. "Locked from the inside. It's a bathroom between the two rooms, Frank. Both doors are locked on the inside."

Sellers looked at me. His eyes were eloquent. Then his big hand gave me a shove. "Out of my way," he said.

He went back a half a dozen steps, lowered his shoulder, braced his elbow, ran forward and hit the door like a football player hitting a line of opposing players.

The seat of the knob pulled out with an explosive, splintering crash.

It was the bathroom. The crumpled figure of a woman lay on the tiled floor. She was dressed for the street, but sprawled now in unconsciousness, the skirts up almost to the hips; the legs, neatly stockinged, bent at the knees; the garters showing a V against the pink flesh. Her head lay face-down and her hair was in complete disarray. One arm was half wrapped around the foot of the toilet bowl, and the other stretched straight out, her fingers extended as though they had been trying to get a fingerhold on the smooth, white octagon tiles.

The bathroom floor was a mess. Evidently the woman had had violent convulsions of nausea after she had become too weak to care what had happened.

I stepped around to feel of her wrist. There was no pulse. The skin felt clammy. I could see one side of her face clearly from this position. It was Daphne Ballwin.

Sergeant Sellers was pouring out a stream of steady profanity, directed for the most part at the stupidity of the so-and-so of the such-and-such who had failed to detect the presence of the communicating bathroom.

I heard running steps on the stairs. Then the officer who had been exploring the pantry came in on the run, his gun in his hand. He had evidently heard the crash as Sellers knocked the door down, and was all ready to gun me out or club me into insensibility as occasion might require.

He saw us standing in the bathroom, saw the broken door, the figure on the floor, and his jaw sagged.

"What have you got, Sergeant?"

"What have I got?" Sellers yelled. "I've got a dying woman. Some guys under me should never have been taken off the pavements. What the hell's the idea of overlooking this bathroom?"

"Cripes, Sergeant, I thought it was a communicating door between two bedrooms and was locked on both sides. I thought maybe it was evidence they'd been having a quarrel or something and the D.A. would want to have the door left locked just the way it was so it would be evidence of the fight."

"How's her heart, Donald?" Sellers asked me, turning away from the apologetic and embarrassed officer.

I said, "I can't feel any pulse, but there's some respiration. She's almost as cold as the floor. I'd say it was touch-and-go."

Sellers said to the officer, "Well, get the lead out of your pants. Get an ambulance. Hell, no, if we wait for an ambulance, she'll die on our hands. Pick her up and load her into the automobile and get her up to the emergency hospital right now. Get her stomach washed out. Get going. Tell the Doc it's arsenic poisoning. Get that through your head!"

The man slowly holstered his gun.

Sellers leaned over the unconscious figure, slid a hand under her legs, one under her shoulders, lifted her without the faintest evidence of effort, carried her down to the street, started to put her in the radio officer's car, then changed his mind, took her across the street to his own car. He called over his shoulder to the officer, "I'll get her to the hospital. You get back to the house and keep on looking for the poison. Don't let anyone in under any circumstances. Do you get that?"

"Yes, Sergeant."

Sellers flung back over his shoulder, "And try to do *something* right. If she croaks, you can see the fix I'll be in. If you let any of this out to the newspapers, I'll break you so fast and hard you'll wonder what struck you."

I was holding the door to the rear of the car open, and Sellers slipped the limp figure in on the cushions, looked at me inquiringly.

I nodded and climbed in through the other door, holding her steady on the cushions.

"You're going to have to hang on," Sellers warned, running around to the front of the car.

I braced one foot against the back of the front seat.

Sellers gunned the motor, turned on the siren and the red spotlight, and we went away from there so fast I felt the cushion flatten out at my back as the car pushed me forward.

A quick glance out of the rear-view mirror showed a car behind us, vainly trying to keep up.

I'd forgotten to tell Jim Fordney that he could go home. He'd been instructed to shadow Mrs. Ballwin, and he was doing his best.

He might as well have been standing still.

Sergeant Sellers kept it in second gear till he passed the second street intersection. Then he went into high, the siren screaming its shrill demand for the right-of-way, the red spotlight blazing, the police car shooting past frozen traffic, rocketing across intersections, now dodging and twisting as the traffic grew more dense, around the wrong side of streetcars, past cars that were stalled in intersections, the frightened drivers not knowing whether to go forward or to try to back up.

I managed to keep myself braced but I couldn't keep Mrs. Ballwin in one place. We rolled and slid all over the back seat of the car, but I kept her up off the floor.

Sellers screamed the car to a stop in front of the emergency hospital. I opened the door for him and tried to help him get the unconscious figure into such a position that he could lift her out.

His big strength brushed aside the futility of my efforts. He circled Daphne Ballwin's waist, pulled her out, and was running up the cement walk before I was even out of the car.

I had to sprint ahead to get the hospital door open for him.

"Okay, Donald," he said. "Get back to the car. Wait for me there."

I went back and climbed into the front seat on the right-hand side.

Fifteen minutes later a car slewed around the corner, braked to a stop behind the police car. I opened the door, got out, and walked back.

It was Jim Fordney.

"Got here as soon as I could," he said apologetically. "She's inside, is she?"

I nodded.

"You want me to wait and—"

I said, "No need to do anything more here, Fordney. One thing I do want, though."

"What?"

"Start in right now. Move fast. Some of the drugstores will

be closed, but some of them will still be open. Start at the Pawkette Building and cover every drugstore in the vicinity that's open. Tell them you want to see their poison register. Get me the names and addresses of anyone who made a purchase of arsenic within the last week."

"Okay," he said; then, as an afterthought: "Don't you want me to start first along Atwell Avenue near the Ballwin residence?"

"Definitely not. In the first place, I don't think you'll find anything there, and in the second place, the police will be covering that. I want my information first. Start at drugstores near the Pawkette Building. Use a little money, if you have to, to expedite matters."

"Okay. You want me to report tomorrow?"

"Call me at my office in an hour," I said.

"Okay. On my way. Just arsenic. You don't want anything else?"

"That's all. You won't have time for anything else. Get arsenic."

"Anything like rat poison or anything of that sort? You know," he prompted, "those things have arsenic—"

"I've got a hunch we're dealing with the pure quill," I told him. "We haven't time to do anything except skim the cream. I want results and I want them fast. Stick to arsenic."

"Okay," he said, and threw his car into gear, making a U-turn in the middle of the block and heading back toward the business district.

I waited another impatient twenty minutes in Frank Sellers's car. Then he came out and said, "Okay, Donald, I guess that's all."

I said, "Cripes, I wanted to bring my car. I didn't want to be marooned like this. Aren't you going to drive me back to the office?"

"No."

"How's she coming?"

"Too early to tell."

"Arsenic?"

"That's what they're treating her for, washing her stomach out and putting in some kind of iron solution to combine with any arsenic that may be left and make it harmless."

"She conscious?"

"You ask lots of questions, don't you?" he said, and turning his broad back, walked back to the hospital.

I climbed out of the car and started walking toward the nearest place where I thought I could get a taxicab.

Chapter Eight
Moonbeams on Flypaper

Bertha Cool was still at the office. I fitted my latchkey to the door and went on in. Bertha had propped the door of her private office open so she could see me when I came in, apparently fearing that I might go to my office without coming in to tell her what was new.

"Hello, Donald," she called, her voice dulcet sweet, in the technique she used when she was either frightened about something or trying to get something from someone.

"Hi, Bertha."

"What did you find out, lover?"

I said, "We found Daphne Ballwin locked in a bathroom. She'd evidently gone in there to be sick, locked both doors, collapsed, fallen on the floor and passed out."

"Poison?"

"Apparently."

"Same kind as her husband had?"

"That seems to be the general supposition."

"Sit down, Donald. Have a smoke. Tell me about Frank Sellers. Is he sore at us?"

"He'd better not be. I found the woman after his men had passed up the bathroom."

"How did that happen?"

"Oh, it's the way the rooms are built. The closets are big and unless you did a little measuring, you wouldn't realize there was a bathroom between the two rooms. It was easy enough to pass her up, I guess. The men were in a hurry to search for poison. They thought they'd find a sugar bowl full of arsenic or something."

"Well, if Mrs. Ballwin got it too, why then she was a victim just as much as her husband was."

"That," I said, "is the thought that is struggling around in Sergeant Sellers's mind."

"What's he going to do about it?"

"He didn't want me to find out. That's why he sent me home."

"What are *we* going to do about it?"

"We're going to try to beat the police to it, if we can."

"Why?"

I grinned and said, "Damned if I know."

"After all," Bertha said, "we're all washed up with the case, aren't we?"

"You may think we're washed up with it. Remember that apparently the poison was in the tube of anchovy paste that I gave to Mrs. Ballwin."

"You don't mean that they'll claim *you* did the poisoning!"

"I don't know what they'll claim. It depends on the quantity of poison and what they find. If they find any poison in the rest of that anchovy paste, we're in a spot."

"How come?"

"Oh, they may figure that I tried to drum up a little business by—"

"By poisoning clients?" Bertha asked.

"By giving them enough poison to make them sick, and perhaps they got an overdose. You can't tell. We won't check out of the case until we know more about it."

"Well, don't spend any money," Bertha cautioned, her eyes getting hard.

"We're still on the credit side of the ledger."

"We won't be if you get messing around with money. A dollar

doesn't mean any more to you than a penny means to a bank president. I don't see why you don't grow up. I—"

Someone was knocking at the outer door, gently at first, then with more peremptory poundings.

"For heaven's sake," Bertha said exasperatedly. "Do you suppose that's another cop—just when I wanted to have a talk with you, Donald."

"What about?"

"Oh, things. See who that is at the door."

I walked over and opened the door.

Carl Keetley, his face smoothly shaven and freshly massaged, clothes impeccably pressed, smiled a greeting and said, "Well, well, well. Mr. Lam himself. I wanted to talk with you a little more about one of those lots, Mr. Lam."

"Come in."

"Who is it?" Bertha called.

"A man who's trying to sell me some real estate," I said.

Bertha's chair gave a shrill, hysterical squeak. "Kick the dope out! Dammit, I want to talk to you and you knock off to have some high-powered, glib-tongued—"

"Come in," I said to Keetley. "I want you to meet my partner."

"Sounds like an amiable individual," Keetley said, following me to the door of Bertha's room and beaming at her.

Bertha's face was flushed. Her little, hard, glittering eyes surveyed Keetley in angry appraisal.

"Mrs. Cool, my estimable partner, Mr. Keetley," I said. "Bertha, this is Carl Keetley."

Bertha said, "I don't give a hoot in—"

"A brother-in-law of Gerald Ballwin," I went on.

Bertha strangled in mid-sentence, gulped, and suddenly extended a hand across the desk to Keetley.

"In the real estate business, are you, Mr. Keetley?" she said ingratiatingly. "I guess that's a very fine business these days. Land is one of the few things that is absolutely proof against inflation. I suppose people are buying right and left, though. But even if prices *are* high, it seems to me that the inevitable steady rise in real estate values and the fact that one can discount inflation is certainly a factor that one should take into consideration."

Keetley shook hands. "Very pleased to meet you, Mrs. Cool," he said, and then went on smoothly: "It's my own idea that only suckers are buying real estate right now. But their money is just as good as that of anyone else. Just what type of real estate are you interested in, Mrs. Cool?"

Bertha sputtered for a moment before her tongue could get enough traction to spit the words out. "Who do you think you're talking to?"

"Of course," Keetley went on, "if you prefer to deal with the hypocritical type who tells lies when he thinks lies will suit his purpose better than the truth, I can oblige you in that respect, Mrs. Cool. After all, as you have so aptly pointed out, real estate is a fixed value. People talk about gold, but gold doesn't mean anything because it can't produce anything. It's only an arbitrary standard of wealth as between nations. The individual can't even have gold in his possession anymore.

"Now you take land, Mrs. Cool, and that's something entirely different. You can produce something on land, and land is more valuable than gold because it is inherently capable of private ownership. Now if you—"

"Get out of here," Bertha screamed at him.

I took Keetley's arm and said, "I just wanted you to meet my partner. We'll go in my office where we can talk."

"I see," Keetley said, and bowed from the waist. "It was a real pleasure to have met you, Mrs. Cool. It's so refreshing these days to meet a woman who really speaks her mind."

"If I really spoke my mind," Bertha Cool said, "I'd burn your ears off."

"Of course," Keetley said as a parting shot, "the only thing that's putting real estate values up at the present time is the scramble of buyers who want to buy something that is inflation-proof. To date, land has not reflected the inflationary increase in prices that is beginning to be manifested in every other line. It is only the natural increases in prices which come from a seller's market. As soon as inflation begins to make itself manifest in real estate prices, you'll really see some fancy prices. However, I'll talk with you some time when you have more leisure, Mrs. Cool. So pleased to have met you. Good night."

"Go to hell," Bertha snapped. "Donald, I want to see you. Don't—"

I said, "I think perhaps Mr. Keetley wanted to call on us with reference to a matter of employment. As I understand it, his real estate activities are purely a sideline."

Bertha gulped a couple of times, then managed to smile and said, "Don't mind me. I'm rather abrupt at times."

"Are you, indeed?" Keetley asked, his voice having a well-modulated, carefully cultivated tone of suave surprise.

"You're damn right I am," Bertha told him, "but we get results. Donald has brains, and I'm a hard-boiled steam roller when it comes to smashing things that get in my way. If you want us to investigate—"

"I'll talk with him, Bertha," I said, and took Keetley's arm.

Bertha managed a wry smile as we walked out of her private office and into my office.

I closed the door. Keetley sat down. I sat on the corner of the desk.

Keetley said, "What's the lowdown?"

"What's it to you?"

"I don't know. I want to find out."

"There are several very good information bureaus in town," I said. "This doesn't happen to be one of them."

"Are you free to accept employment?"

I smiled and said, "I take it your brother-in-law will be a credit reference?"

Keetley pushed his freshly manicured hand into the inside pocket of his coat, came out with a billfold that was choked with money. "My references," he said, "are cash money, folding green oblongs of United States currency. Now, do you want to work or not?"

I said, "We'd have to talk first."

"You do the talking."

"There isn't anything to talk about until you've talked."

Keetley said, "You'd ought to know where I stand."

"Where do you stand?"

"Right in the middle of a damn mess."

"Want to tell me more about it?"

"I guess you know, don't you?"

I shook my head.

Keetley said, "At one time in my life I worked too hard."

I didn't say anything.

"I guess the thing curdled on me. I got tired of work."

"Allergic to it?"

"If you want to put it that way, yes."

"But," Keetley went on, "I can always make money. Sometimes I need a little stake. That's when I've been drinking and start plunging without using my head."

I said, "It must be a great life—only subject to a little worry when it becomes necessary to dig up money for your income tax."

He grinned at me and I grinned back at him.

"Smoke?" I asked.

"Thanks."

"I think there's a bottle around the office some place."

"Hell, no, I won't touch it—until the next time."

I said, "You seem to have recouped your fortunes quite a bit since morning."

"I have."

I said, "As far as I'm concerned, we can keep this up all night."

"Don't hurry me," Keetley said, "I'm fumbling around looking for the proper approach."

"Cards on the table is a pretty good angle with me."

"Yes, I suppose so," he said, and then added musingly, "The trouble with it is that it's so damned inartistic. There's no opportunity for any finesse and that sort of thing."

Keetley waved his hand in an inclusive gesture. "It takes money to run this dump," he said. "It's a good-looking layout. Nice furniture. Nice suite of offices. No ordinary dump."

"So what?" I asked.

"So," he said, "somebody's paying you money whenever you take an interest in a real estate subdivision."

"That should be obvious."

"It is."

"Well?"

"Did Gerald hire you?"

I simply smiled at him.

Keetley shook his head almost sadly and said, "My boy, I'm afraid I've got to indulge in deductive reasoning. I don't like to do that."

"Why not?"

"Oh, it involves concentration and that takes a lot of energy. If a man put in that same amount of concentration on picking a winner in the race, he'd use his time to better advantage. Now let's see, it costs money to hire you."

"Did that take concentration?"

"Hush," he said, "I'm beginning with the basic elemental. A high-class outfit. It takes money to hire you. Someone's hired you to snoop around....No, I don't like that word 'snoop' because you won't like it. Let's be more tactful. Someone has hired you to investigate something in connection with Gerald Ballwin's home life. It couldn't have been Daphne who hired you, because you had a man shadowing her this afternoon. Gerald certainly needed a detective. I didn't think he had brains enough to hire one. Of course, you were blundering around his place there this morning....Wait a minute, I've got it!"

"Got what?"

"Got the whole thing," he said, smiling triumphantly. "You weren't blundering around out there this morning. Gerald knew that I was going to be out there. He had you out there so you could get a line on me. Did you have me shadowed, Lam, to see what I did after I got the money from Gerald?"

I merely smiled.

"So that's it," Keetley said thoughtfully.

"Have you," I asked, "anything to conceal?"

He said, "Don't be silly. Who hasn't? You have. Your partner has. Everyone has. What's more, I didn't like the idea of people messing around in my private life. What's Gerald trying to do? Hook me for blackmail? I've never blackmailed him."

I said, "If you're going on a fishing expedition, you'd better change your bait."

The telephone rang. I answered it. Bertha was also on the line. I said, "I'll take it, Bertha; I think it's for me."

Jim Fordney's voice said, "Hello, yes, Mr. Lam, this is Fordney."

"Okay, Fordney, what is it?"

Fordney said, "I may be sticking my neck out on this thing, Lam, but the fellow who was covering Mrs. Ballwin during the day told me when I relieved him that she'd only made one trip, and that was to the office of Dr. George L. Quay in the Pawkette Building, plus some shopping afterward."

"That's right."

"I'm now here in a booth at the Acme Drugstore," Fordney said. "I've just looked at their poison register—"

"That the first place you been in?"

"No, I've covered four or five. This is—this is the sixth."

"Okay. Found anything?"

Fordney said, "You know, I've always tried to get acquainted around and see if I could pick up any odd bits of information."

"Okay, go ahead. What've you found out?"

"Well, they got the purchase written down here at two o'clock yesterday afternoon. Arsenic trioxite, by a Ruth Otis. She's a dental nurse. That's the only recent sale I've been able to uncover and this is the last drugstore in the immediate vicinity that's open. If you—"

"Come on up to the office," I said. "Come up right away. Can you?"

"Yeah, sure."

I said, "I'm interested in that information; don't let it out to anyone else and come up here just as soon as you can."

He said, "Okay, I'll be right up." I heard him hang up the telephone.

Bertha Cool, who had been listening on the phone in her office, said, "Who the hell's Ruth Otis?"

I said, "Don't mention names."

"Ruth Otis mean anything to you?" Bertha asked.

I said, "This isn't the time to discuss that."

"Why not—? Oh, I see. Okay."

I heard Bertha slam up the receiver.

Keetley said to me, "Very mysterious, isn't it? Very nice window dressing."

"What?"

"These mysterious telephone calls, showing the manner in which you're working—a nice build-up—I presume your partner places those calls from the phone in her office, and you do the same for her when she has a client."

"How did you guess it?" I asked.

He looked at me somewhat dubiously and said, "For the love of Mike, don't tell me it was on the level."

"Why not?"

"It sounds too damn theatrical."

"There's no reason why real life can't be theatrical."

"Not for very long at a time. Life is humdrum. It's monotonous. It's routine. Life is purposely designed so as to be paced to a slow tempo. Human character can't change rapidly. Therefore, nature incorporates all of her changes on a gradual basis. Take fellows like you, who are supposed to be in an exciting and romantic occupation. I'll bet you're bored stiff."

"Fishing again?"

"No, just commenting."

"Go on and comment."

Keetley smiled meditatively. "That butler," he said. "Now there's one for the book. Daphne loves to have him around her. She's made a slave of him. He hates the job of buttling. He doesn't mind driving the car. You know what, Lam?"

"No," I said. "What?"

"She loves to torture him that way, making him do the things that are distasteful to him. She's a cat, a big, savage human cat, and he's her mouse. His infatuation for her makes him helpless. He's her slave. So she loves to torture him."

I said, "I thought you never went to the house."

He regarded me speculatively, then said cryptically, "Would I kill my goose?"

"You are referring to your golden eggs?"

"Do I have to dot the i's and cross the t's?"

"It helps."

"Helps what?"

"Me."

He twisted his face, said, "I believe you really would try to pin it on me to protect your real client. I don't suppose there's any chance of paying you a fee to tell me what you've found out? Now, wait a minute, Lam. Don't get sore. I'll leave you free to represent your client any way you want to. All I want is to have you work for me so as to pass on any information you may get. I want to discuss that evidence. Can you do that?"

"No."

He pursed his lips, said, "Lord, but you're conscientious."

"I can't serve two masters."

"How do you know they are two?"

"I don't."

He grinned.

I heard knuckles on the door to the reception room. Before I could get to that door, Bertha had reached it and opened it. I heard Fordney's voice asking for me and then Bertha in the doorway called to me, "You want to see this guy?"

Fordney peered over her shoulder.

Keetley said, "Well, I'll be going. I just dropped in for a chat."

"Hello," Fordney said. "Want me to wait?"

I said, "No, come on in. Mr. Fordney, meet Mr. Keetley," and then added, "Mr. Fordney is the operative who called me up a few minutes ago. You thought it was an act."

"No kidding?" Keetley asked Fordney.

Fordney grinned. "No kidding."

I said, "I guess you've uncovered what I wanted, Fordney. There's no need of doing anything more. I'll make you a check."

"Oh, that's all right," Fordney said. "I'll fix up a bill and bring it in tomorrow, then you can—"

"No, I'll make you a check right now," I said, and opened the drawer of my desk.

Bertha said, "That's a sloppy way to do things, Donald. Why not let him put in his bill and then settle—"

"Because I may not be here tomorrow," I said shortly.

I held the checkbook on an angle, took a blank check and wrote on it, *I want this man tailed. Go down and get yourself planted.*

I made a big show of signing it and blotting the signature. I handed the check to Fordney.

Fordney glanced at it, and I saw that Keetley was watching his face, but there wasn't the faintest flicker of expression on Fordney's countenance as he read what I had written. He folded the check, put it in his pocket, said, "Well, that's fine, Mr. Lam. Any time you folks have anything for me to do, don't forget to call on me. I try to give satisfaction. I'll always do the best I can on any job."

"Thanks, Fordney," I told him.

He nodded to Keetley and said in a tone of casual indifference, running the words all together, "Pleased't'vemetcha."

He went out and Keetley said, "Cripes, I'm beginning to think you folks are honest. I guess that guy really did telephone. Was he working on this case, Lam?"

I said, very seriously, "No, it was an entirely different matter. We have a client who wants to find out whether the moon is made out of green cheese and this chap was sent out to get some moonbeams trapped on flypaper and take them to a laboratory where they could be analyzed."

"Gee, that's swell," Keetley said enthusiastically. "*I've* always wondered about that myself. I can tell you one thing, though, that after you get the moonbeams trapped on flypaper, you can't get a chemical analysis unless you put the flypaper in a box that has aluminum foil wrapped around it."

I said, "I've thought of that already. We've had the box all prepared."

Bertha said, "Are both of you nuts?"

"Just a little pleasantry," Keetley observed. "Mr. Lam and I understand each other perfectly. Don't we, Mr. Lam?"

"I hope," I said, "that you understand me."

"I do. I'm sure I do. Well, good night."

Keetley bowed low to Bertha, and shook hands with me.

"Good night," he said. "I think I like you people."

We watched him in silence as he crossed the reception room and closed the door behind him as he went out to the corridor.

"Now what did that guy want?" Bertha asked.

"He said he wanted to talk real estate."

"Nuts! What did he really want?"

"I think," I told her, "he wanted to find out if we were still working on the case, or whether now that Ballwin had been poisoned, we'd called it a day."

"Why would he want to know that?" she asked.

I picked up my hat. "I haven't time to speculate, Bertha. I've got things to do."

"Where you going, Donald?"

"Out."

She was standing there, face flushed, eyes angry, as I closed the door behind me.

Chapter Nine
Pretty Powerful Medicine

As I had anticipated, the front door of the apartment on Lexbrook Avenue, being designed to operate with any one of a dozen keys, required no particular skill to manipulate.

I let myself in, climbed the flight of stairs, walked back down the corridor, and tapped gently on the door of Ruth Otis's apartment.

I heard the rustle of motion behind the thin door of the apartment, but nothing else happened; so I knocked again, still using only the tips of my fingers, knocking very gently.

"Who is it?" Ruth Otis asked, from the other side of the door.

"It's about your automobile."

"But I understood you'd towed it to the garage?"

I didn't say anything.

She opened the door a crack. I saw a cautious eye making an appraisal, then her face showed surprise. "Why, Mr. Lam," she said, started to open the door and then suddenly closed it. "I'm not dressed."

"Put on something then."

"I can't. Why do you want to see me now?"

I said, "It's important."

She hesitated for several seconds, apparently weighing several possibilities in her mind. Then she opened the door. She'd put on a robe over pajamas and her feet were encased in fur-lined slippers. There was a newspaper over by the chair, where she had evidently been sitting and reading, after having prepared herself for bed. The wall-bed had been swung out and turned down so that there was but little room in the apartment. The one chair under the light was the only comfortable chair available. The others had been moved over against the wall to make room for the bed.

"What is it?" she asked. "I thought we'd settled everything about the automobile. What's the trouble now?"

I said, "Sit down, Ruth. I want to talk with you."

She flashed me a quick look, then settled down on the bed.

I took the chair and moved the floor lamp a little to one side. "You don't like Daphne Ballwin, do you?"

"Did I say that?" she sparred.

I said, "Please don't play ring-around-the-rosy. This is important. I want some specific information."

"Why?"

"Because it's important. It may be to your interest as well as mine."

"What do you want to know?"

"Exactly how you felt toward Daphne Ballwin."

"I hate her. I simply loathe and detest that woman. And I'm going to tell you something. If anything has happened to her husband and he's been poisoned—well, I know who did it."

"Who?"

"She did."

"I don't suppose you've made any particular secret of your hatred for her, Ruth?"

"No."

"Are you jealous of her?"

"Why? How do you mean? Why should *I* be jealous of *her*?"

"Because the man for whom you work was giving her a lot of attention."

"You mean that I'm in love with George L. Quay?"

"Are you?"

"Heavens, no."

"But you *are* jealous."

She hesitated a moment as though searching her own mind, then said, "It depends on what you mean by jealousy. If you mean that I resented the way she entered the office and completely disregarded my authority, the answer is 'Yes.' If you mean that I'm jealous because perhaps she had a place in Dr. Quay's affections, the answer is 'No.'"

"There was an assurance about her? She acted as though she owned the office?"

"I'll say she did. She came sweeping in there, brushing me to one side, acting as though I didn't have any authority whatever, any place in the organization. You'd have thought I was dirt under her feet. Something to brush to one side. And she didn't take any pains to conceal how she felt. The patients who were waiting could see it. It made me furious."

"So furious that you went out and bought some poison to give to her?"

"Donald Lam! What in the world are you talking about?"

"I'm talking about the fact that Mrs. Ballwin's been given a terrific dose of arsenic."

"You mean that she was poisoned too?"

"Yes."

"Wasn't Mr. Ballwin poisoned?"

"Yes."

She looked at me and I looked at her.

"Well, what do you know about that!" she said.

"Well, what do *you* know about that?" I shot back at her.

"Me?"

"You."

"I know nothing."

"You didn't slip any arsenic in their food?"

"Are you crazy?"

"You don't use arsenic for anything?"

"No, of course not."

I said, "Look, Ruth, I want to give you all the breaks. I'm asking you questions now in a friendly way. When the police ask you questions, their manner won't be friendly and their questions won't be friendly."

"Why should the police ask me questions?"

"Because," I said, "you went down to the drugstore and bought arsenic. Now what did you want it for? What did you do with it? Think fast. Answer the question quick."

"But I never bought any arsenic."

"The poison book says you did."

"Where?"

"At the Acme Drugstore."

She shook her head. "Not arsenic."

"What did you buy?"

"I bought some stuff for Dr. Quay. It had a Latin name."

"Do you remember what it was?"

"I wrote it down somewhere. Let me see, I think I have it still in my purse."

"Let's take a look," I said.

She fumbled through her purse, said at length, "Here it is. *Arseni trioxidum.*"

I said, "That's arsenic in its most deadly form. That's the poison that was administered to Mr. Ballwin and Daphne Ballwin, probably in anchovy paste."

"But—but it's impossible!"

"What's impossible?"

"That there should have been any of that poison given to them. I mean that they simply couldn't have had any of the poison I bought."

"Well, why not?"

"Because when I came back to the office and told Dr. Quay I had the stuff he wanted, he said to put it on the shelf in the laboratory. He was busy working on a patient at the time."

"Now that was sometime yesterday?"

"That's right. Yesterday morning."

"And what did you do with the package?"

"I put it on the shelf in the laboratory."

"You unwrapped it?"

"No, I did not. I left it just as it had been given to me, just as it came from the drugstore."

"Then what happened?"

"I don't know, I—yes, I do too. I remember seeing that same package, at least I think it's the same package, on the shelf in the laboratory, when I was packing my things up tonight. I don't think it had even been opened."

I smiled and shook my head.

"What do you mean?"

I said, "I mean that it will have been opened. The wrapping may have been put back, but you'll find that the package was opened and arsenic taken out. You'll find that that arsenic went into some anchovy paste that was put on crackers that Gerald Ballwin and Daphne Ballwin ate. And tomorrow you'll find that the police will start checking on the poison registers in every drugstore in the city. They'll look for purchases of arsenic that have been made within the last two or three weeks. They'll find your name. They'll look you up and find that you worked for Dr. Quay, and that Dr. Quay was acquainted with Daphne Ballwin; that you had reason to hate her and that this hatred was more than intensified after you lost your job on account of her. What's more, you'll probably find that Dr. Quay denies he told you to buy any arsenic or that he knew anything about any arsenic being on the shelf of the laboratory. That's what *you're* going to be up against. Now then, what's your answer going to be?"

She looked at me with her eyes pathetic and helpless. "I haven't any answer *to that*."

"You'd better think up one then."

"I—I can't. There isn't any answer."

I said, "I think there is."

"What?" she asked.

I said, "Beat Dr. Quay to the punch. Get him on the defensive."

"What do you mean?"

"Go to the police. Tell them the whole story. Beat Dr. Quay to the punch. Tell the police that you were with me this evening, that you heard me telephone my office and learned that Gerald Ballwin had been poisoned.

"Now, remember, and get that straight. You aren't to know anything about his wife having been poisoned, only what you heard Bertha Cool shouting over the telephone, that Gerald Ballwin had been poisoned. Can you get that straight?"

"Yes, I guess so."

"Remember, you're to tell everything exactly as it happened except that you're not to say anything at all about my having come here a second time this evening. The last time you saw me was when I brought your stuff up here to the apartment and left the money on the table for the automobile accident. Have you got that straight?"

"Yes, I guess so."

"You ring up police headquarters," I said. "You tell them that you want to talk to whoever knows anything about the Ballwin case, that you have information you want to give. Then go ahead and tell them what it is."

"Then what?"

"Then you hang up the phone, and whatever you do, don't dress. Stay just the way you are now, in your pajamas, bathrobe, and slippers."

"Why?"

"Because you want everything to fit into that one picture, that you didn't tell the police as soon as you heard about Ballwin being poisoned because you didn't think of it. You didn't think there could possibly be any connection. But you know that Dr. Quay may have reason to wish Gerald Ballwin were out of the way. He's been rather sweet on Mrs. Ballwin, that is, there's been a relationship there that isn't exactly the relationship of a patient and dentist. And above all, conceal any feeling that you may have. Don't be too sweet and namby-pamby. But don't let them feel that you've ever had any hatred for Daphne Ballwin. The only thing that you resented was the way Dr. Quay treated you."

She nodded.

I said, "The recollection of having purchased that arsenic didn't come to you until just as you were ready for bed. Then you thought it over for ten or fifteen minutes, and finally you called the police."

"You mean they'll come out to see me?"

"And how, they'll come! They'll have a radio car on its way here within ten seconds after you've hung up the telephone. The radio car will be here within two or three minutes. You won't believe it's possible for a phone call to get that much action."

"And then what?"

I said, "Then you tell them all about buying the arsenic, all about putting it in the laboratory for the Doctor, and then you go on and tell the officers that you don't *think* that Dr. Quay opened the package, but that you can't be certain, that you can't remember exactly when it was you saw it on the laboratory shelf the last time. But you think they should know about it."

"Then what?"

I said, "Then they'll go to the office. They'll find the arsenic. They'll put Dr. Quay on the carpet. Dr. Quay will be on the defensive. If Dr. Quay is on the square, he'll tell the truth and you'll be in the clear. If he isn't, he'll swear that he never told you to buy any arsenic, that he didn't know it was there on the shelf, and all of that. But the police will be expecting him to lie by that time, and they'll start bringing pressure to bear on him, and they may be able to make him crack. Do you get it?"

She nodded.

I said, "Okay, forget that I've been here. Give me about five minutes to get out of the immediate vicinity, and then put in your call for the police. Remember, wait a good five minutes, because the speed with which a radio car can get here will surprise you. And I don't want to be seen in the neighborhood. There's just a chance that the radio car might spot me. You understand?"

She nodded.

I wrote the address of my apartment and the unlisted telephone number on a card, handed it to her. "This is my address and phone number. If you have any trouble either give me a ring, or just come to the apartment. Okay?"

She nodded.

I said, "Okay, I'm on my way."

She slid off her perch on the edge of the bed and came toward me. She said, with calm confidence, "You ran into my car on purpose tonight, didn't you?"

I met the frankness of her steady eyes and said, "Yes."

"I thought you did. Is that why you paid for it?"

"Yes."

"You aren't going to be stuck for it personally, are you? You'll charge it to expenses in the case?"

"That's right."

"I'm glad," she said. Then after a moment: "Why did you come tonight to warn me?"

"Because I like you. I have an idea that Dr. Quay may be a pretty slick individual, and I didn't want to see you made a fall guy."

I saw her eyes darken with emotion. With a quick, impulsive gesture, her arms went around my neck. There were grateful lips on mine. I could feel the soft contours of her body through the thin pajamas, feel the warmth of her, smell the fragrance of her hair.

My arms tightened and then she was pushing me away.

I took a step toward her as she retreated.

"No, Donald," she said in a voice that was husky with emotion. "Not now. Please. Good night."

I turned and fumbled for the door. "That was pretty powerful medicine," I said.

"Thank you, Donald," she said, still in that same husky voice.

"Thank *you*," I told her, opened the door, ran back down the stairs and out to the agency car.

Chapter Ten
Donald Buys a Lot

The office of Gerald Ballwin, realtor and executive head of the new subdivision on West Terrace Drive, opened up precisely at eight o'clock on the nose.

I knew because I had been sitting out there in my automobile ever since seven o'clock, waiting for action.

The one who opened it was the slender, quiet girl who had been pounding the typewriter, copying the contracts, when I was in there the day before.

I gave her about two minutes to get her hat off, her nose powdered, and the cover taken off her typewriter. Then I opened the door and walked in.

Judging from the way she was banging at the typewriter, she'd evidently settled down and gone to work without any of the usual preliminaries.

She looked up as I came in. "Good morning."

"Hello. Mr. Ballwin in?"

"No, Mr. Ballwin won't be in for at least an hour and a half."

"His secretary—what's her name?"

"Miss Worley."

"Is she in?"

"She comes at nine."

"And how about the salesmen?"

She said, "They're not here right at present. But they come in sometime between eight and eight-thirty, as a rule."

I looked at my watch and said, "I'm sorry I can't wait."

"Is there something I can do for you?"

"I wanted to buy a lot."

"You were in yesterday, weren't you?"

"Yes."

"And didn't you go out with Mr. Keetley?"

"That's right."

"Then you know the lot you want to buy?"

"No."

"I don't understand."

I said, "Mr. Keetley's approach to the subject was rather unorthodox and unconventional."

"Yes," she said dryly, "it would have been."

"My name," I told her, "is Lam. Mr. Donald Lam."

"I'm Mary Ingram. Perhaps you'd like to look over some of the maps. Now that you've seen the property I may be able to tell you something about it from the maps."

"Okay," I said, "let's look."

She pushed back her stenographic chair, walked over to a shelf, whipped out a map, and placed it on the counter.

She said, "I'll try to give you the benefit of such experience as I have, Mr. Lam. That is, if you'd like to know some of the factors involved in selecting a lot in a new subdivision."

"I would very much like to know them," I said.

She took her pencil and traced the contour of a curving line. "Perhaps this wouldn't be considered entirely ethical, but it's my belief that salesmanship consists in making a mutually satisfactory transaction, one in which the customer is entirely satisfied."

"Most commendable," I said.

She glanced at me quickly, but saw nothing on my face.

She said, "Now you'll notice, in scenic subdivisions, the choice property which has the best view is naturally so divided that as many lots as possible are carved from the choice sections."

"Naturally," I said.

"The subdivider finds he can make more money that way. Now I have noticed that in doing this, while there is usually ample room for both a building and a garage, the *approaches* to the garage are difficult, and in wet weather—that's a factor to be considered.

"On the other hand, you'll notice that these lots where there is a good view but a steep slope, present a very peculiar building problem. The back part of the building must necessarily be on several levels. But with a garage to think of, you are again presented with a problem. It's necessary to either have the garage on the front of the house, or to put a driveway down a very steep slope. Such a driveway is always inconvenient and unsatisfactory."

I nodded gravely.

She said, "It's been my experience that if a person will select one of the lots that seems, at first blush, to be less desirable but is more reasonably level, has ample room for putting up a house and also a place where a garage can be located, so that it is really accessible—well, I think that, in the long run, the purchaser is better satisfied with a lot of that type. Furthermore, they are usually quite reasonably priced.

"When a subdivision is first put on the market, people come up and see the driveways and admire the view. And, of course, a view is a big factor, but comfort is also a factor, Mr. Lam. Don't you think so?"

I said, "Look, Miss Ingram, you're a square shooter. I haven't the heart to do this."

"Do what?"

I said, "I'm a detective. Gerald Ballwin and his wife were

poisoned last night and I'm trying to get some information about the business. I thought I could learn more from you than I could from anyone else. And naturally, I used the business approach."

She looked at me without the faintest expression of surprise, but with something of hurt in her eyes. "Do you think that was nice?" she asked.

"No," I said.

She took the map and flipped it off the counter to a flat shelf, and said, "Well, at least, I'm glad you told me."

I said, "Don't put the map away. I want to make a deposit on a lot."

"What lot?"

"Whatever one you suggest."

"Is this simply part of the approach?" she asked.

I took my billfold from my pocket and said, "I only have about a hundred and fifty dollars here. Would a hundred dollars be enough for an initial deposit?"

"It would hold the lot until you could put up the balance of the first payment. We try to sell them for a third down."

"What would a pretty fair lot cost?"

"I'd suggest one at around twenty-five hundred dollars."

"And a hundred-dollar deposit would tie it up?"

"Yes."

"Draw me up a contract," I said, putting five twenties on the counter.

"On what lot?"

"You pick it out."

"Mr. Lam, are you doing this just to—just to be nice?"

I said, "I thought you'd hand me the usual real estate hooey. I was going to see if I could cultivate you and pump you for some information."

"And you changed your mind?"

"*You* changed it. I'm beginning to think I could make money following your advice."

She pulled the map out again, put it down on the counter, looked at two or three of the lot numbers, went over to a filing-case, consulted some cards, came back and marked the outlines of a lot with red pencil. "I think this would make a nice lot."

"What's the price?"

"Twenty-seven fifty."

"Draw up the contract. I'll sign it."

She went over to her typewriter desk, flipped the paper on which she had been typing out of the machine, ratcheted in a form contract, and filled it in with swift confidence. She came back and checked the description carefully with the lot number on the map, and said, "You will note this contract is already signed by Mr. Ballwin. If you will sign here, please, Mr. Lam, and then I'll give you a receipt for a hundred dollars."

I signed the contract.

She went over to the typewriter, tapped out a receipt, signed it, *Gerald Ballwin, per Mary Ingram,* and handed it to me.

"I don't think I'd let you do this, Mr. Lam, if I weren't absolutely certain that even as an investment, this lot is a good buy."

"It's okay by me. Could you give me some information without being disloyal to your employer?"

"Loyalty to my employer consists of doing everything I can to keep the office running straight, to see that the records are properly kept."

"What does Miss Worley do?"

"Miss Worley is Mr. Ballwin's personal secretary."

"She handles matters in connection with the subdivision?"

"In a way, yes."

"His personal correspondence?"

"Some of it."

"How long has she been with Mr. Ballwin?"

"About three months."

"And you?"

"Twelve years."

"You must know the business pretty well."

"I do."

I said, "Pardon me for being personal, but isn't the job of being Mr. Ballwin's personal secretary more remunerative, and generally more important, than the job you're doing?"

She looked at me steadily for a moment, then said, "Yes."

"You must have known the first Mrs. Ballwin."

"Yes."

"And, of course, you know Mr. Keetley."

"Yes."

"And I suppose you hate him?"

"No."

"Miss Worley does."

"I know."

"Doesn't he come out and put the bite on Gerald Ballwin every once in a while?"

"Yes."

"But you don't hate him?"

"No."

"Why?"

"Because, for one thing, Mr. Keetley isn't what he seems. He isn't a periodical drunkard. He just pretends to be. He isn't broke when he comes out to make a touch. I think he just does it to see if he can't goad Mr. Ballwin to a breaking point."

"Why?"

"You can search me."

"So you think he's playing some deep game?"

"I don't know. Oh, Mr. Lam, I wish you'd really get some things cleaned up."

"What, for instance?"

"For one thing, why should Mr. Keetley want to have human hair analyzed?"

"Did he?"

"Yes."

"How do you know?"

"Because he wrote the letter from this office. He wanted to use a business address, he said."

"What letter?"

"One to a firm of consulting chemists."

"Did you see the letter?"

"No. I didn't know what was in it. I only knew he sent it out while Mr. Ballwin was away on his honeymoon—with Daphne. And the reply didn't come until after Mr. Ballwin was back. The girl who was Mr. Ballwin's secretary opened all the mail. She opened this letter, not noticing at first it was addressed to Mr. Keetley. When she read it she saw it was an analysis of human hair. So then she looked at the envelope and saw it was addressed to Keetley."

"Was Keetley angry when he found out she'd opened it?"

"He didn't like it."

"How long has Mr. Ballwin been married the second time?"

She said, "You can consult the vital statistics and get that information."

"And since I can," I told her, "it can't possibly be confidential."

"About two years. Two and a half, I guess it is."

"Did Ballwin's secretary tell him about Keetley's letter—the one she'd opened?"

"I don't know."

"Did the first Mrs. Ballwin die rather suddenly?"

"She was taken sick very suddenly. Then she started to get well, then after two weeks had a sudden relapse."

"What caused her death?"

"Some sort of acute gastro-enteric disturbance."

"Food poisoning?"

"I don't know. Mr. Ballwin said it was a gastro-enteric disturbance. Very severe."

"Was there an autopsy?"

"I believe there was a physician in charge. When there's a certificate of death by a physician, doesn't that eliminate the necessity for an autopsy?"

"I believe so. Do you know whether the body was buried or cremated?"

"Cremated."

"And the ashes?"

"Scattered over the mountain back of the place where they had a mountain cabin. The first Mrs. Ballwin was a nature lover and very much attached to the mountains. She loved to study birds and was quite an authority on them."

"I take it then, she wasn't much of a society gadabout."

"No."

"Mr. Ballwin was quite busy with his subdivisions?"

"Yes."

"And Mrs. Ballwin got more or less occupied with the mountain cabin and her studies of birds?"

"Yes."

"They must have been apart some of the time?"

"Yes."

"Had Mr. Ballwin known Ethel Worley before he hired her, or did he get her through an employment agency?"

"He had known her."

"How long?"

"About two weeks, I believe."

"Met her casually? Or did she apply for a job?"

"Casually."

"Why do you keep on working here if you get the raw end of the deal like that?"

"That's a personal matter, Mr. Lam."

"Of course, it is. It's a personal question."

"I don't choose to answer it."

"Is Miss Worley particularly competent?"

She said suddenly and thoroughly, "Ethel Worley has a beautiful front—and I mean a beautiful front. If you get what I'm talking about. It's nice in a sweater. She has a nice figure. She has all the assurance in the world. She doesn't know a damn thing about the business and she never will. And, because she knows that I know she doesn't know anything about it, she likes to flounce around and lord it over me. But she always calls on me to do her work—never as a favor, but simply coming out with her regal manner and assigning work to me."

Abruptly, Mary Ingram started to cry. I reached across the counter and patted her shoulder. "And you do her work all right?"

She sobbingly nodded her head.

"Couldn't you slip a mistake in it sometime and let her catch hell for it?"

She walked over to her desk, opened a drawer, pulled out a Kleenex, and wiped her eyes. Then she blew her nose and threw the Kleenex in the wastebasket.

"I wouldn't do anything like that," she said. "In the first place, it wouldn't do any good. Ethel would lie out of it in some way. But what do I care? I'm here to serve Mr. Ballwin. I'm doing his work to the best of my ability. He pays me my salary and I do everything I can for him. I think I've—I think I've—I think I've talked altogether too d-d-damn much," she said, and started to cry again.

I said, "Was the human hair Keetley sent in from his sister's head?"

"No. I don't think so. This was over six months after his sister died. Anyway, it wasn't a lock of hair, just a tangle, like hair combings—oh, I'm so miserable. I've talked too much."

"It was good for you to get it out of your system," I told her.

I looked out of the window and said, "Looks like one of the salesmen coming. There's a car driving up. Skip into the powder room, throw some cold water on your eyes, come on back, and we'll begin all over again."

She flashed me a quick look, said, "I don't know why you caught me with my guard down like this. I guess you have a way about you. You look as though you'd understand."

"I do."

She said, "I'm nervous this morning. I'm all upset."

"You'd heard about Mr. Ballwin?"

"Yes."

"How is he this morning? Do you know?"

"Better. Much better."

"And how about Mrs. Ballwin?"

"I didn't inquire. Heavens, is *she* sick?"

"Yes. She was poisoned, too."

"Food poisoning?"

"Arsenic poisoning."

"Oh! I was afraid of that!"

"Of what?"

"Poison. I was afraid someone would try to poison—well, Mrs. Ballwin."

"Why?"

"It was just a feeling I had."

"But you didn't expect Mr. Ballwin to be poisoned?"

"No, just Mrs. Ballwin."

"Why?"

"Oh—the way she treats people."

I said, "Okay, skip in and put some water on your eyes." But it wasn't a salesman who got out of the car that pulled up and parked in the space over to the side of the crazy little real estate structure. It was Ethel Worley.

She came breezing into the office, saw me, and gave me her most magnetic smile. "Oh, good morning, Mr. Lam! You're back."

I nodded.

She glanced over to Mary Ingram's desk and said, harshly, "For heaven's sakes, isn't that girl here yet?"

"Oh, yes," I said. "She's here. She—here she comes now."

Mary Ingram came out of the rest room, said, "Good morning, Miss Worley," and walked over to her typewriter.

"Was there something you wanted?" Ethel Worley asked me, giving me the business with her eyes.

I said, "Yes, I wanted to buy a lot."

"Oh, then you did see something you wanted."

I said, "Miss Ingram has already taken care of me."

"You mean you've signed a contract?"

"Yes."

"May I see it, please?"

I took my copy of the contract from my pocket and showed it to her.

She said, "Oh, this lot—lot thirteen, block seven. Miss Ingram, are you quite sure that lot is available?"

"Quite certain," Mary Ingram said, feeding a paper into her machine. "I looked it up in the card index."

Miss Worley said to me, "Would you mind letting me have your copy of the contract and your receipt, Mr. Lam? I want to check up on this lot, please."

I gave her the contract and the receipt. She favored me with a smile and a glance that was almost a caress.

She vanished into Mr. Ballwin's private office.

Mary Ingram, looking up from her typewriter, said tearfully, "Please don't take any other lot, Mr. Lam."

"Any other lot?" I asked. "Why? Why should I take another lot?"

"In place of this one, I mean. Can't you see what she's doing? She—"

Ethel Worley, sweeping out of the inner office, said regally, "There's a private memo on that in Mr. Ballwin's office, Miss Ingram. That lot is *not* available for sale."

She came over to the counter, took out the printed map, and favored me once more with her smile. "Look, Mr. Lam," she said, "I'm very sorry this happened. The lot which Miss Ingram described to you is off the market. Now, since you've been disappointed, I'm going to tell you what we'll do."

She looked up at me from the map and did things with her lips and eyelids. "We have here a lot which costs seven hundred and fifty dollars more than the lot you picked out. It's much more desirable. But, it happens, we've had a cancellation on that lot after part of the purchase price was paid in. I'm going to let you have that lot at exactly the same price as the one you've selected."

She pulled out a receipt book, said, "I'll give you a new receipt covering a payment of a hundred dollars on that lot," She said to Mary Ingram, "Make out a contract, Miss Ingram, for Mr. Lam, for lot three in block nineteen. And see that the purchase price and the payments are exactly the same as on that other lot."

There was a moment of silence. Then Mary Ingram, giving me one hopeless glance, picked up a printed form of contract and fed it into her machine.

I shook my head. "I don't want that lot, Miss Worley. I want the lot that's covered in my original contract, Miss Worley."

"I'm sorry, but that lot isn't available, Mr. Lam."

I said, "Perhaps it will be by the time I've completed the payments and you are ready to make a deed."

"But, Mr. Lam, can't you understand? This lot is infinitely better. It is on a higher elevation. It has a much better view. It—"

I said, "If I can't have the lot I purchased, then I don't want anything."

She said, "That's going to cause a lot of trouble, Mr. Lam. I—"

"I'm sorry, but that's the piece of property I picked."

She said, "I'd have to telephone Mr. Ballwin and see what the situation is on that lot. There's a stop-order on it in his office."

"I can't help that."

Her voice was dripping ice. "Very well," she said. "I'll telephone Mr. Ballwin." She strode back into Ballwin's private office.

Mary Ingram looked at me gratefully.

"What's the idea?" I asked.

"There wasn't any stop-order on that lot," she said. "I knew she'd come back with some monkey wrench to throw into the machinery."

"Why?"

" 'Cause then she'd make out a new contract with you and give you a new receipt for a new lot, and it would be *her* sale. She'd tear up those other contracts, and, as far as the records were concerned, she'd be the one who made the sale."

"You mean she'd go to all those lengths just to take credit for making a sale?"

"And to keep me from having credit for a sale."

I smiled reassuringly at her and said, "Well, it's all right, I'm sitting tight."

She seemed for a moment to be at a loss for words. Then she blew me a kiss.

It was a gesture of silent gratitude, and somehow it seemed awkward, as though she had seldom had occasion to throw a kiss to any man.

The door from the private office opened. Ethel Worley, coming out, said coldly, "Well, I guess it's all right, Mr. Lam. I had to get Mr. Ballwin on the telephone and get his personal release. However, you may have the lot."

I held out my hand for the contract and the receipt. She pushed them across the counter at me as though I had halitosis, body odor, and had been eating garlic.

"You talked with Mr. Ballwin over the phone?" I asked.

She nodded.

"How was he this morning?"

"Very well," she said, icily.

I said, "That's a relief. They didn't expect him to live the last I heard."

"What's that?" she asked, sharply.

I said, "He was poisoned last night, you know."

I watched the color drain out of her face. Her hands clutched for support at the edge of the counter. For a moment I thought her legs were going to buckle. But she managed to get control of herself, so as to say, "Are you certain it was *Mr.* Ballwin, not Mrs. Ballwin?"

"Both of them," I said.

"You're certain?"

"Yes."

"Thank you," she said, and turning on her heel, walked back to Ballwin's private office, opened the door and went in.

I folded the contract and proceeded to put it into my pocket. This time I was the one to blow the kiss to the puzzled girl who was seated at the typewriter.

Chapter Eleven
Playing for Keeps

It was about twenty minutes past nine when I walked into the office, nodded to the receptionist, and went on to my private office.

Jim Fordney was sitting in there talking with Elsie Brand.

Elsie said, "Mr. Fordney wanted to see you. I didn't think you'd want to have him waiting in the reception room. Sergeant Sellers has been talking with Mrs. Cool on the phone. I thought he might walk in."

"Good girl," I told her. "What's new, Fordney?"

Fordney said, "I tailed that guy all right."

"Did he know it?"

"No. He had a lot of stuff on his mind."

"That's swell. I thought he might be hard to follow. Where did he go?"

"Went to the Pawkette Building."

I whistled.

"He took the elevator and went up," Fordney said. "I parked my car, and when it looked as though he was going to be on the upper floor for a while, I went over to the elevator and said I wanted to go to the sixth floor. The night operator told me to sign the book over in the corner of the elevator. Then he asked me where I was going on the sixth floor."

"What did you tell him?"

"I told him I was going to see Dr. Quay about a tooth. He said Dr. Quay wasn't in. I told him I had an appointment, that Quay had promised to come in and take care of me. Well, the operator said there was no use going up until Dr. Quay came in. While he was talking I was taking a look in the register. The last signature on it was *Alpha Investment Company* with the initials *C.K.*"

"Go on, what happened?"

"I let the elevator operator talk me out of it and told him I'd go out and wait for a while and see if Dr. Quay showed up. I went over and looked at the board. The Alpha Investment Company has an office at 610. Dr. Quay's is 695. Do you suppose that means anything?"

"Damned if I know!" I said. "What happened after that?"

"I went out and parked myself in my car. After a while, a girl went in. That girl didn't sign the register. I don't know how it happened. I only know she didn't sign the register and I didn't ask any questions because I didn't want to make the night man suspicious. I thought if he got suspicious of me, he'd tip off the tenants that a detective was hanging around."

I nodded.

"So," Fordney went on, "I sat back in the car and waited, and after about a minute or two, the girl came out. And when she came out, Keetley came right along on her heels. The girl had a taxicab. Evidently she'd told it to wait. She climbed in the taxicab, and right away I saw Keetley was following her."

"Did you follow them?"

"Yes."

"Where?"

"Down to the Union Station."

"Then what?"

"Then the girl paid off the cab. She went in the station. Keetley parked his car and followed. I took a chance. I just stepped out of my bus and left the motor running. The girl went in and dropped a dime in one of those patent lockers—

you know what I mean, those automatic parcel-checking lockers, where you drop a dime—"

"I know," I said. "Go on, what did she do?"

"She put something in there, locked the compartment, took the key, went out and got on the streetcar."

"And Keetley?"

"Keetley seemed to have lost all interest in her. He got in his car and drove away."

Fordney opened his wallet and took out a red cardboard ticket, which he handed to me. "I got pinched," he said, "leaving my car there with the motor running. Was it okay?"

"It's okay," I said. "The Agency will take care of it."

"Thanks a lot. I didn't know whether I'd done right or not."

"You did right."

"Well," Fordney said, "this guy I was tailing went home and drove straight as a string to the Prospect Arms Apartments. He lives there. I checked him. His name's on the mailbox, Carl Keetley, Apartment 321."

The phone rang.

Before Elsie Brand answered it, she said to me, "Some young woman's been calling for you. She wouldn't leave her name, wouldn't leave any number where you could call her, but said she'd call back. She's been calling about every eight or ten minutes. If this is she, do you want to talk with her?"

I said, "Okay, I'll talk with her," and to Fordney: "What did this woman look like, the one that Keetley was following?"

"A neat little figure," Fordney said. "A gray suit, red hair, and—"

Elsie Brand, who had answered the telephone, gestured to me and said to the instrument, "Just a minute. Mr. Lam will speak to you." I motioned to her to hold it for just a second, and said to Fordney, "About five foot three, around a hundred twelve pounds, gray suit, tan stockings, green shoes, red-head—"

"That's the one."

I picked up the telephone and said "Hello," and Ruth Otis, her voice showing relief, said, "Oh, Donald, I'm *so* glad I got you! I was afraid you might not be in this morning. I've been trying both your office and your apartment."

"I was out for a while, working on an outside angle. What's new?"

"I want to talk with you."

"Did you do what I told you to last night?"

She said, "That's what I wanted to talk with you about."

"Talk now."

"Over the phone?"

"Yes. Don't—"

The door of the private office pushed open. Sergeant Frank Sellers, his hat tilted on the back of his head, a soggy cigar in his mouth, a good-natured grin on his face, barged through the door unannounced.

"It's all right, Donald," he said in his big booming voice, "don't let me interrupt you. You go right ahead. Bertha told me you were in. I just wanted to ask you a question or two."

I said into the telephone, "Just hit the high spots and don't be too specific. I'm in a hurry."

"Did someone just come in, Donald? I thought I heard—"

"Yes. Go ahead."

Sellers seated himself on the edge of my desk and said, "Hello, Fordney. How're you coming?"

"So, so," Fordney said.

"Shut up, you guys," I said. "I'm talking with a wren on the phone."

"Has she got a friend?" Sellers asked.

"How do I know. I've got to talk with her to find out. I can't read her mind and you guys are making so much noise I can't hear what she's trying to say."

Sellers raised one knee, clasped his arms around it, and grinned at Fordney. "Trying to make out he's a sheik," he said. "It's probably the bank on the line. Wants to know what the hell he means by being overdrawn five dollars and ten cents."

"Go ahead," I said to Ruth. "Let's have it."

She said, "You know that package we were talking about?"

"Yes."

"Well, I got to thinking that perhaps it hadn't been—well, you know, used after all, and I still have my key to the office. I was intending to mail it to—well, you know who."

"Go ahead."

"So," she said, "in place of making all that trouble and stuff, I just went up to the office and got the package and put it where it's safe all right, where I can get it whenever I want it."

I said, "You little fool, you've put your head right in the noose."

"No, no, Donald, don't misunderstand me. Before I did anything at all, I was very careful to see that the stuff was just as I bought it. It's just the way it came from the drugstore. If anything happens, I can get it and show—well, you know, that none of it was used. That would put me in the clear. I felt sure all the time that nothing had been taken out and by being able to produce the original package just the way it came from the drugstore—well, I thought that would be the best possible thing to do in case anyone asked me any questions. And I've got it where no one will ever be able to find it unless—well, you know, unless we should want them to."

I said, "I can't discuss it with you now. Look, last night I gave you an address."

"An address?"

"Yes."

"Why, I don't remember—"

"Where you could go in case—"

"Oh, yes, I remember now."

"Go there."

"You want me to—"

"Go there."

"All right, Donald."

"Immediately," I said, "and don't take anything with you. Did you get that?"

"Yes."

"That's all," I told her.

"Thanks, Donald," she said. "I'll see you there. Goodbye."

She hung up. I kept right on the line, saying into the dead telephone, "The big trouble is that he has three witnesses and there's only one of you. Yes, that's right. He has *three* witnesses, himself and the two men who were riding with him.... Of course he will. That's what always happens in those intersection cases. The right of way doesn't have anything to do with it. The man who is on the right claims he has the right of way. The other man claims that he was already in the intersection when the other car came tearing up at a mad rate of speed. Now then, you get out to that address and look around....I know the witnesses have already driven away, but there are people who live there, people who have little stores near there. Get busy."

I waited a moment as though listening to something, and said, "And don't let anyone know that you haven't a whole notebook full of witnesses....Well, I'm too busy now to go all over it again."

I slammed the receiver back on the phone and said to Elsie

Brand, "Elsie, don't ever put through calls like that again. I want to find out who's on the line and—"

Elsie said, "I'm sorry. I thought it was the woman in that embezzlement case."

"It wasn't," I told her. "It was a pest on an intersection traffic accident."

Sellers seemed unusually congenial, unusually naive.

"Well, what's new, Donald?"

"Oh, nothing much," I said. "I feel like hell."

"What's the matter?"

"Didn't sleep last night."

"Guilty conscience?"

I shook my head and said, "Aching tooth."

"Too bad. Why don't you see a dentist?"

"I'm going to as soon as I check in and leave a few instructions."

"Too bad," Sellers said. "An aching tooth can raise hell with your nerves."

"How's Ballwin and his wife?" I asked.

"Last I heard, she was unconscious. He's coming around all right. Guess there's no question but what the crackers and anchovy paste were poisoned. Funny thing, though, the laboratories don't find any poison in any of the tubes. The poison must have been sprinkled on the crackers after the anchovy paste was put on there."

"When was that?"

"We don't know. Mrs. Ballwin prepared them herself. She's unconscious and can't be questioned. The maid says Mrs. Ballwin had just started to prepare the hors d'oeuvres when the cook came into the kitchen. There were about a dozen of them on the plate, little, square, crisp crackers. The cook took over the rest of them, putting the anchovy paste on the crackers in little twists and spirals."

"And they were served how soon afterward?"

"There's the rub," Sellers said. "Ballwin was a little late getting home and the cook put the crackers in the pantry. Mrs. Ballwin had told her they'd be going out for dinner, so the cook didn't bother after that."

"How long were the crackers in the pantry?"

"Perhaps fifteen minutes. Not over half an hour."

"Then what?"

"Then the butler served them after Ballwin came home. Ballwin mixed up a cocktail. Mrs. Ballwin asked him to try the crackers. He did and said he liked them. He seemed to be in a better mood than he'd been for some time."

"How about the butler?"

"Don't worry, we're going over everyone with a fine-toothed comb. We're also working on Mrs. Ballwin's secretary."

I said, "You'll probably have a lot more to go on by this afternoon."

"Probably we will. What do you think of Keetley?"

"What about him?"

"Sort of a ne'er-do-well, isn't he?"

"I wouldn't know."

"Suppose he's working some sort of a squeeze on Gerald Ballwin?"

"If he does," I said, "he would hardly poison the goose that's laying his golden eggs."

"We've thought of that," Sellers said. "He may have been aiming at Mrs. Ballwin."

I said, "If the poisoning was in the crackers and anchovy, it couldn't have been regulated."

"How do you mean?"

"No person on earth could tell who was going to eat what cracker or how many. If Ballwin had been pretty hungry and had eaten half a dozen, and his wife had only eaten one or two,

Ballwin would have kicked the bucket and his wife might only have had a sick tummy."

Sellers said, "We keep thinking that stuff over. I was hoping that perhaps you could help a little?"

"How?"

"Well," Sellers said, "you've got a pretty ingenious mind, Donald. Now suppose you wanted to poison someone, say suppose you wanted to poison a man without poisoning his wife, and you had access to some crackers—"

"Go to hell," I told him. "I've got a toothache. How much poison did they get?"

"Apparently enough to kill a horse. If it hadn't been for Carlotta Hanford's prompt action in saying it was arsenic poison, the doctors could never have saved Ballwin. The fact that they got him in time was the determining factor.

"The wife locked herself in the bathroom and that made things tough for her. She got one hell of a slug of arsenic. Someone sure was playing for keeps."

I said, "Well, if I think of any angles, I'll let you know. Right now I'm going to get my tooth fixed."

Sellers slid down off the corner of the desk. "Well, good luck, Donald. If you get any ideas, let me know."

I nodded to Fordney and said to Elsie Brand, "I'm going to see what a dentist will do for that tooth."

Chapter Twelve
How to Beat the Races

Dr. Quay's office was on the sixth floor. The lighted doors showed two squares of frosted glass marked *Dr. George L. Quay, Dentist, Private,* and one door had a square of frosted glass with the legend *DR. GEORGE L. QUAY, Dentist,* ENTRANCE, and in the left-hand corner the words *By Appointment Only.*

I pushed open the door and entered the little cubbyhole which held a wicker settee, a table, a couple of straight-back chairs, and a basket full of dog-eared illustrated magazines. There was a mirror on one side and a door to the right of the mirror. This door was partially open.

The buzzer sounded somewhere in the inner office as I opened the door, and a man's voice called out, "Come in."

I walked on through the open doorway into a passageway. In a room at the other end of the passageway a woman was stretched out in a tilted dental chair, her mouth propped open.

Dr. Quay, a slender, tall individual, was bending over her, looking in her mouth with a dental mirror.

He looked up somewhat impatiently as I said, "You asked me to come in?"

He raised burning, restless eyes that seemed to take in every feature of my face.

"My nurse quit," he said irritably. "Walked out yesterday without so much as ten minutes' notice. I'm trying to handle things all alone here. It's a mess. What's your name? What do you want?"

"My name," I said, "is Lam. I want to make an appointment about a tooth. If there's any possibility, I'd like to have you make a preliminary examination and—"

"Go out there and sit down," he said. "I'll see you in about five minutes. I'm just finishing up here."

I walked back to the reception room and waited.

In about three minutes the woman who had been in Dr. Quay's chair came out. She was a trim, young matron, somewhere around the early thirties, a big engagement ring and a diamond-encrusted wedding ring glittering on her left hand.

She was smiling, a sophisticated little smile, and she looked me over as she went out.

I could hear the sound of running water as Dr. Quay washed his hands.

From where I was sitting, I could see a dark shadow form on the door to the corridor, the shadow of a man standing there, apparently trying to screw up nerve enough to enter the doctor's office, or else waiting for something to happen.

Dr. Quay stood in the door in a short-sleeved smock, his hands smelling of some perfumed antiseptic.

"All right, young man," he said, "let's see what you need."

The outer door opened. The buzzer sounded and Dr. Quay looked up, frowning.

The man who stood in the doorway was Carl Keetley.

"Good morning," Dr. Quay said.

"Hello," Keetley said, and then looked at me in surprise. "Well, well, well, it's Donald Lam! And how are you this morning, Mr. Lam?"

"Not too good," I said.

Keetley came over and shook hands.

Quay stood to one side, waiting for me to come in, looking courteously at Keetley.

Keetley said, "Be gentle with him, Doctor. It isn't often you have a first-class private detective as a patient."

Quay stiffened.

"I want to see you when you're at liberty," Keetley went on to Dr. Quay.

Dr. Quay's face was as expressionless as a piece of virgin white blotting paper. "Lie down. I'll see you in just a few moments.

"What was your name again?" he asked me.

"Donald Lam."

"Your address?"

I gave him one of my cards. "Cool and Lam," I said. "We're private investigators."

"Oh, yes. What did you want to see me about?"

"My teeth."

"What about them?"

"I'd like to have you look at them."

"Come in here and sit down."

I sat down in the dental chair. Dr. Quay put a towel over my collar and necktie, fastened it in the back with a snap, tilted back the headrest, ran a mirror around the inside of my mouth, took a long, thin metallic probe, and started in picking around in between the teeth.

"How long since you had any dental work done?"

"I never have had very much."

"So I see. When was the last time you had your teeth examined?"

"Oh, it must have been two years ago."

"Have them checked every six months. Any trouble in particular?"

"I've got a toothache."

"Where?"

"This one over here on the right."

"How long has it been aching?"

"It's a dull, constant, throbbing aching. It's been with me all night."

Dr. Quay probed around. "Yes," he said, "I think you've got a bad nerve there. That tooth may have to come out. You've got two or three more that need filling. I'd rather take an X-ray to see just what needs to be done."

"You mean there are others besides that one tooth?"

"Oh, definitely."

"How many?"

"Well, let's see. Here's one and, as I remember it, I saw a slight cavity over there....Yes, here it is."

"How much is all this going to cost?"

"Does that make any difference?"

"Naturally."

"Well, I can't tell yet. I'd better treat this aching tooth a little. Perhaps I had better take it out."

"It isn't aching so much now."

Dr. Quay took a syringe full of hot water, squirted it on the tooth. "That bother you?"

"That makes it feel better."

He squirted cold water. "That bother you?"

"Not very much."

"That tooth had better come out."

I said, "Gosh, Doctor, I've got a lot of important matters I'm working on today. Can't you give me something to deaden the pain a little and let me come back later on for the extraction? If you have some pills—"

"Not if you've got a lot of important work to do," he said. "Here, here's some Anacin. Take those as directed on the box. Come back here tomorrow morning at ten o'clock, and I'll take that tooth out."

I struggled up out of the chair.

"At that time I'll go over the rest of your teeth. I think you're going to need quite a bit of work."

I heard the buzzer sound as the door opened and closed. Dr. Quay said, "Excuse me, I guess that's another one. Damn not having a nurse. I've telephoned the employment agency. I'm going over there and interview four or five prospects. Breaking in a new nurse is always a job. Excuse me a minute."

Dr. Quay stepped out to the reception room and I jerked the towel off from around my neck, got up, and started out after him.

Quay said, "It was just someone going out. That man who was in here. I suppose he'll be back. You said you knew him?"

"Yes."

"Who is he?"

I said, "His name's Keetley. He's Gerald Ballwin's brother-in-law."

"His brother-in-law? Why Mrs. Ballwin is a patient of mine—I didn't know—"

"Brother-in-law by a former marriage. The first Mrs. Ballwin."

"Oh, I see," Dr. Quay said.

"Nice chap," I commented.

Dr. Quay said, "Tomorrow morning at ten o'clock I'll take out that tooth. Be here promptly at ten, because I happen to have a canceled appointment for that time. Otherwise I couldn't possibly get at you for three weeks."

Carl Keetley was waiting for me at the elevator.

"How's the tooth?"

"Better."

"Get it pulled?"

"No."

"You're lucky."

"Why?"

"Dr. Quay probably didn't want you hanging around."

"Yes, after your very tactful introduction, I thought myself that Dr. Quay was becoming unnecessarily violent. I gathered he wouldn't be too disappointed if I didn't show up tomorrow."

"Dr. Quay," Keetley assured me, "is not exactly a fool. It wouldn't be wise to play him for one."

"Was I playing him for a fool?"

"Well, you'll have to admit that when a man who is a private detective suddenly decides to buy a lot in a subdivision operated by Gerald Ballwin, when he suddenly has a toothache and goes to the dentist who takes care of Mrs. Daphne Ballwin's teeth, it *is* stretching the long arm of coincidence rather far."

"No farther," I told him, "than the fact that the Alpha Investment Company happens to have an office in such an advantageous position that you can keep an eye on the corridor and see who goes to Dr. Quay's office."

"Oh, so you know about that too, do you?"

"Yes."

"Interesting," Keetley said. "You *do* get around."

"I was intending to come to the Alpha Investment Company later on today to say that I had some investments I wanted the company to handle."

"Well, well, that would have completed the circle. Well, let's not stand here talking. Let's go on down to my office and discuss these investments."

He led the way down the corridor to a spacious office at the far end of the hallway. He unlocked the door, opened it, and then instead of waiting for me to enter first, said, irritably, "Dammit, I've gone out and left the radio on again. Trying to handicap some horses."

He rushed over to an oblong box, clicked a switch which put out a green light, indicated a comfortable chair, said, "Sit down there, Lam. I'll sit over here."

I sank into the deep leather-covered cushions and looked around me at the peculiar "office."

The walls had pictures of race horses, pictures which, for the most part, were eight by ten enlargements on glossy paper and suitably framed, pictures which showed a wealth of detail. The far side of the office was given over to a huge chart.

There was a big drawing-table under the window, a T-square, some colored inks, and the floor was littered with scraps of colored Celluloid.

"I see you're interested in my workshop," Keetley said as he moved the radio he had just switched off over to one side.

"I was just wondering what you did here."

"I handicap the ponies."

I motioned toward the drawing-table.

"Because you're a suspicious guy," Keetley said, "I'm going to let you in on a secret. Do you want to know something?"

"What?"

He said, "Pick up the paper. Tell me what horses are entered in the second race this afternoon."

I read off the names of the horses. Keetley made a list of numbers. Then he opened a long drawer in the bottom of the table below the drawing-board and selected some long strips of colored Celluloid.

He laughed and said apologetically, "This will show you what a man can do when he has unlimited leisure and a restless disposition."

He picked out various numbered strips of Celluloid, then placed them all together, one on top of the other; then dropped them one at a time into slots in a queer boxlike affair on a table under the window. Carefully he manipulated little knobs which moved the strips of colored Celluloid by fractions of an inch. At length he had the strips adjusted to his liking.

"Now watch," he said.

He clicked on a switch which illuminated an oblong behind the colored Celluloids with an intense illumination. Evidently it was a quartz light which ran the full length of a slot in the machine.

As the light came on, I could see a half-dozen wavy lines stretching up to peaks and down to lows.

Keetley once more began a process of adjustment with micrometer screws. Each strip of Celluloid, I saw now, made almost imperceptible motions as Keetley made his careful adjustments.

There were certain cabalistic marks upon the edges of the Celluloid strips, marks which apparently referred to weight, distance, and track conditions.

In the end when Keetley had the colored strips of Celluloid all adjusted to his satisfaction, he pressed them together and followed the wavy lines which showed through the sheets of Celluloid.

"This is going to be a pretty close race," he said. "You can see all of these lines are pretty much together. But notice the way this one line over here on the right comes to a peak that's just a little bit higher than those of the other lines."

I nodded. "What does that mean?"

"It means," he said, "that that's the winning horse."

He smiled at the expression of perplexity I purposely put on my face.

"For most people," he said, "working out a handicap on a horse is a slow and laborious process. Now I've worked out certain standard factors which cover the performances of every horse on the track. And I can raise or lower those standard tabs of performance to suit conditions.

"For instance, when I have a horse that likes a muddy track, I elevate his curve of performance by turning this knurled knob a certain graduated percentage, depending on the condition of the track. If a horse doesn't like a wet track, I twist the knurled knob which controls that particular action another way. Every time a horse runs a race, I evaluate his performance in that race in terms of his performance as compared with his standard curve of performance. Or, you might say, his general average. Then I make the appropriate extension on his curve of performance.

"Of course," Keetley went on, "a horse race isn't a mathematical proposition, something that you can reduce to an *absolute* certainty. There's always an element of chance in it. There are certain unknown factors. There are certain imponderables. But, taken by and large, I'm able to do quite well.

"Of course, you understand, the secret of the efficiency in this business lies in correctly evaluating the performance of the horse each time he runs so that the performance of each horse is translated into uniform terms that apply equally to all other horses. But, after all, that's only what every race track fan tries to do when he sits up nights plodding away with a pencil. This is just a short-cut—a sort of perpetual inventory on what each horse has to offer to the betters.

"Some of the sports writers also handicap the horses, and when they arrive at the same conclusion I do, I don't bet because the odds are against me. If a horse is a strong public favorite, it doesn't pay to back him."

"And you make money at it?"

He laughed and said, "It's a lot of work, but it's a lot of fun, and it pays off. Now, for instance, take this second race this afternoon. The curve shows that Fair Lady will win by about— well, it's going to be close. I'd say that she wouldn't win by more than a length, and it may be quite a bit less than that. Now, let's see what the professional handicappers have to say."

Keetley picked up one of the papers, ran his thumb down the listing, and said, "Well, this writer picks Satellite." He picked up another paper, said, "And this one is Satellite. Now let's see what the dope sheet is. Here we are, Satellite, the favorite."

"And what does that mean?"

"It means that Fair Lady is a good bet. The odds will be right. Now, what's the idea of snooping around Dr. Quay's office? Do you have anything on him, Lam, or are you just tabbing everyone?"

"Is it just a coincidence that *you're* in the same building on the same floor?" I asked.

"Hell, yes."

"You mean you don't know he's Mrs. Ballwin's dentist?"

"Of course I do. What's wrong with that?"

"If you wanted to, you could leave your door open, look down the corridor, and see everyone who came and went to his office."

"My God," he said, "if I wanted to know that, I'd walk down and take a look at his book of appointments and know who was scheduled to come for the next three weeks. Don't be silly. I have this office because I want a place to work where I can be undisturbed. I enjoy sitting here in an atmosphere of quiet, and devoting my attention to trying to outsmart the other fellow."

"And occasionally you run into a series of hard luck?" I asked.

"Occasionally," he said, "I go out on a hell of a binge. When I do, I make a damn fool out of myself. My reason ceases to hold sway."

"And then you make a touch from Gerald?"

He said, "At times, Lam, you have a very obnoxious personality."

"I have a job to do. I'm trying to do it."

"What is the job?"

"Right at the present time, I'm trying to find out who gave Mr. and Mrs. Ballwin the poison."

"So are the police."

"Well?"

"The police," Keetley said, "are better organized. They have more efficiency and they have more power. Why don't you leave things to them?"

"Sometimes they make a wrong guess."

"Not very often."

"Sometimes I uncover something that helps the police."

"Yes, I suppose you do."

"Who do you think slipped them the poison?"

"Well," Keetley said, "it had to be an inside job. As I understand it, the tubes of anchovy paste which you took out there weren't poisoned. And now, looking at it from a cold-blooded, dispassionate standpoint, it looks almost as though you were anxious to put temptation in someone's way."

"It wasn't that at all. I was trying to get Mrs. Ballwin interested in—"

"In what?" he asked, as I hesitated.

"In maintaining her home life in *status quo* for a while."

He thought that over and said, "It's surprising what damn fools people are."

"Meaning what?"

"Meaning that I personally think the police will have the poisoner in jail within three hours."

"Want to bet on it?" I said.

He said, "Hell, yes. I'll bet you—now wait a minute—give me a break. I'll bet that the police have found out who put the poison in the food and have enough evidence to get a conviction within three hours. I'll bet you even money on it."

"Do you," I asked, "have inside information?"

He grinned and said, "*You* have inside information, don't you?"

"Not particularly."

He said, "All I have is confidence in the police. We like to think of the cops as being dumb because we analyze them as individuals. You can't do that.

"In the first place, cops aren't dumb. A lot of cops don't have the education that a scientist would have. That is, it isn't the same type of education. But we overlook the fact that there's power in unity. When we think of the police, we shouldn't think of a collection of individual policemen, we should think of the entire police force."

"I know they're good," I said. "You don't need to try to sell me."

"You're damn right they're good," he went on. "They're a lot better than most people think. And on the other hand, people who try to commit murder are, for the most part, damn fools."

"What makes you say that?"

"Hell," he said. "Look at the record. Pick up your newspaper almost any Friday morning. What do you see? Tucked down in the corner of an inside page there's a paragraph about some poor guy being electrocuted or hung or stuck in the gas chamber. The trap was sprung at 10:01. The man was pronounced dead at 10:16.

"Every Friday there's a sorry procession of them, stumbling up the thirteen stairs to the scaffold, being led into the gas chamber between two attendants, marching the last grim mile down to the electric chair. They're fools. They've started out for eternity on Friday, the last grim stroke of torture that our civilization can think up. Not only do they deprive the man of his life, but they try to make him feel he's starting on his journey to eternity on an unlucky day. Damn it, they make me sick. The thick-headed incompetency of them!"

"Of whom?"

"Of the fools who die on Friday," he said, his eyes glittering with strange intensity. "They're the stumble-bums among the murderers, the ones who lost their heads, the ones who are incompetent."

"And sometimes the ones who are unlucky," I pointed out.

"Yes," he conceded, "every once in a while there's someone who had the breaks go against him. But that's true in every profession, in every phase of life's activities. Right now there are good automobile drivers headed toward the coroner's office. They've always got by all right before, but within the next few minutes they're going to be unlucky. A chap will come out of a side street, or they'll meet a drunk driver and—*CRASH!* There'll be the sound of splintering glass and a happy, carefree motorist will be an exhibit for the coroner's jury.

"That's the way it is all through life, so you can't pick on the poor murderer. Some of the best of 'em are unlucky. Some are lucky. They cancel each other out. The really good murderers don't go stumbling up the thirteen steps on Friday—only the dregs of the profession, the fools.

"Well, I guess there's a disappointed would-be murderer around today, hating Carlotta Hanford's guts. And I don't think he's a clever would-be murderer. I think the police are going to get him.

"Not that they'll be able to do a hell of a lot with him when they do get him. I guess Ballwin and his wife are just damn sick and that's all. They say he's out of danger and apparently she's improving."

He got to his feet, said, "Well, it's nice having you drop in, Lam. I've got to start work on tomorrow's races. The trouble with this system is that you have to keep it up. You can't let the thing get away from you. I like to read about murder and I like to talk about murder, but I make my living guessing which horse is going to be first under the wire."

"Well, good luck to you," I said, and shook hands.

The door clicked shut behind me. I walked halfway down the corridor, then suddenly turned back to see if he was watching.

The door was closed. He wasn't even interested enough to see whether I went back to Quay's office or if I took the elevator.

Chapter Thirteen
A Bear by the Tail

Ruth Otis was waiting in front of my apartment house. She was looking in the other direction as I drove up and slid my car into a parking place at the curb almost directly in front of her.

She turned around as she sensed the presence of the car, frowned slightly, then saw me.

"Donald!" she exclaimed.

I slid across the seat, opened the door, and she put her hands on my arm and squeezed until I could feel the tips of her fingers pressing hard against the flesh. "Oh, am I glad to see you," she said.

"Been here long?"

"Not very. About five or ten minutes, but every minute seemed like an age. Tell me, did I do something wrong?"

"Yes."

"But, Donald, that package is where no one can ever find it, yet I can get it whenever I want it. It's in a place where no one will ever think to look."

I said, "I'd have been here sooner, but I've been having a conference with Carl Keetley."

"Who's he?"

"Mr. Keetley," I said, "is a brother of Gerald Ballwin's first wife."

"Oh."

"And," I said, "he happens to be the man who followed you last night when you left Dr. Quay's office carrying the package of poison."

"He—he followed *me*?"

"That's right."

"But, Donald, he couldn't. I—you mean—"

"Exactly," I said. "Two people were following you. One of them was Keetley, and the other was a detective I had employed to shadow Keetley."

"But did Keetley know—you know, know what I had in the package?"

"I have an idea he did."

"You've been talking with him?"

"Yes."

"What does he say?"

"Nothing. He plays 'em close to his chest."

"Then perhaps he doesn't know who I am. Perhaps he—"

"Don't be silly," I said. "He was sufficiently interested in you to follow you from Dr. Quay's office down to the station where you checked the package in the locker-check compartment."

She looked as though her knees might be going to buckle under her right there on the sidewalk.

I said, "I don't like to rub it in, but if you had done what I told you to, the situation would have been a lot less complicated. As it is, I don't know just what is happening or just what's going to happen."

She said, "Then if he should turn me over to the police—if he should tell them—"

"Exactly."

"But, Donald, that package hasn't been opened. It hasn't been tampered with."

"How do you know?"

"It's in the same condition as when I bought it from the drugstore."

"How do you know?"

"I opened the package and looked at the little vial, and then sealed it up again."

"Wipe it off?"

"What do you mean?"

"Your fingerprints."

Again there was dismay on her face. "No, I was so certain it hadn't been tampered with."

"You didn't weigh it on scales?"

"No."

"How much did you order when you went down to get the arsenic?"

"Two hundred grains is what Dr. Quay told me to get."

I said, "Well, we've got a bear by the tail. If there were two hundred grains of arsenic in that bottle, you certainly couldn't tell whether a small dose had been taken out."

"Couldn't I go and get that arsenic?"

"And do what with it?"

"Gosh, I don't know. Throw it away. Destroy it. Get rid of it some way. Or call the police like you suggested?"

I said, "You can't tell whether Keetley has talked or not. It may be Keetley has gone to the police and the police have set a trap. They may be sitting there waiting for you to come and get that arsenic. Just about the time you get the locker compartment open and start out with the arsenic, there'll be a little tap on your shoulder, and when you look up a man will pull back the lapel of his coat so you can see a gold shield, and say—"

"Donald, don't! My nerves are raw enough already."

"Well," I said, "that's the situation. We just don't know what the score is. We're playing along in the dark."

"Oh, Donald, I'm *so* sorry. I thought when I saw that poison there on the shelf and it hadn't been opened that I could just get rid of it, get it out of the way and—"

"And when they found your name on the poison register, what did you intend to say?"

"I intended to tell them exactly what had happened. Can't we do that now?"

I shook my head.

"Why not?"

"Because now it sounds like a story that you've concocted, something that you've thought up to give yourself an alibi."

"But I don't get it."

I said, "Suppose you *had* poisoned Gerald Ballwin and his wife. You had been fired from the dental office where you worked. You suddenly realized that the poison you had used had been left on the shelf in the laboratory, that when the police examined it, they would find a certain amount of it had been used. You intended to replace the amount that had been used. You probably intended to do it today, but because you were fired yesterday, you realized you weren't going to have a chance. So just before you surrendered your key to the office, you went up and got the poison off the shelf. You took it down to the Union Station, checked it there last night. Then early this morning or perhaps later on last night, you went to the locker and took the package out, put in enough poison to make it come up to the original prescription, then you called the police.

"Once you admit knowing about the poisoning, knowing that the arsenic you purchased might have figured in that poisoning, you're licked. You can't give any satisfactory explanation to the police which will account for going to the Doctor's office in the dead of night, taking the package off the shelf, keeping it in your possession for twelve or fifteen hours, and *then* notifying the police."

She nodded. Her eyes looked big and pathetic.

"Get in the car and sit down. Rest your hands and feet. We've got some thinking to do."

"What can we do?"

I said, "There is only one thing to do—you're going to have to keep out of circulation for a while until we can get some additional information."

"Do you think the man who followed me has told the police?"

"I'm darned if I know," I told her. "He's playing a funny game and he's smart. Don't make any mistake about that."

"But how can I hide? Where can I go?"

"That's something we're going to have to think about."

She'd put her hand over mine, said, "Anything you say, Donald, I'll do."

I heard the shouts of a newsboy, listened for a moment to hear what he was saying, and gently disengaged Ruth's hand to reach in my pocket for a nickel.

The boy came around the corner shouting, *"Poiper, poiper, all about de moider. READ about it."*

I leaned across Ruth, beckoned the newsboy over to the car, handed him a nickel, and took the paper.

There were headlines on the right-hand side of the page: *Daphne Ballwin Dies*. Ruth's eye caught the headline. She gave a half-suppressed scream.

I placed the newspaper across the steering wheel where we could both read it.

"Donald," she said, "does this mean— Oh—!"

I said quickly, "Save it. There's no time for dramatics."

Evidently the news had come in at the last minute and the paper had thrown in a few paragraphs of lead-off on a story which had been prepared and set in type earlier.

When death came suddenly and unexpectedly to Mrs. Gerald Ballwin this morning, police knew they were confronted with one of the most baffling murder cases of the decade.

Daphne Ballwin, admitted to the hospital last night suffering from a case of arsenic poisoning, had all but passed through the most critical period when a sudden relapse, together with the complication of a weak heart, brought about her death.

Her husband, Gerald Ballwin, prominent realtor, had been admitted to the hospital considerably over an hour before Mrs. Ballwin's illness was discovered, although police believe that both were poisoned at the same time. The fact that Gerald Ballwin was given prompt hospitalization is, in the opinion of physicians, responsible for his speedier recovery. At a later hour this morning he was reported making very satisfactory progress and was able to telephone business associates, directing the activities of his large real estate business.

He was talking over the telephone with his secretary this morning when news of his wife's death reached him. Immediately he ordered his office to be closed until after the funeral.

The exact circumstances surrounding the poisoning of Gerald Ballwin, 34, and his wife, Daphne Ballwin, 32, residing at 2319 Atwell Avenue, are still shrouded in mystery, although more than twelve hours have elapsed since police started working on the case.

Ballwin, prominent in real estate circles, was seized with a sudden spasm of sickness shortly after eating hors d'oeuvres which had been prepared by his wife. Rushed to a hospital for treatment (continued page four)

Quite obviously the article had been written earlier in morning and with the death of Mrs. Ballwin, those first paragraphs had been revised. I folded the paper, tossed it into the back of the car, said, "Well, that's that. It's murder now."

"Donald."

I reached across and opened the door of the car. "Get out."

Without a word she stepped to the sidewalk. I got out after her and closed the door.

"Where are we going?"

"We're going to walk," I said.

I took her arm, marched her across the sidewalk, up the four steps to the little cement porch, fitted my key to the door, and hurried her along the hall and into the automatic elevator.

"Your apartment?" she asked.

I nodded.

She looked at me speculatively for a moment, then moved over into the corner of the elevator.

I punched the button for the third floor and the door slowly closed. The elevator creaked up the shaft.

Ruth said nothing.

When the elevator stopped and the door slid open, I took her arm, piloted her down the corridor, fitted the key to the lock of my apartment, and all but pushed her through the door.

I said, "The place is a mess. I don't have maid service, only once a week. You won't be disturbed here. If the telephone rings, don't answer it. If anyone knocks at the door, don't go near it.

"Now, here's a code for the telephone. If I should want you I'll dial the apartment. You'll hear the phone ring. Don't pay any attention to it. Don't go near it. Just look at your watch.

"I'll let the phone ring about four or five times, then I'll hang up. Exactly two minutes later I'll call you again and do the same thing. Then exactly two minutes after that, I'll call you for the third time.

"You can keep an eye on your watch. If the three calls come through spaced exactly two minutes apart, you answer the third call. Is that clear?"

She nodded.

I said, "There's only one way out of this for you. I don't know whether we can make it stick. It depends on how good an actress you are."

"What do you want me to do?"

I said, "There's only one thing we *can* do, and we've got to do it fast."

"What?"

I said, "You can't go to the police and tell them about that package of poison now, because you can't account for the delay."

"You covered that before."

"I'm just pointing the thing out to you again. I'll have to go get that poison and turn it over to the police."

"How do you mean?"

I said, "I'll go down to the Union Station. I'll make certain that I'm not being followed. I'll *try* to make sure no one is watching those lockers waiting to pick up the person who takes the poison out. Then I'll walk over and take out the package of poison."

"But can you tell if they're watching? There are so many people around there and—"

"I can't tell," I told her. "That is, I can't guarantee anything, but I'll do the best I can."

"But suppose you miss it?"

"If I miss it," I said, "then someone taps me on the shoulder when I'm taking the package of poison out. I'll tell them that you came to me, told me that you remembered Dr. Quay had sent you out for some arsenic. That you didn't know what to do. That you didn't want to consult the police without talking to me first. That you tried to get me last night and couldn't; that you went to the office, got the poison, put it in the locker, and then when you got in touch with me, you immediately turned the key to the locker over to me and made a full report and asked me if I would tell the police.

"I told you that I'd make an investigation. If the package of poison was in the locker as you said, and if it appeared that you had purchased it and taken it to Dr. Quay's office, I would then notify the police. But that I wasn't going to go running around with a story that turned out to be a false alarm.

"Do you get that?"

She nodded.

"In other words," I said, "I want to establish a position of a certain skepticism on my part. I told you I wasn't going to stick my neck out and be made the laughingstock of the police. I said I'd have to investigate your story before I could go to them."

She said, dubiously, "Would the police believe that?"

"No, but a jury might."

"It's too dangerous, Donald."

"No, it's the only way out."

"I'm afraid of it. Oh, Donald, I'm afraid of everything."

"In order to put that across," I went on, "I'll have to adopt an attitude of bored indifference to you personally. You will have to adopt the attitude of being absolutely fascinated by me. I have won your confidence. You are a shy, retiring, modest girl. You can't bear to think of going to the police, but you want to see justice done, so you came to me. Do you get the sketch? You'll have to be absolutely crazy about me. All wrapped up in worshipful affection. Do you understand?"

She nodded again.

I said, "That's where the part comes in that you have to act out. Everything depends on it. I'm all steamed up over the murder case. I can't see you at all. You're nuts about me. You'd only ask for the chance to die for me. I wouldn't lift a finger for you. I'm busy and preoccupied. Do you think you can put a sketch like that across?"

The corners of her mouth twisted in a faintly wistful smile. "I think I can do it convincingly, Donald," she said quietly. "My part at least."

I said, "Remember, there can't be any slip-up. You came to me and poured your heart out. I was skeptical. I wouldn't even go to the police until after I'd made an investigation. But I put you here in the apartment and told you not to leave; that if I found the poison and things were as you said, I was going direct to Sergeant Frank Sellers of Homicide and bring him here to listen to your story. Can you remember that?"

"Certainly."

"That's all there is to it."

"But, Donald, you're taking a terrific risk."

"Not if things work out the way I hope they will."

"But suppose they don't work out that way?"

"Then I'm taking a risk."

"Why?" she asked. "Why are you doing all that for me?"

I said, "I'm damned if I know. I guess it was that kiss last night."

"Donald, I don't want things that way."

"What way?"

"I wasn't trying to vamp you."

"I know it."

"I like you. You're nice."

"Thanks."

"And I don't want you getting into any trouble on my account. I can't ask you to do this for me."

"You're not asking me. I'm doing it."

"I think you're taking more risks than you say you are."

I shook my head and said, "Give me the key to the locker."

She opened her big purse, looked in the coin purse, frowned, then smiled and reached for the side pocket in her tailored suit.

I saw the sudden dismay in her eyes. "What's the matter?"

She said, "I left it in the pocket of the coat of that other suit. I put on another suit this morning."

"What did you do with the one you were wearing last night— send it to the cleaners?"

"No, it's in my closet."

"And the key's in it?"

She nodded, then said after a moment, "Shall I go get it?"

I shook my head.

"You're not even going near your apartment. Give me the keys."

She handed me a key from her coin purse.

"Where's the suit?"

"You go into the apartment. The closet door's the first one on the left. The suit is on a hanger, and the key is in the left-hand side pocket of the coat."

I said, "Okay. Wait here until I get back. Remember what I told you about answering the phone."

"Donald, I—" She was up out of her chair, coming to me, her lips half-parted, her eyes swimming.

"Donald," she said, chokingly.

And then suddenly she turned away.

"Well?" I asked.

She had her back to me, looking out of the window. She shook her head.

"What is it, Ruth?"

"I can't," she said. "I shouldn't have last night. It—it did things to you and now you're running a risk on my account just because of—well, of that."

I said, "That was last night, and I've already decided on running the risk. This isn't going to make it any greater."

She kept her back to me, looking out of the window.

"Donald, don't," she said, and I knew then from the tone of her voice she was crying.

I walked over to her, put my hands on her shoulders, started to turn her around.

"Don't, Donald. Can't you see that—it does things to me, too."

Chapter Fourteen
Murder Keeps on Happening

I slammed the agency car to a stop in front of the apartment house on Lexbrook Avenue and dashed across to the entrance. I fitted Ruth's key to the door.

As the lock clicked back and I pushed the outer door open, I looked back casually over my shoulder.

I couldn't see anyone taking the slightest interest in what I was doing. There were cars parked here and there along the block, but I couldn't see anyone sitting in any of them.

I took the steps two at a time, walked down the corridor to Ruth's apartment. Without any preliminary knock, I fitted the key to the lock in the door, paused, looked up and down the corridor to make certain no one was watching, and then clicked the lock back, pushed open the door, and stepped into the apartment.

Some instinct warned me. I ducked.

I wasn't quick enough. It felt as though the roof had caved in on me. I felt the strength ebbing out of my legs. The faded red carpet was rushing up at me. It hit me on the face, and blackness engulfed me.

In a vague way, I knew that time had passed. I couldn't tell how much time. Time didn't mean anything. I was sick, and something kept boring into my brain, a peculiar drill that sounded loud for a while, then subsided. It was like a dentist's drill, only it was fully automatic. It didn't need anyone to work it. It kept boring away in my brain.

I managed to get my eyes open. Slowly my senses came back to me.

I was lying on the thin carpet of Ruth Otis's apartment. The smell of floor dust was in my nostrils. The noise I had been hearing which sounded like a dentist's drill was the droning of a big green fly that buzzed in circles around my head, then settled down for a moment, only to start droning away in circles again after a few seconds.

I tried listening to see if anyone was in the apartment. Outside of the buzzing fly, I couldn't hear a thing.

I couldn't see anything except the legs of chairs, the legs and underside of the table.

I tried flexing the muscles of my arms and legs. I had a terrific headache, my stomach felt sick, but my muscles all seemed to respond.

I took a deep breath, listened for a moment, then gathered my strength, and suddenly got to my hands and knees, then jumped to my feet.

Nothing happened.

I seemed to be alone in the apartment. The place had that deserted, dejected air which clings to a vacant apartment during the middle of the day.

There was an atmosphere of gloomy unreality about the place. The apartment seemed barren now that Ruth's personality had been withdrawn. It was like seeing the clothes of someone you loved empty and dejected on a coat hanger.

My head was getting clearer all the time, but it still ached. I walked to the bathroom door and jerked it open.

No one was inside.

I pussyfooted up to the closet, whipped that door open, and jumped back.

Nothing happened.

I had the apartment to myself.

I diffidently reached in the closet and found the gray coat Ruth had been wearing the night before.

I slid a tentative hand down into the left-hand side pocket, then the right-hand side.

I hadn't expected to find anything; so it was a shock to me to feel the cool touch of flat metal against the tips of my fingers.

Halfway expecting some booby trap, I fished the key to the locker at the Union Station out of the pocket.

I think I was surprised when I had the key in my fingers and no gun had been fired, no brazen-throated gong had broken into staccato alarm, no whistles had been blown.

I waited, looking at the key for a moment, then reached an abrupt decision and dropped it into my vest pocket.

I stood there for a moment, making a last-minute survey of the apartment, and decided that if I was going to make a thorough job of the place, I'd better take a look at the place where the wall-bed was kept.

I opened the door; the bed swiveled smoothly outward, all nicely made up, the top sheet neatly folded back. There was an end space in the back. A shoe protruded from this end space. I looked at that shoe. A leg was in it.

I jumped back.

Nothing happened. The leg remained motionless. I switched on a light. A feminine figure was slumped in the corner, a motionless feminine figure that looked inert.

I felt of the wrist. It was still warm but lifeless. I tilted up the head.

The light shone on the dead face of Ethel Worley. A Nylon stocking had been twisted around her neck.

I made certain she was dead; then I backed out of the closet-like space, gently swung the bed back into position and latched the door shut.

I walked over to the corridor door, put my handkerchief around the doorknob, very slowly twisted the knob. Then I used my other hand gently to turn the knob of the spring lock.

When I had them both back, I jerked the door open.

There was no one in the corridor.

I pulled the door shut behind me, ran down the steps to the lobby. There was a phone there. I dropped a nickel, dialed Headquarters, asked for Homicide, and inquired for Sergeant Sellers.

A moment later, I heard Frank Sellers's voice.

"Donald Lam, Sergeant."

"Hello, Donald. I want to see you. Where are you?"

"1627 Lexbrook Avenue," I said. "You'd better get here fast."

"What's the idea?" Sellers grumbled. "Suppose you come to me for a change. I—"

"The body of Ethel Worley, Gerald Ballwin's secretary," I said, "is lying in the place where the wall-bed is kept, in an apartment that's in the name of Ruth Otis, and—"

Right in the middle of a sentence, I pressed the hook for the receiver down so that it broke the connection and left the line dead.

I slid the receiver into place, opened the door of the phone booth, jerked open the street door to the apartment.

When the blaze of outer sunlight hit my eyes, I winced from the pain in my tortured head.

A moment later my head had cleared enough so I could take in the sunswept street with its parked automobiles, its air of noonday indifference.

The Agency heap was still parked at the curb right where I had left it.

I shook my head, trying to clear it, and decided that was a mistake. I ran down the stairs, crossed to the car, opened the door and jumped in.

No one followed me as I drove away.

Chapter Fifteen
The Contents of a Locker

I found a stall for my car at the parking station at the Union Depot.

No one seemed to be following me.

I walked back along the hot sidewalk through the glare of the intense sun, joined the trickle of people who were moving into the station, and once inside, worked my way over to the crowded soda fountain.

I had a Coke and took two aspirin tablets.

No one seemed to be paying very much attention to me.

I walked over to the phone booth.

As nearly as I could tell, there was just the ordinary bustle of people coming and going. At this hour of the day the depot wasn't particularly crowded. The morning trains had disgorged their passengers and it would be another three or four hours before the afternoon trains began to wend their transcontinental way, carrying their streams of travelers.

I found an empty phone booth and dialed my bookmaker.

"How does Fair Lady look to you in the second race this afternoon?" I asked.

"Five to one shot. Want any?"

"A hundred bucks?"

He whistled. "That's plunging for you, Lam."

"Faint heart never won fair lady," I said.

"Another crack like that and the odds will go down to two to one," the bookie said over the phone. "God, I believe you just picked the horse so you could pull the gag. All right, you're covered. Goodbye."

I strolled out of the phone booth.

No one seemed to care where I went or when.

I walked over to the section where the parcel lockers were located, spotted the location of number twenty-three.

No one seemed to be watching the place.

I took a deep breath and remembered what I'd told the broker: "Faint heart never won fair lady."

I slipped the key out of my pocket, walked directly up to the locker and fitted the key.

The key wouldn't slip into the lock. Then I noticed the sign above the lock which said there was a charge of ten cents for each twelve hours. Parcels left more than twelve hours required an extra ten cents.

I dropped a dime into the slot and heard the click as the time-lock mechanism was set back.

I twisted the key.

The locker opened.

There wasn't a thing in it.

I pushed my right arm into the locker, felt around the inside, then stooped so I could get my head on a level with it and see every inch of the space.

Not a thing was in there.

I left the key in the locker, closed the door, and walked away.

Chapter Sixteen
Hotter Than a Stove Lid

I hoped that Bertha would be out for lunch.

She wasn't.

The new receptionist said, "Mrs. Cool wants to see you right away. She's waiting in her office."

I said, "All right. I'll go in and see her in a minute."

"I'll tell her you're here."

"No, don't. I'll go in and see her."

"But she wanted to know just as soon as you came in."

I said, "I have something to do first. It will only take a minute. I'll go in and see her as soon as I've done that. Don't tell her I'm here."

The receptionist looked at me with a puckered brow. She looked as though she might break out crying.

I laughed and said, "All right, go ahead and tell her, if you have to," and walked into my private office.

Elsie Brand said, "My God, Donald, you look terrible. What's happened?"

"I've had a jolt."

"Want to talk about it?"

"No."

I saw the sympathy in her eyes and said, "Someone cracked me on the back of the head and put me out like a light. I've got a headache and my whole spine is beginning to feel stiff as a board."

"Why don't you go to a Turkish bath?"

"I haven't got time."

"Well, *take* time, then," she said. "You can think in a Turkish bath as well as—"

The door jerked open and Bertha said, "You chiseling little runt. What do you mean running out on me right when this thing begins to get hot?"

"I've been working on the case."

"Working on the case!" Bertha Cool screamed at me. "*You* don't even know what the case is! *You're* working on *yesterday's* case. What kind of a dump are we running anyway, when we can't even get in touch with each other when something like this breaks? Why the hell don't you tell me where you're going to be? Why don't you call up the office?"

I walked over to my desk, sat down in a swivel chair, leaned back and put my feet up on the desk. I winced as the back of the chair pushed against my spine.

"What's the matter with you?" Bertha asked.

"He's got a headache," Elsie Brand said.

"A headache!" Bertha yelled. "A headache? What does he think *I've* got?"

I said to Bertha, "Shut up. I want to think."

"Want to think?" she said. "Why, you don't even know what there is to think about, yet."

I said wearily, "All right, tell me what there is to think about. I'd rather listen to it than have your voice rasp holes in my eardrums. What is there to think about?"

"Our client," Bertha said. "She's in a jam. She needs us bad and she needs us right now. And me having to sit here and stall her along."

"Who is our client?" I asked.

"Are you nuts?"

"No, I want to know who our client is."

"The same one we've always had. Carlotta Hanford."

"What does she want?"

"She's in a jam. She wants you to get her out. What do you suppose she wants? Why do you suppose she walked in here and plunked down every cent she's been able to raise? Five hundred and eighty-five dollars! Cold hard cash."

"Did she do that?"

"You're damn right she did. She wanted to make it two hundred and fifty, but I put the screws on her and squeezed her for five hundred and eighty-five bucks. And all the time keeping one eye on the clock and telling her what a smart little detective you were and then she gives me the money and I give her a receipt and there I am, sitting with my hands on my lap, not knowing where the hell you are—trying to run a partnership without any merchandise to deliver."

"Why didn't *you* go to work on the case?" I asked.

"Work on it!" Bertha screamed. "I was working on it. Didn't I tell you I boosted the ante from two hundred and fifty to five hundred and eighty-five smackers. Don't be silly. If you think that isn't work, try it sometime."

"What did your receipt say, Bertha?"

"It said that we'd received five hundred and eighty-five bucks."

"For what?"

"For representing Carlotta Hanford."

I said, "You shouldn't have done that."

"Oh, I see, you don't like the color of her hair or something. Is that it?"

I said, "You'd better find out what the score is before we go sticking our necks out."

"Well, I know what the score is. The score is five hundred and eighty-five bucks and somebody is trying to frame that little girl."

"Who's trying to frame her?"

"That's for you to find out."

"What are they framing her with?"

"Fabricated evidence. And Frank Sellers makes me so damn sore. He just can't tell an innocent person when he sees one."

"Where's Carlotta now?"

"I sent her out to get some lunch. I told her you'd be back. My God, I got so nervous I couldn't even finish a cigarette, once I started to smoke it. Fifteen cents' worth of cigarettes only half smoked!"

"Fifty percent of fifteen cents is seven and a half cents," I told her wearily, still keeping my eyes closed.

"You're damn right it is," Bertha said. "And it's time you realized it."

There was silence for two or three seconds while Bertha was gathering her strength for another onslaught.

"Well," I said wearily, "I'm glad we agree about something."

Bertha said, "Frank Sellers has been out snooping around that Ballwin house, and what do you think he's found?"

"What did he find?"

"A demitasse cup with anchovy paste and arsenic still stuck to the sides."

"Where did he find it?"

"On an upper shelf in the pantry."

I said, "Well, that's nice. It makes a nice piece of evidence for him. A good feather in Frank Sellers's hat. Now give me ten minutes, Bertha, ten minutes, just to sit here and think something out, and then I'll go to work on that cup."

"Ten minutes!" Bertha yelled. "You've had the whole damn morning to do your thinking."

"Just ten minutes," I said.

"She's coming back here any minute," Bertha went on. "I've

stalled and stalled and stalled. I've even told her to go out and dictate a lot of facts to the secretary out there in the reception room so we'd have everything down in black and white. I stalled her every way I could think of, and she's getting mad. She wants action and—"

I said to Bertha, "I'm going to take ten minutes to think. Now, if you get out and leave me alone, I'll do my thinking. If you don't, I'll do it somewhere else, and you won't see me again all afternoon."

Bertha sucked in a deep breath, then slowly exhaled. "Now, listen, lover," she pleaded, "you can't do that to Bertha. Bertha has been up here running the business all by herself. Bertha's been taking in the money so that you could buy all those nice new clothes. Bertha's been working her fool head off. What happens? You come breezing in here—"

"I've got to think something out, Bertha. There's a mix-up. Something doesn't fit together, and in a few minutes I'm going to have to tell a story to the police."

"Well, in a few minutes we're going to have to tell a story to—"

There was a knock on the door. The frightened office secretary pushed her head through the door and said, "May I come in?"

Bertha started to yell at her, but the secretary slipped through the door and said in a hushed whisper, "Miss Hanford is out there and your voices are very loud. I—I didn't know what to do—I—"

"Send her in," Bertha said.

"Ten minutes, Bertha," I said. "Take her in your office. Keep her there for ten minutes. This thing is important and—"

"I've stalled her as long as I'm going to," Bertha snapped.

She shoved the frightened office secretary to one side, jerked the door open, and, in a voice that was all honey and syrup, said, "Oh, *there* you are, Miss Hanford. Mr. Lam and I have been having a conference about your case. We've gone over it very thoroughly. He came in just after you'd gone out. I tried to catch you in the corridor, but you'd already gone down in the elevator. Did you have a nice lunch, dearie? Well, come in. Mr. Lam wants to talk it all over with you, and then he's got a plan which we've been working on."

Carlotta Hanford entered the office. The secretary darted out through the crack in the door. Bertha slammed the door shut, and Carlotta smiled at me. "Hello," she said.

"Hello."

She sat down in the client's chair and crossed her knees.

I closed my eyes.

"He's thinking," Bertha said, in a hushed voice.

I heard the rustle of motion as Carlotta Hanford adjusted her skirts and shifted her position a little in the chair.

"Well," Carlotta said, "what's the score? What conclusion have you reached?"

Bertha said, "He wants you to tell the facts. He wants to hear them in your own words."

"But I dictated everything I knew and it was all written down."

"Oh, not all *those* details," Bertha said. "Mr. Lam is familiar with all the general stuff; but he wants to hear you talk, wants to hear the tone of your voice when you tell him about the teacup— don't you, lover?"

I said, "Yes."

Carlotta sighed wearily. "It wasn't a teacup, a demitasse. Someone has pegged me for a fall guy."

"They have for a fact," Bertha sympathized.

"And I don't like it."

"I wouldn't think you would, dearie. Tell Mr. Lam about the teacup."

She said, "That nasty, snooping, nosy, sarcastic Sergeant Sellers!"

"I know just how you feel, darling," Bertha said soothingly.

"He messed around the place and found that demitasse with anchovy paste and arsenic in it, and then he found the little spoon."

"Where were they?" I said.

"The cup was on the top shelf in the pantry, behind some dishes that were very seldom used. Someone had put it up there to get it out of the way, someone, apparently, who was trying to conceal it and didn't have much time to find a better place."

"Go on," I said.

She said, "The cup is one that I had used. That is, it has my fingerprints on it."

"Oh, oh," I said.

"I had been using it," she went on. "I'd gone up to my room after dinner the night before, and had taken this demitasse up with me. I like a sweet demitasse after dinner. I put lots of sugar in and make it almost a syrup. Then I sip it, just a bit at a time."

"The spoon," I asked. "Where was that?"

"In the drawer of the writing-desk in my bedroom."

"Any other prints on the cup except yours?"

"I don't know. Sergeant Sellers didn't say anything about that. He simply showed me photographs of my latent finger-prints that were on the cup."

"He's enlarged those latent fingerprints?"

"Yes."

"And he's letting you compare them with your fingerprints so as to convince you that he isn't trying to run a bluff?"

"Yes."

"What did you tell him?"

"I told him at first that I simply couldn't understand it. I kept trying to think, and then I remembered about leaving the cup in my room. Anyone could have taken it."

"You told Sergeant Sellers about that?"

"Yes."

"You're not trying to think up a story that will pass muster?"

"No, I'm telling the truth."

"You're certain it's the whole truth?"

"That's right."

"You haven't made up a single thing?"

"No."

"You have no idea who put the cup on the shelf in the pantry?"

"No."

I said, "Well, if your story's true, you've got the one perfect means of proof."

"How do you mean?"

I said, "There's one thing in the evidence which will absolutely demonstrate that your story is true. Something that will confirm it."

"What's that?" she asked hopefully.

Bertha muttered cooingly, "I told you he was brainy."

I said, "The anchovy paste in the cup will have poison in it because that's where the poisoner mixed the arsenic into the anchovy paste."

"Naturally," she said.

"But," I said, "when Sergeant Sellers checks the spoon, he'll find there is no anchovy paste on it. That will substantiate your story. The cup was used to mix the poison. If you'd done it, you'd have used the spoon that was already in your room. A person trying to frame you wouldn't think of the spoon, but would take the cup with your fingerprints on it and use another spoon."

"That's the dope, lover," Bertha Cool muttered approvingly.

Carlotta Hanford didn't say anything.

"Well?" I asked.

She shifted her position.

"Go on," I said.

She said, "I guess whoever framed me wasn't very dumb."

"Why?"

She said, "Bits of anchovy paste were stuck on the spoon when Sergeant Sellers found it. They also contained arsenic."

"Fry me for an oyster!" Bertha muttered in an explosive undertone.

I said, "It's too bad you couldn't have thought up a better one before you had to tell it to Sellers."

"Shut up," Carlotta Hanford snapped at me.

Bertha said, "Get to thinking, lover. Please get to thinking. We've got to get her out of this some way."

I said to Bertha, "Our license is to operate a detective agency."

"What do you mean?"

"If," I told her, "you want to be an accessory after the fact, you'll have to get another type of license."

Bertha just glared at me.

"I think you're horrid," Carlotta said.

Bertha said, "Look, Donald, you've done it before."

"Done what?"

"Pulled a rabbit out of the hat."

"The hats I've had, in those cases, had rabbits in them. It was just a question of knowing where to look."

"Well, start looking," Bertha said.

"I'm telling you the absolute truth!" Carlotta insisted.

Bertha said, "Look, lover, we can't leave her here like this, the way the case is right now. Frank Sellers would be—well, he'd be difficult to handle."

"Yes, I can understand just how Sellers might look at it," I said.

"Well," Bertha snapped. "*Do* something!"

"What do you want me to do?"

"The first thing we have to do is get Miss Hanford out of the way until we can—well, until we can explain the facts in the case."

I said, "We find the facts. It's up to Carlotta to make the explanations."

"Haven't I made them?" she asked.

I said, "You satisfied Bertha. You haven't satisfied me, and I don't think you're going to satisfy the police."

"I tell you I was framed."

Bertha said, "Take her some place where she'll be safe until we can get things straightened out, Donald."

"Where?"

"How do I know—take her—take her to your apartment."

I said, "No."

"I don't know why not," Bertha went on. "You have a nice little apartment and there's no one at the desk to see who goes in and who goes out."

"I wouldn't want to compromise her good name," I said.

"Phooey," Carlotta observed.

"That's it, lover," Bertha pleaded. "Take her to your apartment."

"Why don't *you* take her to *your* place? It would look better."

"My place?" Bertha screamed. "What the hell are you talking about! She's hotter than a stove lid. If Frank Sellers caught me hiding her in my apartment, he'd—he'd—"

"What would he do to me if he caught me hiding her in my apartment?"

"He wouldn't do a thing. In the first place, he'd never find out you had her there and, in the second place, if he did, you could talk your way out of it."

Carlotta said, "If you folks don't want to represent me, just give me my money back, and I'll find some other detective agency—"

Bertha said, "Of course we want to represent you. Donald is going to take you up to his apartment, but he wants to make sure first that you understand just what he's doing. You may have to stay there for—well, you know, quite a while."

"I'm not saying anything," Carlotta Hanford said. "I'm in a jam. I want out! I've come to you and paid you money to get me out."

Bertha Cool looked at me and nodded. "Your apartment, lover," she said. "And we haven't much time, you know."

I said, "Let me think for just a second or two, will you, Bertha."

"You can think after you get her up to your apartment. That'll be a swell time to think. The way things are now, you'll be sitting here thinking and Frank Sellers will walk in, and then we'll be in a real fix."

I got up out of the swivel chair. "Come on," I said to Carlotta. She was on her feet with a swift, lithe motion.

"Thank you," she said to Bertha Cool.

"Okay," Bertha told her. "We'll take care of you."

I saw Elsie Brand looking at me solicitously as I walked across her office, opened the door to the reception room, and stepped to one side for Carlotta to go out.

She walked with quick, nervous strides, as though it took an effort of the will to keep from breaking into a run.

We caught an elevator almost as soon as we pressed the button, got down to the street, and I piloted her across to the parking lot and into the Agency car.

"How far is your apartment?" she asked.

"We aren't going there."

"What?"

I said, "Don't be silly. Bertha Cool is a swell egg, but this is too important for me to trust to her discretion."

"What do you mean?"

I said, "Suppose she should make some crack inadvertently and the police would know where you were."

"She wouldn't be that indiscreet, would she?"

"I don't think so."

"Then why not go to your apartment?"

"Because I can't afford to take chances with you. I don't *think* there's any possibility that Bertha would let the cat out of the bag, but in case she should, I would never forgive myself and you'd never forgive me."

"Where are we going?"

"To an auto camp."

"Why?"

I said, "For several reasons. One of them is I can't afford to have you register under a fictitious name. That would be an indication of guilt, if they should try to build up the case against you."

"Well, they're trying that already."

"Therefore, you can't afford to resort to flight. They can use that against you."

"How are you going to work it?"

I said, "I'm going to an auto camp. I'll convey the impression there are several people in my party. I'll register under my own name, 'Donald Lam and party,' and I'll give the correct number of my automobile.

"Then in case there should be an investigation, I'll say that I was trying to get all of the witnesses together so I could get them to compare their stories. I wanted to have them where we wouldn't be interrupted, and I got you as the first witness, took you out there and parked you, and then went back to round up some of the others. Bertha and I intended to get all the witnesses there for a conference sometime late this afternoon."

She thought that over and said, "Damn it, you *are* clever. That's a good idea."

"Okay by you?" I asked.

"Okay by me," she said.

I eased the car out into traffic. She straightened her stockings. I said, "Sellers has enough to warrant making an arrest. The fact that he's letting you run loose shows he's laying some sort of a trap. We've got to be careful."

"I'm leaving it up to you, Donald."

I nodded and did some more silent driving.

"What," she asked, "is the matter with you? The last time I saw you, you were full of biology. Now you're the soul of discretion."

I said, "I've got a hell of a headache."

"Well, *isn't* that too bad!"

I took my eyes off the road to glance at her.

She was grinning up at me. "I've used that one once or twice myself."

I said, "Mine is a traumatic headache."

"What kind is that?"

"That's a medical term."

"What does it mean?"

"A headache induced by violence."

"You mean someone hit you?"

"Across the back of the head with a sap."

"When?"

"A couple of hours ago."

"Where?"

"I told you where. In the back of the head."

"Why, Donald? Why did they hit you?"

"I think they didn't like me."

She relapsed into silence and didn't say anything more until I had driven over the bridge, got to the outskirts of town, and stopped at one of the larger auto courts.

"A double cabin with accommodations for six people?" I asked.

"We can let you have one. It'll be eighteen dollars."

"Is that the best you can do?"

"Absolutely. That cabin is—"

"I'll take it."

I signed the register, "Donald Lam and party." The man took a look at the license on my automobile and wrote it down.

"Where are the rest of them?" he asked.

"They're coming."

"There are three double beds," he said.

"That's okay."

"All right. I'll show you where it is. Number six."

He took the key and led the way down to a big cabin. A nice place with two tiled showers, a living room, and two bedrooms.

"This okay?" he asked.

"Just what I want," I told him.

He went out. Carlotta Hanford came over to stand beside me.

I said, "Well, that's that. You'll just have to wait here. Promise me you won't go out for anything."

"I promise. What are you going to do now?"

"Going back to the office."

"You poor boy, don't you think you should lie down a little while?"

I said, "There's work to be done."

She reached up to stroke the back of my neck with gentle fingers. "Does it hurt?"

"It's sore. Down underneath, all along the spine. I guess I got quite a rap."

"That's a shame," she said. "Perhaps you'll be feeling better when you—when you get back here tonight. I like you better when you're more like your old self."

I said, "You didn't act that way when I was my old self."

She smiled. "Women never do."

"I suppose not," I said, and made for the door.

"When will you be back?"

"I don't know exactly. There are cooking facilities in the little kitchen there. I'll bring some food with me. Don't go out under any circumstances. Stay right there. Keep the door locked. If anybody knocks, answer the door but tell them you've been taking a bath and are undressed."

She moved so as to be directly in front of me as I started for the door. "Donald," she said, "you've been awfully good to me."

"It's all in the game."

"Awfully good to me. I'll never forget it. You—you're a dear. You knew that I—well, that I needed to think up some more details. I could fool Bertha Cool, but I couldn't fool you. Could I, Donald?"

"Don't worry about fooling me," I said. "The one you have to fool is Frank Sellers," and I pushed past her to the door.

Chapter Seventeen
Dead-to-Rights

Elsie Brand had the door of her office propped open so she could watch the entrance door. As soon as I came in, she started making signs, winking toward Bertha Cool's office and motioning with her hands for me to back out.

I was just stepping back, letting the door shut behind me, when the door of Bertha Cool's office jerked open, and I heard Frank Sellers say, "Well, as soon as he comes in—"

The slow action on the automatic door check held me trapped. Before I could get out of his line of vision, Sellers had seen me and said, "Here he is now."

I pushed open the door, went in, and said, "Hello, Sergeant."

Bertha Cool, her face hard and grim, said, "Come in here, Donald."

I walked nonchalantly over to Bertha Cool's office and said to Sellers, "You found the body all right?"

"Yes," Sellers said, "I found the body all right."

We all three sat down. Sellers, his hat on the back of his head, his forehead creased into a frown, mouthed the soggy cigar, biting at it nervously, twisting it from one side of his mouth to the other.

"Well?" he asked.

I looked at him in surprise. "Well, what?"

He said, "What's the idea? You report a corpse to the police and hang up in the middle of the conversation. You don't tell

me where you are, or how I can find you, or how you happened
to stumble on to this corpse. You act as though you might have
been reporting a stray dog somewhere. Then you come up to
your office, you make no attempt to get into communication
with the police, you don't even tell your partner about finding
the body. Now, what the hell's the idea?"

I said wearily, "There are a lot of different questions."

"Well, start talking."

I said, "One at a time."

"Didn't you hang up on me?"

I let my face show surprise. "Me hang up on you! I thought
maybe you wanted to get on the job fast. I'd given you all the
essential information so I wasn't surprised when you hung up
on me."

"You didn't tell me where I could reach you or that you'd be
waiting. When a person finds a body, he's supposed to communicate with the police and tell them who he is and all about it."

I said, "I communicated with the police within ten seconds
of the time that I found the body. I told them who I was. Then
you hung up on me and—"

"We were cut off."

"How was I to know?"

"You could have called back."

"And got my head snapped off," I said. "You had all the
information."

"Why didn't you tell Bertha about it?"

I said, "I didn't have a chance. I didn't want to talk about it in
front of our client. I thought you might prefer to let the police
do their telling in their own way; then if it should turn out that
the guilty person made some slip and let it appear that he knew
of the murder, he couldn't explain that he'd learned about it
from us."

"Considerate, aren't you?" Sellers said.

"Yes."

"How did you happen to be there?"

"I wanted to see the girl who lives there."

"Ruth Otis?"

"Yes."

"Why?"

I said, "She's a nurse for Dr. George L. Quay."

"What's that got to do with it?"

"Dr. Quay is Mrs. Ballwin's dentist."

"Go ahead," Sellers said.

"And she'd bought some poison at the Acme Drugstore."

"So you knew about that?"

"Yes."

"Anything else?"

"Isn't that enough?"

"What did you do?"

"Drove up to the apartment house where she lives."

"Ring the doorbell?"

"No."

"How did you get in?"

"The door of her apartment was slightly open."

"How did you get in the outer door?"

I raised my eyes to study the ceiling. "I simply pushed the door and it came open."

"Baloney," Sellers said. "You'd better come clean, my boy."

I said, "Okay, if you have to get personal, I used a passkey."

"That's better. What were you looking for?"

"Evidence."

Bertha said angrily, "You didn't tell me anything about this, Donald."

"I haven't had time."

"You've got time now," Sellers said.

I looked at my watch. "Speaking of time, I've got something red hot in the second race. I want to get on the phone as soon as the race is over and collect."

Bertha said, "Frank is on our side now, lover. Our client is in the clear. We're all working together. What's your horse, Donald?"

"The winner."

"How do you know?"

"Because I've found a way of really beating the races. It's a wonder someone never thought of it before."

"How much have you got on this horse, lover?"

"A hundred smackers."

"A hundred bucks!" Bertha exclaimed. "Hell, it *must* be hot. I've never known him to go beyond ten bucks before, Frank."

Sellers said, "Seems to me like we keep getting farther away from the stuff *I* want to talk about. Tell me what you wanted in that Otis girl's apartment. Well, if you have anything on the second race—give."

I said, "It isn't anything. I found a fellow who has a brand-new scheme for picking the winners. Something that's mathematical."

Bertha Cool's chair creaked as she leaned forward.

"What's the horse?" Sellers asked.

"Fair Lady."

"I don't like her," Sellers said, shaking his head. "She's a goat."

I said, "You should see the way this fellow works out his handicaps. He has every horse tabulated on the basis of past performance. He has a machine with a light in it so he can superimpose all the curves of performance on Celluloid cards, snap on a light behind them, and see which horse is going to win."

"Just like that, eh?" Sellers asked.

"Just like that, a perpetual inventory of what any horse has to deliver."

Bertha said with awe in her voice, "You pungled up a hundred bucks in cold cash on the nose of one pony on the strength of it?"

"That's right."

Bertha grabbed up the phone, said to the operator in the outer office, "Give me an outside line." Then she dialed frantically, said, "Hello, Fred? Look, this is Bertha Cool. I've got something hot in the second race...No, that's all right...Well, hurry up, I want to get it on. I know I have to hurry. It's Fair Lady. I want twenty bucks right on her nose."

Sellers said, "Get twenty for me too, will you, Bertha."

"Make it forty," Bertha snapped.

Again there was an interval of silence. Then Bertha said, "Make my bet thirty, and my friend's bet twenty. That'll make it an even fifty....Sure, put the whole bet in my name. As far as you're concerned, you're dealing with me and that's all. That's right. Fifty bucks. Five to one. That's swell. Okay, goodbye."

Bertha hung up the telephone.

"Who is this guy?" Sellers asked.

I said, "He has a downtown office and apparently doesn't do a darn thing except sit there and study records. He does a real job of handicapping, has knurled knobs that raise and lower the Celluloid cards on which he has the performance of the horses listed. It's a slick idea."

"Why should he raise them or lower them?" Bertha asked.

"Because, if a horse likes a wet track, he can adjust the card for that particular horse in relation to the other cards. Every time a horse runs, he evaluates its performance, and carries on his curve of performance, as he calls it. Then by taking a card for each horse that's in a race, putting them all together, adjusting them so they're in their proper positions for the condition of the track and all that, he simply flashes on a light, and there's your winner, standing out in bold relief, absolutely mathematical."

Bertha said, glancing at Sellers, "It sounds as though it could be done."

"Why not?" I asked. "After all, that's what every handicapper tries to do, laboriously and with a pencil and paper. Only there are too many factors to work out and you can't coordinate 'em all. By reducing everything to a standard graph and then superimposing those graphs you get an instantaneous answer."

Bertha said, "I don't know a damn thing about that. What sells me is that you put a hundred bucks on this goat. You sure must be sold."

I said, "Don't blame me if she doesn't win. I didn't tell you to bet on her. I wasn't even going to tell you what horse I was betting on until Sergeant Sellers made me."

"But you did put a hundred bucks on her?"

"Yes."

"That's good enough for me," Bertha said. "We've got fifty on her."

"I've got twenty-five of it," Sellers said.

Bertha's eyes glittered. "You only wanted twenty dollars, Frank."

Sellers said, "I thought I was splitting the bet with you. I'm in for twenty-five."

"You said twenty bucks," Bertha told him. "The bookie said he'd give me five to one if I'd make it an even fifty."

"I know. You said twenty bucks too. When the bookie boosted the ante on us, I expected to go my share."

"It's all right," Bertha said. "I've got the thirty dollars. I'll take care of it. You're just in for the twenty which is just what you wanted."

"But I'm telling you I *want* that other five," Sellers said.

Bertha took a long deep breath. "Okay, it's twenty-five apiece."

"Five to one?" Sellers asked.

"Five to one," Bertha told him.

"We'd ought to go take a look at this card-indexing thing," Sellers said.

"I can go any time you want," Bertha chimed in.

Sellers said, "Damned if it doesn't sound like a swell idea. The more I think of it, the *better* it sounds."

I said, "It got a hundred dollars of my money."

"How did Fair Lady look in the test?" Sellers asked.

"It's going to be close. It wasn't a walkaway. Figure probably a length. That's the reason you can get five to one."

Sellers said, "It doesn't make any difference if it's only an eyelash. Just so she gets her nose across. Well, let's get back to that Ballwin case. We've got it cracked."

Bertha Cool said, "Well, you can't always trust to circumstantial evidence, Frank. You know that. There are lots of times—"

"We've got her this time dead-to-rights."

"What I can't understand," Bertha went on, "is that thing you were telling me about—that murder of Ballwin's secretary."

"She probably knew too much. That's the way it looks now."

"And you think that's tied up with the Ballwin poisoning?"

Sellers laughed grimly, said, "Tied up with it? I'll say it is."

"Who did it?" I asked.

"Ruth Otis," Sellers said.

"Do you mean the poisoning and the other murder, too?"

"Yes."

Bertha glanced significantly at me. "I thought you were trying to pin it on Carlotta Hanford."

"Not trying to pin it on anyone," Sellers said. "We were just getting evidence. Now I want to see that Carlotta Hanford. If she should get in touch with you, you tell her I want to see her quick."

Bertha looked at me.

I didn't say anything.

"You're sure Ruth Otis is the one that did the poisoning?" I asked.

"Hell, yes," Sellers said. "When we got to her apartment, we had the whole thing all blueprinted for us. We even found the package in which she had bought the poison. Now we know exactly how much she used."

"How much?" I asked.

"One hell of a lot," Sellers said. "Authorities agree that anything above two grains may be a lethal dose, under two grains you get sick as hell, but that's all."

"How much was missing out of what she'd bought?" I asked.

"She got two hundred grains. Thirty grains were gone."

"And you found what was left in her room?"

"Found what was left of the poison in her room," Sellers said. "And found a tube of anchovy paste, about half of it gone. As a matter of fact, she resents Mrs. Ballwin. Hates her guts."

"Why? Was she jealous?"

"No, it wasn't that, but it was through Mrs. Ballwin she lost her job. Mrs. Ballwin was Dr. Quay's patient. As a prominent, wealthy patient, she had certain privileges. Ruth Otis didn't like that. Ruth wanted to be the queen of the office. She was rude to Mrs. Ballwin. I guess she thought Dr. Quay would back her up, the little fool."

"And what did Dr. Quay do?"

"Backed up Mrs. Ballwin, naturally, and fired the nurse."

"So the nurse decided she'd poison Mrs. Ballwin?"

"Uh huh."

"Did she think that would get her her job back?"

Sellers twisted his cigar around a couple of times, his eyes bored into mine. "What the hell are you trying to do? Get sarcastic?"

"I was just asking."

"I didn't like the tone of your voice."

Bertha Cool said, "But how about this other evidence? The evidence that you had—well, you know, the other evidence."

"What other evidence?"

"The cup with the poisoned anchovy paste in it and Carlotta Hanford's fingerprints."

"Oh, so that's it. Carlotta Hanford is your client."

"I didn't say so."

Sellers grinned and said, "You didn't need to. Where is she now? I want to get in touch with her."

Bertha said cagily, "How about the cup you found—"

"She was framed," Sergeant Sellers said. "Damn near fooled me too. I'm telling you, if it hadn't been for that murder of Ethel Worley, I'd have really gone to town on that Carlotta girl. I was going to ask for a warrant. Just shows how facts can twist themselves around."

"What have you found out about Ethel Worley?" I asked.

"Well," Sellers said, "we're still working on the case. In fact, the men were still fingerprinting the apartment when I left. I left them because I wanted to see where the hell you were. Damn it, why didn't you wait there until we arrived?"

"Because you didn't tell me to."

"You should have known I wanted you to. Naturally I wanted to see you."

"You're seeing me, aren't you?"

Sellers flushed. "Don't get so damn flip. You *could* be in a jam on this thing. I want to know about this passkey."

"Well," I told him virtuously, "any time you want to locate me during office hours, all you have to do is to drop in or just give the office a ring and—"

"Shut up," Sellers said.

I kept quiet.

"You were going to tell us about Ethel Worley and Ruth Otis," Bertha said.

"Well," Sellers said, scraping a match on the sole of his shoe and making a futile attempt to light up the end of his soggy cigar, "Gerald Ballwin is coming along all right. He's as good as new right now. In fact, if it weren't for the mental strain, the doctors would let him out of the hospital. If his wife had only received as prompt attention as he did, she'd have been okay, too. Funny thing about that. The guy who acts as chauffeur and butler took it a lot harder than the husband did. He blubbered like a baby."

Sellers crossed his legs, said, "I don't mind telling you, we had this guy, Wilmont Mariville, his name is, pegged for being it. After all, he served the poisoned crackers. If it had been only the husband that had died, we'd have given that guy the works. But when the husband got well and the wife croaked—well, that shot our motive all to pieces and if you could have seen the way the guy broke down and went all to hell when he learned Mrs. Ballwin had kicked the bucket, it told the whole story."

"It wasn't an act?" I asked.

"Act, hell! He had real tears cutting channels down his cheeks."

"The husband didn't take it so hard?"

"He had better control," Sellers said, "just reached for the phone and called his office, told them what had happened and told them to close the office for the day."

"Whom did he talk with?" I asked.

"Ethel Worley, his secretary."

"Then what happened?" Bertha asked.

"There are two girls working out there, this Ethel Worley and Mary Ingram. I guess they're not too cordial—maybe a little office jealousy between them. Something of that sort.

"As soon as Ethel Worley got the news that Mrs. Ballwin was dead, she told Mary Ingram that that settled it. If it was a murder case, there were certain things she knew that she couldn't keep to herself, that she was going to do something."

"Did she say what?"

Sellers said, "I'm coming to that. Ethel Worley's car was on the blink. She couldn't get it started. Mary Ingram had her automobile out there, and Ethel Worley asked Mary to give her a ride uptown."

"And Mary did?"

"That's right. She was going to take Ethel Worley home, but Ethel Worley wanted to go to this address on Lexbrook Avenue."

"Then what?"

"So Mary Ingram took her to that address on Lexbrook. Ethel Worley asked her to wait a few minutes. Mary sat outside and waited for half an hour. Then she got mad, thought she was being imposed upon and the Worley girl was being a little too high hat, so she simply drove off."

"Having no idea Ethel Worley was in danger?"

"That's right. She thought Ethel Worley had simply gone up to talk to a witness. That was what Ethel said she intended to do."

"Was Mary watching the door of the apartment house? Could she tell who came and went?"

"No, that's the bad part of it. She's the studious type. She's studying Spanish and she had her Spanish book with her. She was sitting there in the car studying and not paying very much attention to the apartment house. Not for the first twenty minutes, anyway. Then she got a little restless, and started looking, and after a while, got too mad to stay. She closed the book and waited for about another five minutes, then stepped on the starter and drove off."

"What do *you* think happened?" I asked.

Sellers gave me a withering glance. "How the hell do I know? I'm no brilliant young genius like you are. But as far as I'm concerned, when one woman hates another, and that other one gets poisoned, when you find that the woman that did the hating bought the poison, and when someone who knows about it goes to her apartment to check up, and gets strangled, even a dumb cop can begin to put two and two together."

I said, "Ethel Worley wasn't any puny weakling. She had lots of beef and lots of curves. She might object if someone who wasn't a lot bigger and stronger—"

"That," Sellers said, "was taken care of by a nice little blow on the side of the head. It was struck from behind, evidently when she wasn't looking, and wasn't expecting anything. A nice little contusion along the back of the skull, just above the right ear. A blow with a blackjack."

"Well," Bertha said, "the point is that Carlotta Hanford is in the clear now. Is that right?"

"Yes, she's in the clear," Sellers said. "But I sure want to talk with her."

Bertha looked at me. I shook my head.

Bertha said, "Why not?"

"What the hell are you two trying to do?" Sellers asked.

"Nothing," I said.

Sellers said, "Now for some time I've had reason to think Carlotta Hanford is your client. I don't know what she was trying to do. But from all I can put together, she knew that there was apt to be a poisoning out at the Ballwin house, and wanted to prevent it. I thought for a while she was soft on Gerald, but apparently she's just a good kid who is trying to keep peace in the family and keep from having a crepe wreath on the front door. The trouble is, I can't figure why she would want to pay money to see that nothing happened to Gerald Ballwin. I don't think it was her money she was paying out. That means someone in the background knows a lot of things that I want to know. Therefore, I want Carlotta Hanford and I want her quick."

No one said anything.

"Is she your client?" Sellers asked.

I said, "I told you once we can't hand out information like that, Frank."

"Oh, nuts," he said, "you can tell me now, particularly when I'm telling you she's absolutely in the clear. I want some information from her and that's all."

Bertha Cool blurted out, "She's in Donald Lam's apartment."

"The hell she is!" Sellers said, sitting up straight.

"No, she isn't," I said.

Sellers threw back his head and laughed. "Well, well, Donald, that's pretty slick! Makes it nice for you, doesn't it? Well, we'll just go up right now and have a talk with Carlotta Hanford."

I said, "I tell you she isn't there."

"Bosh," Bertha said. "Don't be so damn cagey, Donald. Frank Sellers wouldn't double-cross us. He's told us that Carlotta Hanford is in the clear. You always do want to cut corners with the police. I don't. I want to cooperate with them. They can give us all sorts of breaks if they want to and, on the other hand, they can make things tough for us. You know that and I know it."

I said, "All right, I'll take you to where Carlotta is. She isn't in my apartment."

"Yeah, I know," Sellers said. "Take us out on some wild-goose chase until you can get a chance to telephone or work some prearranged warning. What are you trying to keep her out of circulation for?"

"I'm not."

Bertha said, "Don't be silly, Donald. If you're not going to come clean, I am."

Sellers looked inquiringly at Bertha.

"Carlotta was in here just about forty minutes ago," Bertha said. "She told her story. Donald Lam decided to keep her out of circulation for a while. We talked over the best thing to do and the best place where we could put her, and finally decided on Donald's apartment and he took her up there."

"No, I didn't," I said. "I took her to an auto court."

Sellers laughed.

"Come on and I'll prove it to you."

"Sure, sure," Sellers said, "but we'll go to your apartment first."

"With a search warrant?" I asked.

Sellers flushed. "I could throw the book at you on this case, Lam. As far as you're concerned, I don't need no warrant. Get that straight. You squawk and I'll start teaching you manners."

Frank Sellers pulled the soggy cigar out of his mouth, looked at it disgustedly, banged it down into Bertha Cool's waste-basket.

"Don't you do that!" Bertha screamed at him. "I've told you a dozen times those damn stogies of yours stink up the whole office."

Sellers laughed. "Come on, Bertha, let's get going."

Bertha got up out of the big squeaky chair, strode around the corner of the desk.

Sellers gave her hips a resounding slap. "Come on, old gal!"

Bertha whirled to glare at him. "Keep your hands off of me."

Sellers said, "Don't be a pill, Bertha. I know you like it. Come on, let's go take a look into Donald's love life."

Chapter Eighteen
All Head and Some Heart

I said, "I want to take my car, because I've got some other places to go. I suppose you want to go in yours."

"That's right."

I said to Bertha, "Do you want to ride with Sellers or with me?"

"I'll ride with Frank."

"Just a minute, just a minute," Sellers said. "Don't think you're going to get away and try any funny business on the telephone."

I said wearily, "My God, I tell you she isn't out there, but you want to go take a look. It's okay by me, but if you think I'm trying to work any funny business on the telephone, ring up the damn apartment. You won't get an answer, because no one's there."

"It's a good idea," Sellers said. "What's his number, Bertha?"

Bertha gave Sellers the number of the apartment. Sellers called it, hung onto the phone for eight or ten seconds. When he had no answer he dropped the receiver back into place and looked at me in a puzzled way. Then he said, "All right, Donald, we're going out. I want to take a look just for the fun of the thing."

"Suit yourself," I told him. "I'll be tickled to death to take you out there and buy you a drink. Here, you can take the key. I suppose you'll get out there a few minutes before I do, if you're going to use the siren."

"Don't worry, darling," Sellers said. "I'm not going to use the siren, if you're going in your car. I'm going to put you right ahead of me, so I can keep my eye on you, and you're going to lead the way right out to the apartment. Bertha and I are going to be right behind you. Is that clear?"

I nodded, and then managed to yawn.

As we walked out through the reception room, I remembered an old-fashioned bill file Elsie always kept on her desk, one of those steel spikes mounted in an iron stand on which papers can be impaled until ready for disposal.

Sellers walked out first. I stepped gallantly to one side to let Bertha walk past, then swiftly grabbed the spike file from the desk, scooped off the papers that were on it, and let them flutter to the floor.

As I looked back, Elsie Brand was watching me curiously. But she didn't say a word, didn't even move from her chair to pick up the papers until after I was out of the door.

I pushed the spike on its iron mounting down inside my coat and rode down in the elevator with Sellers and Bertha Cool. Sellers's car was parked in front of a fire plug at the entrance to the building.

Sellers climbed in behind the wheel. I escorted Bertha around to the other side of the car, held the door open for her, and closed it.

Such gallantry tickled Bertha to death. I could see her beaming.

I walked around back behind the car, took the spike from inside my coat, leaned over and pushed it hard into the right rear tire. Then I pulled it back out, put it behind my coat, walked around the car, and said to Sergeant Sellers, "Well, I'll get the Agency heap."

"Okay," Frank Sellers said. "Lead the way."

I said, "*I'm* not going to try to keep track of *you* now. You'll have to keep track of me."

"Don't bother about me," Frank Sellers said, tapping the siren. "I've got this little persuader here. Any time you get going too fast, I'll catch up with you. Don't worry. Just go as fast as you want. I'll even square a pinch for you."

"Okay by me," I said, and went over to the stall where we kept the Agency car.

Sergeant Sellers was lighting a fresh cigar as I drove out. He was in no particular hurry to get started.

I drove fast through the traffic, and got nearly a block and a half head-start and one traffic signal the best of them; but I hadn't gone four blocks after that before Sellers's police car was rolling right along behind me, Frank Sellers sitting at the wheel as big as life, his fresh cigar tilted up at a forty-five degree angle.

We went another half-dozen blocks before I had a chance to make a left-hand turn. When I did, I saw that Sellers's car swayed pretty much to one side. Then suddenly Sellers was jolting his way toward the side of the road with his tire flat.

I stepped on my throttle.

I heard Sellers's horn in a series of expostulatory blasts before I had gone half a block. At the end of the block I heard his impotent siren.

I kept right on going, and going fast.

I slammed the car to a stop in front of my apartment house, dashed out of the car holding my latchkey in my hand as I sprinted for the door. I fitted the latchkey and prayed that I'd find the elevator at the bottom of the shaft.

It was. I went up.

The elevator door had the tendency to stick unless it was given a little momentum. I was careful to see that it stuck open just about half an inch from making the contact that would be required to work the elevator. That would force them to take to the stairs and give me a few seconds.

I ran down the corridor to my apartment, unlocked the door, burst in and said, "Come on, Ruth, we've got to get out of here. Quick!"

I heard the thud of bare feet and a little scream.

Ruth stood in the door of the bedroom holding a bath towel in front of her.

I said, "Of all the times for you to be taking a bath!"

"Donald, I had to do it. I cleaned the place up. It was a mess. What's the matter?"

"Sergeant Sellers is on his way up here. They found the package of arsenic in your apartment."

"What?"

I said, "You've got to get dressed and get out of here."

"I can't get dressed while you're standing there looking at me."

I walked over to the window, said, "I'll turn my back. Get your clothes on. Don't bother with stockings. Just put on enough to cover yourself, and get out. I've left the elevator door so it won't work. The first thing you do when you get to the corridor is to go to the stairs and run *up* one flight. If anything should happen that you're caught, don't make any statement. Now did you know Ethel Worley?"

"Who's she?"

"The secretary to Gerald Ballwin."

"Yes, I met her once."

I said, "She was found dead in your apartment."

"Donald!"

"Murdered. Some one had tapped her over the head and then strangled her with one of your Nylon stockings. Did you know she knew about Dr. Quay?"

"Yes."

"How well did you know her?"

"Not well. She came to my apartment once. She'd looked me up."

"What did she want?"

"She tried to pump me about Dr. Quay and Mrs. Ballwin. I wouldn't tell her anything."

I said, "Keep on with your dressing."

"I'm—I'm dressed."

I turned around. She had her skirt, blouse, and jacket on. She finished with her shoes as I turned.

"Did you have a hat?"

"Yes."

"Where is it?"

"I'll get it."

"Your stockings?"

"They're in my purse."

"You haven't left a thing?"

"No."

"All right. Get out of here. Go up the stairs, remember that."

"Donald, what will happen if they should catch me?"

"They'll catch you if you stick around here," I told her. "Get up the stairs. Hang around the upper corridors until I come after you. They'll never think of looking for you up there. Beat it!"

I hurried her to the door, held it open for her, pushed her out into the hall, said, "There are the stairs, back of that fire door. Now get started."

I watched her open the fire door and start climbing the stairs. Then I went back to the apartment and started to look around to see if she'd left anything. I hadn't much more than got started when I heard a terrific banging on the door.

I went over and opened it.

Sergeant Sellers pushed the door back so hard that it banged against the door stop.

I stepped back to let him into the apartment.

"How long you been here?" Sellers asked.

I showed surprise. "Just got here," I said. "I thought you'd be right behind me."

"You didn't hear my siren?"

"Siren? Sure I heard it."

"Why didn't you stop?"

I said, "Weren't you using it to clear traffic out of your way?"

"I wanted you to stop. I had a puncture."

"The hell you did."

Sellers reached out and grabbed the shoulder of my coat; his big hand spun me around. He slammed me back against the wall and glared at me. "Damn you," he said, "you're just a little *too* lucky or a little *too* smart."

Bertha, puffing and blowing, said, "Leave him alone, Frank."

I said, "What's the idea? Am I to blame for your puncture? Are you kidding me? You couldn't have got here this quick if you'd had to change a tire."

Bertha stopped breathing through her mouth long enough to say, "We didn't change it."

"Commandeered the first car that came along until I could get a taxi," Sellers said. "Even that way, you must have had four or five minutes' start on us."

I shook my head. "I don't think I've been here that long. Wait a minute, perhaps I have, too. I can't see why it's important, though. When I stopped the car and didn't see you, I waited down there for a minute or so looking around. Then I came on up here."

Sellers said, "Damn it, Donald, if you're lying to me, I'll—I'll put you out of business. I'll have your license."

"Look here," I said angrily. "You two told me to go ahead and drive and to keep ahead of you. You said you'd—"

"Oh, forget it!" Sellers said angrily. "Where's the dame?"

I said, "Bertha's the one who thought she was here."

"You mean she isn't here?"

I said, "Carlotta Hanford isn't here. I told you that before you came here. Look around if you want."

Sellers looked around the apartment. Then he turned to Bertha. "What kind of a song and dance were you giving me, Bertha?"

Bertha, still huffing and puffing, said, "Donald, don't think you're going to play *me* for a fool."

I shrugged my shoulders.

Sellers said, "Well, don't either one of you think you're going to keep stringing me along. There's no dame here, Bertha."

Bertha said, "The elevator was out of order. We had to walk upstairs. Think *that* was a coincidence?"

"What do you mean?" Sellers asked.

Bertha said, "Don't look at me like that, Donald Lam. By God, *I'm* not going to take the rap." She stopped for a moment to get her breath and then went on. "Frank says he hasn't anything against her. Why the hell don't you surrender her?"

I took out my cigarette case, handed it to Sellers.

Sellers said, "To hell with those coffin nails," and fished another stogy from his vest pocket.

I said, "I've got some whisky in the kitchenette."

"I'm on duty," Sellers said. "Go on, Bertha, keep talking. I like the sound of your voice. I think Donald is trying to change the subject."

Bertha said, "The elevator was out of order. We had to walk up, but the indicator showed the elevator was on *this* floor."

"You may have something there," Sellers said.

I said to Bertha, "Why don't you join the cops and be a real detective."

Bertha glared at me. I surreptitiously closed my eye in a slow wink.

Bertha said, "The hell with you. I'm not going to be the goat."

Sellers said, "That elevator business makes me think you've really got something there, Bertha."

"The little pest took advantage of you having the puncture," Bertha said. "He came tearing up here and jimmied the elevator so we'd have to walk up the stairs. That gave him more time. The thing I can't understand is why he did it. You told him Carlotta Hanford is in the clear. That's all we want."

"She your client?" Sellers asked.

"Yes."

"The only one you got?"

"Yes, that's right."

Sellers looked at me and said, "I don't get it."

I said, "The reason it doesn't fit together is because Carlotta Hanford wasn't here in the first place. She's never been here."

Bertha started looking around. Abruptly she said, "The hell she hasn't been here. Look at the way this joint is cleaned up. They only give Donald maid service once a week and look at the place! The ashtrays all cleaned out. Everything dusted. Look here." Bertha ran her finger over the top of the bookcase.

Sellers was watching her thoughtfully.

Bertha went to the bathroom door, looked inside, and said to Sellers, "You're a fine detective."

"Never mind the compliments," Sellers shot back at her.

Bertha said, "God almighty, look at the mirror in the bathroom. It's still covered with steam. The bathmat is damp. What does that mean to you?"

Sellers gave a low whistle, turned suddenly to me, and said, "All right, Lam, where is she?"

I shook my head, "Carlotta wasn't here."

"You're not talking to me," Sellers said. "Look at the dump. Bertha's right."

"There's no law against a man having a woman visitor, is there?"

Sellers scratched his head. "That could be it," he said to Bertha. "That's why he didn't take Carlotta here in the first place. He had a dame up here."

"Let's take a look at her then," Bertha said. "Let's find out who she is."

"That's probably what he doesn't want and what she doesn't want," Sellers said.

"Well, damn him, he isn't tongue-tied. He can talk fast enough when he wants to."

Sellers said, "Okay, suppose Donald rushes up here. He jimmies up the elevator. His lady-love is taking a bath. He pulls her out of the bathtub and—"

"The closet?" Bertha asked.

"I've looked there," Sellers said.

"He's smart," Bertha told him. "He wouldn't do the obvious thing."

"Wait a minute," Sellers said. "Put yourself in his fix. Why did he jimmy up the elevator?"

"So it would take us that much longer to get here. We would have to come up the stairs."

Sellers said, "He gained a little time that way. Say perhaps a minute or two, while we're climbing the stairs. But he's in danger there. If the elevator's running, we'd take it and wouldn't ordinarily use the stairs. Therefore, he'd want to have the elevator running when the girl left. Then she could go down the stairs and in that way she wouldn't be apt to meet us on the road up."

"I don't get it," Bertha said.

"The minute Donald put his girlfriend out, he'd go over and put the elevator back in commission. Then we'd use the elevator and she could take the stairs. That stands to reason."

"Yes, I suppose it does," Bertha said.

"But he didn't do it," Sellers said. "Why?"

I said, "You're making a lot of mountains out of a half of a molehill, Sellers."

"Shut up," he said. "I want to think."

Bertha said, "Perhaps he intended to go out and fix the elevator—"

"He would have if he had time," Sellers said. "That's what he originally intended to do. But something happened to change his plans. It must have been that he found the jane in the bathtub. That doesn't leave him time to get her out of the house before we get here."

"Then what *would* he do?" Bertha asked.

Sellers chewed at the unlit cigar, his eyes thoughtful and moodily surveying my face.

I met his eyes with steady innocence.

Suddenly Sellers said, "Hell—of course! Why didn't I think of it in the first place?"

"What?" Bertha asked.

Sellers strode to the door of the apartment, jerked it open, walked out into the corridor, turned and said to me, "Where's the door to the stairs?"

"You came up," I told him. "You ought to know—"

"I don't want the stairs down; I want the stairs *up*."

I pointed to the door.

Sellers said, "Thanks, Donald," and pushed open the door and started upstairs.

I turned to Bertha. "This is a hell of a way to run a partnership."

"Don't think I'm going to be the fall guy! Why didn't you tell me you were keeping a jane up here?"

I said, "I didn't want to take Carlotta Hanford here in the first place. We can't run a detective agency and still hide people out who are keeping out of the way of the police."

Bertha said angrily, "I don't know what makes you so damned conscientious all of a sudden. The trouble is with you, you haven't any financial sense."

"What do you mean?"

"You won't work for money," she said. "But some damned little floozy comes along and makes sheep's eyes at you and you go overhead and take the partnership whizzing around the walls of San Quentin prison. My God, when I think back on the chances you've taken just because some skirt has made goo-goo eyes at you, I get cold chills chasing up and down my spine. Every time I wake up in the morning I wonder what the day is going to hold in store for me. I—"

The door pushed open. Sergeant Sellers came in leading Ruth Otis by the hand.

"Look what we've got," he said.

"Fry me for an oyster!" Bertha ejaculated.

Ruth said, "I don't know what right you have to drag me down here. Who are these people?"

Sellers said, "Now don't get all excited, sister. You mean to say you've never been in this apartment before?"

"Certainly not."

"Then how does it happen your fingerprints are over everything."

I said, "That's a hell of a bluff. You haven't taken—"

"Shut up," Sellers said. "I'll do the talking."

"This is my apartment."

"That's right," Sellers said with elaborate courtesy. "You're living here, Mr. Lam, but you're only living here temporarily. Your permanent residence is going to be in a nice big house with lots of rooms. But you'll only be occupying one of them and that will have bars on the window."

I said, "I suppose it's a crime to have a babe come in and do housework."

Ruth said, "All right, I'll come clean. I met Donald about a month ago and fell for him. My divorce isn't final and we can't get married—yet."

"So you've been living here?"

"Not very long," Ruth said. "Just the last week or so."

Sellers walked over to the closet door, pulled it open, and said, "Where are your things?"

"Donald has maid service and he didn't want the landlady to know I was in here with him."

"Where's your toothbrush?"

She looked helplessly at me.

Sellers said, "This is the damnedest thing— Say, wait a minute. Red hair, five foot four, weight a hundred and twelve, good figure. Why, dammit, this is the girl I'm looking for! This is the murderess! This is Ruth Otis!"

I said, "Okay, Ruth. Sit down. We may as well face it. He'd have had your driving-license out of your purse in another minute."

"I'll be a son of a gun!" Sellers said.

"Kipper me for a herring," Bertha announced under her breath.

I said, "All right, folks, let's sit down and talk things over."

"Well, I'll hope to tell the world we'll talk things over," Sellers said.

I said, "I'm trying to get this thing straightened up. I think I can do it inside of two or three hours."

"Well, isn't that nice," Sellers said. "Old Master Mind, himself, on the job. You're going to beat the whole damned police force, aren't you, Donald?"

"Yes."

"Modest, isn't he?" Sellers said to Bertha.

I said, "Sit down and don't go off half-cocked, and I'll prove it to you. The trouble with the police is that the minute they pick someone up, the newspapers are on their tail and the next thing anyone knows the whole thing is smeared all over the pages of the press. The cops won't fall for bribery, but how they do lap up publicity! All a newspaper has to do is to take you off into a corner and say, 'Look, Sellers, give me the dope on this and I'll play it up big, how you went out and followed clues everyone else had overlooked and captured the gal you wanted singlehanded.' You fall for that like a ton of brick, and spill everything you know."

"Go on," Sellers said. "Go right ahead."

I said, "I'm going to tell you the truth."

"Well, well, well!"

"Dr. George L. Quay sent Ruth Otis down to get some arsenic. She brought it back and put it in the laboratory the way he told her to. Ruth told me about it and asked what she should do. I told her to go back to Dr. Quay's office, get that package of arsenic before he had a chance to conceal it or tamper with it, and put it in some safe place.

"Ruth got the arsenic last night, put it in a locker at the Union Station. She told me about it. I told her she should have notified the police. She said she wanted me to do it. I told her to wait here and I'd go get the arsenic. She said the key to the locker where she'd put the poison was in her other suit. She gave me the key to her apartment. I went to her apartment to get that locker key. When I opened her door, using the key she'd given me, someone conked me. And when I came to, there was the corpse in back of the wall-bed. I went down and reported the corpse, but before I did that, I took a look through the suit Ruth described. The key was in the pocket just like she had said. I took it down to the Union Depot, opened the locker where the poison was supposed to be. It wasn't there."

"So you rang up the police right away and told them all about it!" Sellers said sarcastically. "That puts you in the clear. I'm glad you did it."

I said, "I wanted to ask Ruth some questions and get the thing straightened out before we had all the publicity that was bound to result from calling the police."

"Well," Sellers said to Bertha, "I guess that means you go it alone from here on, Bertha."

"What do you mean?"

He said, "On the strength of what Donald himself has said, he's an accessory after the fact. He's going to be out of circulation for fifteen or twenty years."

"You mean that, Frank?" she asked.

"Damn right I mean it," Sellers said. "I'm going to throw the book at him. I've had enough of this masterminding."

I said, "Sit down, and take the load off your feet. Let's talk a little sense."

"Talk sense, hell," Sellers said. "You've talked already."

I said, "Hold your horses. I didn't have a damned bit of corroboration, didn't have a thing to go on. I simply had to know I was right before I got you in on it. I didn't want to give you a bum steer."

"No," Sellers said sarcastically. "You wouldn't give *me* a bum steer. Not a-tall."

"Look, Sergeant, leave this girl here. She won't try to get away. The newspapers won't know anything about it. Work with me two hours and we'll have this case solved."

Sellers grinned and said, "As far as I'm concerned, I've got it solved now. You folks are going to Headquarters."

"Sellers, have a heart!"

"Phooey," he said. "I've got a head. I don't need a heart."

"You take this girl into custody and spread all this stuff in the newspapers, and you'll *never* get your murderer."

"I've got my murderer right now. I may have two of them. You know what I think, Donald?"

"What?"

"I think you went to this jane's apartment, and I think Ethel Worley caught you there. I think you tapped her over the head just trying to make a clean getaway, and you tapped her a little bit too hard. You thought you'd tie her up so she wouldn't make a noise and—hell, you may have strangled her deliberately. I don't know. You're no tin angel as far as that's concerned. Bertha has had nothing but trouble ever since you joined the partnership."

"She's made nothing but money."

"She isn't making any money out of this case," Sellers said.

"Just two hours," I pleaded.

"Not a damn minute."

I said, "Let me make one phone call."

He laughed at me.

"Just one phone call."

"Who to?"

I looked at my wristwatch and said, "My bookie. I want to see what happened in that race."

Sellers said, "Is it that late already?"

"It's that late."

"I'll find out," he said. "I'll call— No, I won't, either. Bertha, you make the call."

Bertha went over to my telephone, dialed the number, said, "Hello…hello…let me speak with…oh, it is, is it? Well, you know who this is. How did I do on Fair Lady?"

I watched Bertha's face with more anxiety than I'd ever felt over the outcome of any horse race in my life. When I saw it light up, I let my knees buckle me into a chair and groped for a cigarette.

"The little runt," Bertha said, hanging up the phone, admiration in her voice.

"How much?" Sellers asked.

"Won by a neck," Bertha said. "Five to one. Two hundred and fifty smackers. You've got a hundred coming, Frank."

"A hundred, hell!" Sellers said. "I told you I was going to split that extra ten with you."

"Oh," Bertha said, meekly. "I thought there was some misunderstanding about it. I thought you only wanted twenty."

"Nuts," Sellers said.

"Well," Bertha told him, "we aren't going to get in an argument over fifty bucks."

"You're damn right we aren't."

I said, "There you are. Go ahead and be a dumb cop all your life."

"What the hell are you talking about?"

"You take this girl into custody and the whole story comes out."

"Won't that be too bad?" Sellers said. "I can just see it in headlines in the paper: 'Sellers Arrests Murderess. Modern Lucretia Borgia Nabbed By Shrewd Detective Work on Part of Sergeant Frank Sellers.'"

Sellers grinned at me, said, "How do you like it, Master Mind? You're the one that threw it at me. I'm throwing it back at you."

"Sure," I said. "You'll get a lot of newspaper notoriety. Then what?"

"Then maybe I'll get boosted. I might get promoted, and my

pay would be raised. Wouldn't that be terrible? Give me a handkerchief, Bertha. I'm going to bust out crying."

I said, "You'll ruin the only absolutely mathematical system of playing the horses that was ever invented. This guy is mixed in the case up to his necktie. Soon as he reads about Ruth and me in the papers, he'll take a powder. Then, soon as I tell my story, the police will have to go after him. They'll raid his place. You might be smart and make the raid, but even if you did, you know what would happen then.

"As soon as the brass hats learn what you have, the Captain will come in and say, 'Sergeant, let me have that evidence.' And about the time the Captain gets his hands on it, the Chief will come in and say, 'Captain, bring that evidence into my office.'"

Sellers scratched his head.

I said, "You've got this girl. You've got me. Sew us up any way you want to, but use your head and you'll be able to have this whole handicapping system where you can use it. All you have to do is to put some Celluloid slips in a chart, turn a couple of disks, press the button, and read the answer."

Bertha Cool said, almost tearfully, "Five to one, Frank. Cripes, if we'd bet five hundred it would have been twenty-five hundred!"

Sellers walked over, sat down, pulled a match from his pocket, scraped it on the sole of his shoe, and held the flame to the end of his half-chewed cigar.

For four or five seconds, he puffed out blue smoke; then he said to me, "Where is this dump, Donald?"

I laughed at him.

Sellers said, "It isn't going to do you any good. You can't play the horses for a long, long time."

"It won't do you any good. It won't do anyone any good, except maybe the Chief."

"I could go right to the Chief with it," Sellers said, "and—"

"You could if you got hold of it."

"I'll get hold of it all right, don't worry."

"You and the newspapers," I said.

Sellers shifted his position, ran his fingers through his thick, wavy hair, looked at Bertha.

Bertha said, musingly, "Just by pressing a button. I'll be a dirty name!"

Sellers turned to Ruth Otis, said, "I haven't heard your story yet, Ruth. Let's hear it."

I said, "Shut up, Ruth."

Sellers flushed, said to me angrily, "Who the hell do you think you are?"

I tried blowing a smoke ring. "I'm the guy that told you to put your money on Fair Lady."

Sellers and Bertha exchanged glances. Sellers said, "How much time do you want?"

I said, "You can leave Bertha here with Ruth Otis. You know damn well Bertha will play ball with you. I'll go with you and show you where this place is."

"Then what?"

"Then we raid the dump."

"*We* do!"

I said, "You're looking for evidence. I'm a material witness."

"Witness, hell!" Sellers said. "You're my prisoner."

"Okay, have it any way you want, only make your investigation the way I tell you to."

"Why should I do that?"

I said, "Why did you bet on Fair Lady? Because you wanted to make some jack, didn't you?"

Ruth said, "As far as I'm concerned—"

"Shut up."

She kept quiet.

Bertha said pleadingly to Sellers, "You know you can trust me, Frank. If the little devil tries to pull any shenanigans on me I'll flatten her out like a bookmark. And I'm the baby that can do it."

Sellers looked admiringly at Bertha's broad shoulders.

"Damned if you ain't," he admitted thoughtfully.

Chapter Nineteen
Voices of Death

We walked down the corridor in the Pawkette Building and passed the office of Dr. George L. Quay.

Sellers looked at me, curiously. "Quay isn't the guy?"

"No."

"I thought he was. You wouldn't try to string me, would you?"

"No."

"No, you made a deal. I think you'll shoot square. Where are we going?"

I paused before the door of the Alpha Investment Company.

"Here."

I knocked.

After a moment I heard steps and then Keetley opened the door. "Well, well, how are you, Lam? Didn't expect to see you back so soon. Still snooping?"

I said, "Meet Frank Sellers, Mr. Keetley."

Keetley looked him over, shook hands, and if he knew Sellers was a cop, gave no indication.

"We want to talk to you a minute," Sellers said.

Keetley, who had been standing in the door, stepped back, said, "Just a moment," and slammed the door shut.

"What the hell!" Sellers said as the door clicked shut. He grabbed the knob, rattled the door, and then threw his weight against it. "Hey," he shouted. "Get this door open."

Keetley opened the door.

Sellers swept back his coat, showed Keetley his badge, and said, "What the hell's the idea?"

"I had forgotten something," Keetley said. "I didn't intend to slam the door in your faces."

"Well, if you didn't intend to do it, it was a funny accident," Sellers said.

"To what am I indebted for this visit, Lieutenant?"

"Just Sergeant, so far," Sellers said. "I'm checking up a little bit. What are you doing here?"

"I have an office—just a hobby."

"What sort of a hobby?"

"Frankly, I play the races occasionally, Sergeant."

"How do you play them?"

"The same way anyone else does. I pick the winner and put money on him. Sometimes he wins; sometimes he doesn't."

"How do you pick them?"

"By handicapping."

"What's that machine you got over there with the light in it?"

"That's something I use in helping me arrive at my conclusions."

"Mind showing me how it works?"

"Certainly, I do," Keetley said coldly. Then looking at me, said, "What's the idea, Lam? Can't you keep anything under your hat?"

I said, "Personally, I'm on my way to jail. We're just stopping by. I'm under arrest."

Keetley raised his eyebrows.

Sellers said, "I'm not entirely satisfied with some of the things in this case."

I said, "Keetley knows that Ruth Otis took that poison out of Dr. Quay's office last night. He followed her, saw what she did with it."

"The hell he did," Sellers said.

Keetley looked at me and said, "What is this? Are you trying to pass the buck in some way?"

"Never mind him. Talk to me," Sellers said.

Keetley said, "I'm awfully sorry, Sergeant, but it's all news to me. I don't even know Ruth Otis."

"She's Dr. Quay's nurse."

"Oh, yes. Dr. Quay. He has an office here on this floor."

"Well, what about it?" Sellers asked. "Did you follow her?"

Keetley laughed and said, "Certainly not. I have something else to do with my time. I can't go around following women over the city."

I said to Sellers, "Let's get this straight. Pin him down on it. Be sure there isn't any misunderstanding. Get him to make a definite commitment, one way or another."

Keetley looked at me coldly and said, "I think I'm going to dislike you, Lam."

"Probably you are," I said, "but the question right now is whether you followed Dr. Quay's nurse last night."

"I tell you I didn't."

"Didn't follow her to the Union Depot?"

"No."

"Didn't see her put a package in a parcel-check locker?"

He laughed and said, "No, definitely not. Absolutely not. I'm sorry, Lam, but you can't use me as a red herring."

Sellers said, "Understand, I'm just checking up, that's all. And I'll tell you something. Ethel Worley, Ballwin's secretary, was found murdered in Ruth Otis's apartment this morning. What's more, that package of poison with about thirty grains missing was found in Ruth's apartment. Now if you know anything about Ruth or about that poison, you start spilling right now."

Keetley licked his lips. "I know nothing about Ruth Otis. I tell you I didn't even see her last night."

I eased my way around behind Keetley, close to the radio

outfit that was on the table, as Keetley and Sellers locked eyes in a mutual and somewhat antagonistic appraisal. I twisted the knob which turned the switch.

I said, "All I wanted to do was to catch you in a complete falsehood, Keetley. One of my operatives was following you last night."

"You mean he *said* he was," Keetley sneered. "He probably was in a saloon some place and made his report up out of thin air."

I said to Frank Sellers, "It was Jim Fordney. You know him. You know how much chance there'd be that he'd fake a report."

I saw interest on Sellers's face. He said, "You mean Fordney followed this guy and knows that he was following Ruth Otis?"

"That's right."

Keetley said suavely, "And how does anyone know it was poison Ruth Otis had in the package, Sergeant?"

Sellers said, "That's a point, Donald. How does anyone know?"

I said, "Fordney can describe the package."

"In other words," Keetley said, smiling, "it's Ruth Otis's word and that's all."

"What do you expect a detective to do?" I asked. "Stop her? Ask for a teaspoonful of the poison so he can make sure that's what it is?"

Sellers started to say something, but checked himself as a voice filled the office: "Open up a little wider, please."

"What the hell?" Sellers said.

Keetley turned, reached out for the radio.

I caught his wrist.

"Now spit," the voice said.

Keetley threw me to one side.

A woman's voice said, "Doctor, that hurt—"

Keetley switched off the radio.

"What the hell?" Sellers said again.

Keetley said, "Sergeant, I'll meet you at Headquarters or any other place for any questions you may wish to ask; but this office is private. I'm engaged in handicapping horses and I don't care for divulging the secrets of my system. And as far as Lam is concerned—"

He whirled to me, his eyes glittering with anger. "You get the hell out of here," he said venomously.

I said to Sellers, "I suppose you know what that was?"

Keetley made a swing at me.

I got my head out of the way just in time.

Keetley, his face white with anger, said, "Damn you, I'll—"

Sergeant Sellers reached forward a big, capable hand. His fingers gathered up a fistful of necktie, coat lapel, and shirt. He shoved Keetley back against the wall and said, "Stay there! Let's get this thing straight."

I reached over and switched on the radio again. Keetley made a grab at me and Sellers slammed him back against the wall.

Once more the voice filled the office. "Well, I think that's all the drilling we'll have to do. It was pretty hot in there, but we're past all the decay now."

"What the hell is it?" Sellers asked.

"Dr. Quay preparing a patient for an inlay, I judge."

Sellers whistled.

"Both of you fellows can get out of this office," Keetley said. "You don't happen to have a search warrant, do you, Sellers?"

I said, "He doesn't need one. You're not a peace officer. You have a Dictograph running into Dr. Quay's office. That's a crime. When premises are being used for the commission of crime, a peace officer doesn't need a warrant."

Sellers looked at me and nodded gratefully.

Keetley said, "And to think I've been palling around with this guy! I gave him a right steer on those lots in Ballwin's subdivision so's he wouldn't get stuck. I gave him a tip on Fair Lady this afternoon. Win anything on it?" he asked.

"We all did," I said.

"That's what comes of letting out information about a race horse," Keetley said.

"Never mind all that," Sellers told him. "I know Jim Fordney personally. If he said you followed Ruth Otis, I know damn well you followed her. Now what's the idea?"

Keetley spread his hands in a gesture of surrender. "I'm trying to work this thing out, so I'll have a perfect case which I can put into the hands of the police. A premature disclosure will ruin it."

"Oh, my God, another one," Sellers groaned.

"Another what?"

"Another damned amateur, trying to stand between the police and their folly," Sellers said. "If some of you guys who have information would turn it over to us, and let us get this case cleaned up, it'd be a big relief. But no, every damned mastermind on the job has to freeze onto what he knows. What do you know? Tell me all you know, and tell it fast!"

"Why should I?"

Sellers pointed toward the receiving unit of the Dictograph and said, "You heard what Lam just said."

Keetley said, "I don't want you to jump the gun on this thing."

"Put your cards on the table," Sellers told him. "And where the hell do we sit down? Okay, now let's get going."

I said, "Just to help your recollection a little, Keetley, I'm going to tell you where you can begin."

"Where?"

"Several months ago you sent a hairbrush containing some

strands of human hair to a firm of consulting chemists. You wanted an analysis made for traces of arsenic. Now suppose you begin there."

He kept looking at me for as much as ten seconds, apparently trying to find out just how much I knew.

Sellers said, "Well, come on. Get started."

Keetley pushed papers away from the corner of his desk, cleared a place where he could rest one hip, and sat there, one foot on the floor and one foot swinging like a pendulum, slowly, methodically, the only outward evidence of nerve tension.

"Go ahead," Sellers said.

"All right. I'll give it to you straight. My sister married Gerald Ballwin. She had been very close to me. We loved each other deeply. I was opposed to the match with Gerald. He looked to me like a weak sister and a chaser.

"He *was* a chaser. He started in playing around with Daphne. Then Anita got sick. It was a pretty bad stomach upset. Apparently a case of food poisoning. She was sick for a long time. Then she began to get well. Then suddenly she died. There was no autopsy. The doctor gave a death certificate, death from complications following a gastro-enteric disturbance due to food poisoning. The body was cremated.

"Gerald married Daphne. Damn fool that I was, it was six months before I began to suspect anything. And then I began to think of lots of things. Well, it was too late. The body had been cremated. The ashes were scattered over a whole mountainside. But I began to look around. I began to read up on things."

Keetley walked over to his shelf, took down a book entitled *Forensic Medicine,* said, "This is the fourth edition of Sydney Smith. Here's what he has to say about arsenic. Arsenic is a peculiar poison. It will appear in the nails and in the hair long after there's no trace of it in any other part of the body. Here's what Smith says: *It has been shown that arsenic is not found in the hair until about five days after ingestion, that it continues to be excreted into the hair for several months, and that it may be demonstrated there after its complete disappearance from the rest of the body.*

"Among the personal effects of my sister which had been turned over to me was the hairbrush she had used in her last illness. I had it analyzed. The hair contained distinct traces of arsenic."

"Why didn't you go to the police?" Sellers asked.

Keetley snorted. "Go to the police? They'd claim a frameup. They'd claim that the hair on the brush wasn't from Anita's head. It was the only evidence that was left. You couldn't get another damn bit of evidence. I've tried. I covered drugstores. I looked into poison registers. I prowled around. And in order to make it a little more effective, I pretended to be a drunken bum, a chap who played the ponies, sometimes having a winning streak, and then going on a bat and losing it all."

"And all the time you were trying to get evidence?"

"That's right."

"Against Gerald Ballwin?"

"Don't be silly," Keetley said. "Against Daphne."

"Against Daphne? But she's dead."

"You're damn right, she's dead."

Sellers's eyes narrowed. "Let's hear the rest of it," he said.

"Daphne's dead. I shouldn't say things against her, but she was no good. She was a rat. She was a tramp. While I was looking for evidence, I contrived to keep her under pretty close observation. I found out she was taking an interest in Dr. Quay. And then, for some reason or other, perhaps it was just a hunch, I got the idea that this Dr. Quay might have been instrumental in getting the poison she used on Anita. I looked up poison registers and found that Dr. Quay used arsenic from time to time. Well, it was only a step after that to getting this office and putting a microphone in Dr. Quay's office. That called for making all of the elaborate setup which you see here."

"What did you find out?" Sellers asked.

Keetley hesitated perceptibly and then said, "I'm going to tell you what I've found out. I certainly hope you have sense enough not to spill it until you're ready."

"Let's have it."

Keetley walked over to a big filing-cabinet, took a key from his pocket, opened a drawer, and disclosed a rack filled with wax cylinders.

He said, "These are wax cylinders containing conversations which came over the Dictograph from Dr. Quay's office. I'd put the important ones on cylinders. Whenever I had to be out of the office, I'd set the Dictograph so that it would record on wax cylinders everything that was said in Dr. Quay's office. Lots of the cylinders were simply blank, lots of them had only routine conversations on them, such as you heard just now. Here's one, however, I think you'll be interested in."

Keetley selected one of the wax records, said, "The whole thing is right here on this record. There is, of course, some distortion due to microphones and all of that, but you can still recognize the voices, I think."

He opened the closet door, took out a transcribing machine, plugged it into a socket, slipped the wax cylinder on, and said, "Listen to this."

For a moment we could hear only the faint surface noises made by the transcribing needle as it moved over the cylinder. Then suddenly Ruth Otis's voice, sounding, all things considered, quite natural and lifelike, said, "Dr. Quay, Mrs. Ballwin is here. I told her she'd have to wait. She insists upon seeing you."

"Send her into the laboratory."

"I'm sorry, Doctor. The other patient who is waiting has been there ever since—"

"Send her into the laboratory."

"The patient in the office," Ruth Otis said firmly and clearly, "is complaining that he has an appointment, yet several people have been run in ahead of him and—"

"Send her into the laboratory."

"Very well, Doctor."

There was a moment's pause. Then Dr. Quay's voice, sounding exceedingly unctuous, said, apparently to the patient in his chair, "I'm terribly sorry, but this patient happens to have a very acute condition that requires emergency treatment. Whenever she comes up here, it means she's suffering terribly. If you'll excuse me for just one moment, please."

There followed an interval of silence and Keetley explained, "I have microphones planted in Quay's different offices. He's leaving now to go to the laboratory. The next pickup will be the laboratory mike. Here it is."

There was the sound of a door opening and closing. Then Dr. Quay's voice saying to Daphne, "I'm terribly busy. I—"

"I wish that you'd fire that little bitch," Daphne Ballwin's voice said.

"She's loyal. She's just trying to do her best, Daphne. After all—"

"I want her fired!"

"Let me explain, Daphne. You see, there was a patient—"

"Are you going to fire her?"

"Yes, sweetheart."

"That's better, darling. Kiss me."

There was no sound of the kiss. Keetley said parenthetically, "Those kind are silent."

Sellers shifted his position.

The voices came in again from the recording machine. "Darling, I had to see you," Daphne said. "The break we've been waiting for has come. I'll have to give it to you fast because I think we can put the whole thing across tonight."

"Go ahead," Dr. Quay said. "Hit the high spots, sweetheart. What is it?"

"The Zesty-Paste people, who make anchovy paste, want to do some advertising. Their representative called on me this afternoon and left me a carton of the paste. He wants me to try it out. Then they're going to send down photographers and have photographs taken for use in their advertising campaign. It is to be in all the magazines. God, I'd like to go through with it, but I know that if I wait, Gerald is going to change his insurance, change his will, and that damn Ethel Worley is going to get her hooks into him."

"Of course," Dr. Quay's voice said, "he's very vulnerable as far as Ethel Worley is concerned. After all, if you—"

"Don't be silly, darling. Ethel Worley isn't such a damn fool. She's had detectives on us and knows about that weekend. Damn it, if it wasn't for that, I certainly would— Well, anyhow, no one has any suspicion about this other thing, so I think that now is the time to go through with it."

"You mean, use this anchovy paste to—"

"That's right."

Dr. Quay's voice said, "Now remember, Daphne. There can't be any slip-up on this thing. You've got to do *exactly* as I say. The tolerance for this type of poison varies with the individual, but all authorities agree that there has never been a fatality on a two-grain dose. Now there are two grains in this capsule. Be sure nothing happens to it."

"And when do I take it?"

"You take it just before you give the other to your husband. It will take the capsule a little while to dissolve in your stomach, so that your husband will be the first to get sick. You can telephone the doctor, and describe your husband's symptoms, and be sure you describe them just as I've told you. He will diagnose the case as food poisoning and tell you certain things to do.

"Now about the time he is finished giving you those instructions, you'll be getting sick too. That will excuse you from doing anything more about it when your husband gets worse instead of better. Now you've got that all straight?"

"I should have. We've been over it often enough."

"All right," Dr. Quay said. "Now here's something else. Don't think that you're going to double-cross me on this. We're playing for keeps now."

"What do you mean?"

Quay said, "You mean a lot to me, darling, but still somehow I don't trust you. Who's this chauffeur?"

Her laugh sounded harsh and metallic as it came from the wax cylinder.

"Who is he?" Dr. Quay insisted.

"No one that needs worry you, darling. I'll fire him in a minute if you say so."

"Well, I say so. I don't like him. I think he's snooping."

"Oh, don't be silly! The boy is just trying his best to get along. Poor fellow. I sympathize with him."

"Well, I don't."

"Heavens, George, do you think anyone like that could— Darling, kiss me."

Again there was an interval of silence.

Then Dr. Quay said, "Now, remember, Daphne, you're going to have two grains of arsenic in your stomach. If you get even the least bit more, it may prove fatal. Fix the crackers that you want your husband to take on one side of the plate. Keep the ones that you can afford to eat on the other side of the plate. It won't hurt anything if Gerald takes crackers from both sides, but you can only afford to take crackers from the one side. You understand?"

"Yes, darling. I know. Don't think I'm so stupid. And remember to fire that bitch in your reception office!"

The machine went silent and Keetley said, "That's all there is on this record. The record which follows has just the tag end of the conversation, nothing particularly significant. I think this gives you the sketch."

Sellers looked at him with eyes that showed astonishment and elation in spite of anything he could do to keep his self-control.

"Now then," Keetley went on, switching off the machine, "I can tell you the rest of it."

"Go right ahead," Sellers said.

"Daphne Ballwin took the poison and went out and mixed up arsenic with the anchovy paste. She was smart enough, however, to leave herself an alibi in case anyone ever suspected that it wasn't just a case of food poisoning. She secured a cup that Carlotta Hanford, her secretary, had used in drinking demi-tasse. It had Carlotta's fingerprints on it. Daphne mixed the poison in that cup. She fixed up some crackers with the poisoned anchovy paste and some crackers that weren't poisoned. Then she left the plate with the crackers and anchovy paste on it, while she went to greet her husband. It was up to the butler to serve the hors d'oeuvres.

"Now here's a little irony of fate. Daphne had picked up this green kid who knew something about driving a car but didn't know very much about anything else. Daphne had him to play around with, just something to keep her occupied during the spare moments of her time. In due time she probably would have poisoned Dr. Quay, in order to have enjoyed life with this chauffeur, but right now she was keeping him around her because he amused her. His dog-like devotion flattered her. The fact that she could make him work at something that was obnoxious to him gave her a sense of power, a sense of command that was a tonic to her.

"But the butler apparently was inept. When he picked up the plate, he slid some of the crackers off the plate, either to the pantry shelf or perhaps to the floor. He retrieved these crackers, put them back on the plate, and, in doing so, inadvertently changed the entire arrangement.

"Daphne had duly taken her two-grain capsule of arsenic. When the poisoned hors d'oeuvres came in, she selected one that she knew was loaded with poison, fed it to her husband while he was busy with the cocktail shaker. Then she settled down and had a few hors d'oeuvres with him. In doing so she must have taken an additional one or two of the poisoned crackers. That, on top of the two grains she had taken, was enough to do the trick.

"Everything would have gone according to schedule if it hadn't been for that and if it hadn't been for the fact that Carlotta became suspicious almost immediately, telephoned another doctor, and then notified the police. So that in place of becoming merely terribly ill as Daphne and Dr. Quay had intended, Daphne collapsed. She'd taken a fatal dose of arsenic.

"There, gentlemen," Keetley said with a little gesture, "is your story of the murder."

"And how about Ethel Worley?" I asked.

"It happens that I know what happened there," Keetley said. "As a matter of fact, I did follow Ruth Otis. The little fool couldn't let well enough alone. You see, Dr. Quay is smart. From time to time he makes it a point to use arsenic. He knew that a check of the poison registers would show that. He knew that sooner or later his friendship for Daphne Ballwin would be investigated.

"This is where Dr. Quay was smart. Knowing that he might be questioned and knowing that the books would show that he had purchased arsenic in the past, he sent his nurse out about the time he thought things were getting ready for a blow-off to get a package of arsenic. He didn't need that arsenic at all. It was his idea that when the police questioned him about it, he would be able to say, 'Why, yes, gentlemen, I did send the nurse out for arsenic. I've been out for the last two or three weeks and I like to keep it on hand because I use it for this and that. But the arsenic that we bought couldn't have any connection with anything that happened to Mr. Ballwin because that arsenic is still on my shelves untouched.' And then he'd lead the way into his laboratory, and let the police open the package and see that nothing was missing.

"But Ruth Otis had been the one to buy that arsenic. She was afraid that she might be connected with the case, so she went to Dr. Quay's office last night, and removed the arsenic, taking it to the Union Depot where she concealed it in a parcel-checking locker. I didn't want to see the evidence distorted that way because it would mean that under those circumstances, suspicion would be directed toward Ruth Otis either as a principal or an accomplice and I knew that Dr. Quay was perfectly capable of swearing that she was bitter and vindictive and had stolen the bottle of poison and used it to kill a woman whom she hated.

"So, gentlemen, I rectified that mistake just as soon as I had an opportunity."

"How did you rectify it?" Sellers asked.

"Why, by taking the arsenic out of the locker where she'd concealed it and putting it right back where it belonged in Dr. Quay's office. Those lockers aren't too hard to open."

"You have a passkey to his office?" Sellers asked.

Keetley grinned. "How do you suppose I installed those Dictographs?"

"Then you put the poison back on Dr. Quay's laboratory shelf?"

"That's right."

"Then how did it happen it was found in Ruth Otis's apartment?"

"You can figure that one out for yourself," Keetley said. "As soon as Dr. Quay learned that Mrs. Ballwin had died, he knew he had to get himself in the clear and by that time he knew also an autopsy would be performed on Mrs. Ballwin's body.

"Dr. Quay decided that what he needed was a fall guy. He felt sure that Ruth Otis would be out this morning looking for a new job. He decided he'd take that poison she had purchased for him, dump about thirty grains of it down the sink, and put the rest of it in her apartment."

"You can prove this?" Sellers asked.

Keetley looked at him scornfully. "For God's sake," he said, "I've tied the whole damn case up in a pink ribbon for you, put it on a silver platter and handed it to you. You should be able to do *some* of the stuff for yourself."

"In other words, this business about Ethel Worley is pure deduction on your part. Is that right?"

"My God, I can't expect to have *everything* for you. There should be some—"

"Never mind the sarcasm," Sellers interrupted. "I want to know what you *know* as distinguished from what you *think*."

"All right, I know that Dr. Quay planned to murder Gerald Ballwin. I know that he and Daphne were in on the deal together. I know that Daphne poisoned Anita. I know that there was a mix-up and that Daphne got an overdose of her own poison. I *surmise* that Dr. Quay wanted to put the arsenic in Ruth Otis's apartment. I *know* that I put that package of arsenic on his laboratory shelf at about eleven-thirty last night. I *surmise* that Dr. Quay dumped out about half of that poison, took the rest of it out to Ruth Otis's apartment to plant it. I *surmise* that while he was in that apartment, Ethel Worley, trying to get Ruth Otis lined up as a witness, caught Dr. Quay either in the apartment or just coming out of the apartment.

"That was something Dr. Quay hadn't counted on. He knew Ethel Worley suspected him and he knew she hated him. You can see what had to happen after that. Once Quay had opened that arsenic and dumped out part of it, it had to be either Quay or the girl in the long run."

Sellers chewed away at his cigar for several seconds, then suddenly said, "Donald, I'm going in and talk with Dr. Quay. I'm going to leave you here to see that nothing happens to this evidence."

"Don't worry," Keetley said. "Nothing will happen to it."

"I know," Sellers said. "But that record you have there means the difference between life and death for Dr. Quay. It means the difference between a promotion and a demotion for me. I can't take that record with me where I'm going and I can't call in any assistance. Not right now."

Sellers looked at me. "Can I depend on you, Donald?"

"You can depend on me," I said. "Give me the record, Keetley."

Keetley handed me the record.

I said, "Better frisk him for a gun, Frank."

Sergeant Sellers ran his hands over Keetley's unresisting contours. "He's clean," he said.

"Okay. I'll keep him that way. I don't want any misunderstanding about this, Keetley. We're mixed up in a murder case now. No monkey business."

"You damn fools," Keetley said. "I'm trying to solve the case. I hope you don't go barging in on Dr. Quay now, because I don't think he's ripe for a confession. I think if we get a little more evidence—"

"If he isn't ripe for a confession now," Sellers said grimly, "I'll soften him up and make him ripe. I'm going to have this case all cleaned up, and I mean *all* cleaned up. You guys wait here."

Sellers turned and strode past me. He paused on the threshold. "I'm depending on you, Donald."

"Okay," I told him.

The door marked *Alpha Investment Company* clicked shut.

"I think it's too early to try for a confession," Keetley said to me.

I said, "You don't know Sellers. He's a nice boy, but when he gets hard, he's *hard.* What do you say we turn on that Dictograph, Keetley?"

"Why?"

"I'd like to hear Sellers's technique."

Keetley's face lit. "Gosh," he said, "so would I."

He clicked on the switch.

"Better put on a wax record too," I said. "We may want to have some evidence of this."

Keetley nodded, turned a switch, and said, "Everything is recording now."

I settled back in the comfortable chair.

I hadn't much more than got a match to the end of my cigarette when the Dictograph started spewing words out into the office.

"I'm sorry, sir. I'm short of a nurse today. My nurse just quit yesterday without any notice whatever. If you'll just wait out there— Huh?"

Sellers's voice said, "Sergeant Sellers. Homicide squad. Anything you say will be used against you. Get that patient out of there. I want to talk with you."

"We can talk in the laboratory."

"Okay, get in there."

Dr. Quay said, "May I ask the meaning of this intrusion. You—"

"You knew Daphne Ballwin," Sellers's voice said.

"Yes, she was a patient of mine."

"Just a patient?"

"That's all."

"How much work did you do on her?"

"Why, I—"

"How much? Bring out your books."

"I'm afraid that I didn't put her work on the books, as an old friend—"

"How often was she in here?"

"Why, several times."

"How often?"

"More or less frequently."

"How often in the last two months?"

"I can't tell."

"Do your books show?"

"No."

"In other words, she came in to see you from time to time without having appointments?"

"Yes."

"And without making any appointments when she left?"

"No."

"She just had the run of your office?"

"Well, not exactly—"

"Your nurse says she did."

"The nurse was jealous. She thinks she lost her job on account of Mrs. Ballwin."

"Did she?"

"Absolutely not. She was discharged for insolence."

"Mrs. Ballwin didn't have anything to do with it?"

"No."

"You give Mrs. Ballwin any arsenic?"

"Arsenic? Good heavens, no!"

"Never did?"

"No."

"You sent your nurse out to buy some arsenic?"

"I did not. If my nurse bought any arsenic, she did it without my knowledge or consent. And quite evidently for the purpose of poisoning someone. Good heavens, do you suppose there is any possibility that vindictive girl, with her warped mind and starved personality, could have poisoned Daphne Ballwin?"

"No," Sellers said, "I don't suppose there's a bit of possibility of it. I do know that you went to her apartment to try and plant some evidence, and while you were there, Ethel Worley came in."

"What are you talking about, Sergeant?"

"Don't kid me," Sellers said. "And I know damn well that you planned with Daphne to poison her husband."

"You're crazy!"

"The hell I'm crazy," Sellers said.

We heard the sound of something ripping and then Sellers said, "Look at that! Do you see that!"

"Yes, what is it?"

"It's the microphone of a Dictograph," Sellers said. "We've had a Dictograph in your office. We heard the whole conversation when you and Daphne planned to murder her husband. You gave Daphne a two-grain capsule. Didn't you?"

There was a long period of silence.

"Come on," Sellers said, "*out* with it!"

Dr. Quay's voice was quivering with fear now. "I swear to you, Sergeant, that all I did was give her enough arsenic to make her sick. She wanted to simulate the symptoms of food poisoning. If you had a recording of the conversations which took place in this laboratory, you know that."

"Yeah, we know it," Sellers said. "You were trying to kill her husband. Weren't you?"

Quay thought for a moment and then said, "Well, what if we were? Her husband is getting well, isn't he?"

"And," Sellers said, "you went out to Ruth Otis's apartment to plant some evidence. You were surprised by Ethel Worley out there."

"Definitely not! You can't substantiate a bit of that."

"The hell I can't!" Sellers said. "How do you suppose Ethel Worley got to that apartment? Mary Ingram, who works in the same office with her, drove her down there. She was waiting for Ethel Worley to come out. And while she was waiting, she was sitting in the car studying Spanish, but she happened to look up when you went in. She happened to look up when you went out. After half an hour when Ethel Worley didn't show up, Mary Ingram went up to the apartment and knocked. She didn't get any answer, so she called the police. You know what the police found. Now then, by God—"

The microphone suddenly sounded as though someone was moving furniture around the other office. Then Sellers, with a grunt of satisfaction, said, "Try some more of that and see what happens to you! Now get up here—get up on your feet, you yellow-livered liar. Get up and tell the truth!"

And Dr. Quay started telling the truth, a quavering confession which lasted for some ten minutes.

Sellers put Dr. Quay under arrest. We could hear the click of the handcuffs. Then we heard Sellers telephoning for the squad car to get there on the run.

I went over to Keetley's phone and dialed the number of Dr. Quay's office.

Sellers answered the phone.

I said, "I did a job for you, Frank."

"Who is this talking?"

"Lam."

"Where are you?"

"Right here in Keetley's office. I say, I did a job for you."

"Damned if you didn't!"

I said, "You don't know the half of it. I did something you forgot to do."

"What?"

"Have Keetley turn on his recording machine on the Dictograph," I said. "Every word of Dr. Quay's confession is down here on wax cylinders. You can take the evidence in with you when you go to Headquarters."

There was a moment's silence and then Sellers said, "By God, I owe you one on that!"

I said, "Better turn your prisoner over to the squad car when it comes, Frank, and then you can come in here and collect the evidence. That will give you an opportunity to confer with Keetley here, and of course neither you nor Keetley would want his system of handicapping horses to become public."

Sellers said, "Remind me, Lam, to give you a courtesy card, which may come in handy when you get pinched for speeding."

"That's swell," I said. "In the meantime you can ring up Bertha Cool at my apartment and tell her Ruth Otis is in the clear. Tell Bertha to get the hell out of there and leave Ruth alone."

"What's your number?" Sellers asked.

I gave it to him.

"Okay," Sellers said. "It'll be done."

I hung up the phone.

Keetley said, "I thought you said you were a prisoner when you came in here."

"Just a gag," I told him, holding up my two crossed fingers. "Frank Sellers and I are just like that!"

Chapter Twenty
Cupid Closes a Case

I went out to the auto cabin where I'd left Carlotta Hanford, parked the car, and tried the door of the bungalow.

It was locked. I knocked on the door. After a minute Carlotta's voice from the other side of the door said, "Who's there?"

"Donald Lam."

"Oh," she said, and opened the door. "Come in. Make yourself right at home."

"Thanks."

I kicked the door shut behind me. She walked over to the davenport and sat down. I found an easy chair and lit a cigarette.

"Tired?" she asked.

"Yes."

"Been working?"

"Uh huh."

She said somewhat coyly, "How are you now? What's your present mood? Professional or biological?"

"Professional."

She made a little face and said, "I liked you better when you were biological. I put on my very best stockings today and haven't had a word out of you."

"There were more important things to think about."

"That's what irritates me."

"What?"

"That you *would* consider other things more important."

"Who's being biological now?"

She laughed a throaty, nervous little laugh. "I am."

I said, "Carlotta, when you came to the Agency, you weren't using your own money."

"What makes you think I wasn't?"

I smiled and said, "I don't think you're in love with Gerald Ballwin. Even if you had been, I don't think you'd have dug down in your savings and gone to a detective agency to try and keep him from being poisoned. I think that was someone else's idea and someone else's money."

"Oh, do you?"

I said, "They *are* nice legs, aren't they?"

She stretched out her legs on the davenport, ran the tips of her fingers up the sheer stockings, bringing the skirt up to the top of the stockings. "*I* like them," she said, and then asked archly, "Do you suppose I could pose for a stocking ad?"

"I don't see why not. Whose money was it, Carlotta?"

"Oh, for God's sake, are you going to keep harping on that?"

"Yes."

"It's none of your business."

I said, "I'm sticking my chin out for you. There's quite a bit of circumstantial evidence against you. You know that you mixed that poison in the demitasse cup."

"What if I should tell you the whole truth?"

"I might give you some good advice."

"What if I didn't?"

I said, "It would be a shame for a girl with nice legs like yours to spend so much time in prison that when she got out she'd be an old woman and no one would notice her legs."

I saw the panic in her eyes.

"Was it Carl Keetley who got you to do it?"

"Why do you ask that?"

"Because I think it was."

She hesitated for several seconds and then nodded her head.

"He became acquainted with you after you got your job?"

"No, he planted me in the job. I had been—well, I had been friendly with Carl for quite a while. He wanted me to get that job because he wanted to know some of the things that were going on in Ballwin's house."

"Do you like Carl?"

"Yes, I like him a lot. At one time I—well, you know Carl. He's not the marrying kind."

"So he gave you the powder and told you what to do with it?"

"Yes, he telephoned me and told me to come to his office right away. He gave me this powder, told me that it was an antidote for arsenic poisoning, that Mrs. Ballwin was going to take some poison so that she could appear to be very innocent. You know, later on she intended to poison her husband, but first she wanted to have it appear that someone had tried to poison her. Probably the same one who had tried to poison her husband."

"So, what happened?"

"Carl told me to mix the powder that he gave me in some anchovy paste, to put it on a cracker, then to enter the room where Daphne and her husband were and to wait until she had taken a cracker with anchovy paste on it, and then I was to distract her attention and switch the cracker off her plate, putting in its place the one I'd prepared with this powder. Oh, Donald, what am I going to do? I thought, at the time, it was just an antidote that would keep her from having any of the symptoms of poisoning and would block her plan. But I know now it—well, you can see....And no one is ever going to believe me."

"I believe you," I said.

"But will the police believe me?"

"No."

She said, "I'm in a spot. I've got to take the rap. I—I don't even know whether Carl Keetley will come forward to protect me. I don't suppose he will, because if he did, he'd be putting his own neck in a noose, and I—I don't want to drag him into it, but—"

"No one will believe the story you're telling. They'll think that you deliberately poisoned her."

She nodded ruefully.

I said, "I set a trap for you, Carlotta. I guess you didn't walk into it."

"What?"

I motioned toward the telephone. "I thought that as soon as I left here, you'd telephone to the person who had been backing your play. You were marooned out here without a car. It's way out in the country, and I didn't think you'd want to take a chance on hitchhiking with police looking for you. Didn't you telephone?"

"Yes, I did, and a lot of good it did me."

"What?"

"I told Carl where I was, and he said he'd come to get me. That's the reason I've been telling you all this. It looks as though he's run out on me. Donald, I wish you'd help me."

"I am helping you."

"Well," she said, "perhaps I need a microscope. As far as the naked eye is concerned, your help isn't perceptible."

I started to say something else when I heard the sound of quick steps on the graveled driveway outside, then knuckles on the door.

"Do you suppose that's the police?" Carlotta asked.

"If it is, promise me one thing."

"What?"

"That you won't say a word. Keep absolutely quiet. I don't think it's the police. I think I'm getting you out of it all right, but if it *should* be the cops, don't make a single statement. Seal your lips and keep them sealed."

I walked over to the door and opened it.

It was Carl Keetley on the threshold.

He recoiled in surprise at sight of me.

"Well, well," I said, "you're a little late. Come on in."

He hesitated a moment, then shrugged his shoulders and came on in. He tossed his hat on the table and said, "Hello, Carlotta."

"Hello, darling."

I said, "A most interesting opportunity presented itself for murder. I was wondering if you'd take advantage of it, Keetley. As soon as I heard that record of the conversation between Dr. Quay and Daphne Ballwin, I thought that a person with an ingenious mind like yours—"

"Tut, tut," Keetley said. "Sit down, Lam; let's talk things over. You're a smart young chap, but you talk too much. Your friend, Sellers, has the case all sewed up now. He has it all solved to his satisfaction."

I said, "You'd been trying for a long while to get evidence against Daphne. You'd about given up. Then you saw this priceless opportunity. You not only knew she was going to take poison herself, but you knew you could prove it. You had the record of the conversation between her and Dr. Quay. All you needed to do was get Carlotta to see that she got a double dose of poison. And, of course, because Carlotta called the turn just as soon as Gerald Ballwin had his so-called food poisoning, she managed to save his life."

"Interesting, very interesting," Keetley said.

"More than interesting," I told him, "because Carlotta has told me—"

Carlotta Hanford's voice cut like a knife. "No, Donald, please!"

I settled back and waited.

Keetley looked quizzically at Carlotta Hanford and then at me.

"What I don't understand," I said, "is why you had Carlotta spend money coming to consult us."

"I know the answer to that," Carlotta said. "Because he really wanted to protect Mr. Ballwin and—well, you see he had me hire you *before* he heard that conversation between Dr. Quay and Daphne."

Keetley was silent for several seconds. Then he looked at me with narrowed eyes. "You've talked with your partner, Bertha Cool, about this?"

"No."

"With Sergeant Sellers?"

"No. So far, it's all in the family."

Keetley grinned. "In that case," he said, "the answer is simple."

"I thought you might get the idea," I said.

"What?" Carlotta asked.

I said, "Don't look at me like that, Carlotta. I'm Cupid."

Keetley said, "Of course, Lam, once it is established by evidence such as I have that Daphne Ballwin took arsenic of her own free will, no one can prove a damn thing. No jury would ever convict anyone. Even if anyone could prove Carlotta gave her arsenic, no one could say how much. What Carlotta gave her may have been a non-fatal dose. What Daphne took after that may have killed her."

"It's an argument," I said, "but that's all. A district attorney could punch holes in it."

He said, "You're an insistent cuss, aren't you?"

"Yes."

"After all, Daphne was a murderess. The law says she should be punished with death."

I smiled at him.

Keetley said, "Oh, well, if you insist. As I've told you before, Lam, it's only the fools who go to the execution chambers on Friday."

"What in the world are you two talking about?" Carlotta asked.

"I've studied the penal code of the state," Keetley said. "Very interesting. Section thirteen twenty-two provides that neither husband nor wife is a competent witness for or against the other in a criminal action. Darling, will you do me the honor?"

"What?" Carlotta gulped. "For the love of Mike!"

"I'm proposing marriage," Keetley said. "After all, the smart man always picks a female accomplice, not that I'm making any concessions to your wild-eyed theory as to what happened, Lam. But just in case you *did* happen to be right, having chosen a female accomplice, it only needs a very brief trip across the state line and the mumbling of a few words by a justice of the peace to seal her lips forever. Carlotta, my sweetheart, will you marry me?"

"You mean you're trying to make an honest woman out of me?"

"Exactly."

Carlotta said, "Well, I don't like it. Any time I start playing for keeps, it's going to be with someone who really loves me. I'm not going to marry someone just to put a muzzle on my face."

Keetley sighed, said, "Lam, I'm afraid you've forced me to go about this in the most unromantic manner. Here's the afternoon newspaper. Would you mind reading it while I make a more formal and romantic proposal?"

He handed me the newspaper, walked past me to sit on the davenport beside Carlotta.

"Look, sweetheart," he said, "you and I know each other

pretty well. You did things for me. You did them competently and you did them loyally. And I've been doing a lot of thinking, sitting up there in that office in the Pawkette Building, listening to Dr. Quay say, 'Open—now close—now spit—' Hang it, Carlotta, you're a good girl. You've been a square shooter. I'd like to make it permanent.'"

I kept my eyes on the newspaper, but said, "Tell her about her legs, Keetley. She's proud of them and they're damn good-looking."

"Oh, nuts," Carlotta said, "what chance does a girl stand against both of you wolves? Okay, Carl, when do we go?"

"We go right now," Keetley said, "and we go fast. My car to an airport, then a plane."

Carlotta got up off the couch. "You want to kiss the bride?" she asked me. "You've passed up two opportunities, and this is the last chance you're going to have."

I kissed her.

Chapter Twenty-One
Chain Reaction

Bertha Cool said, "Well, it's about time you were getting here! What's the idea? Frank Sellers phoned you were out in the clear. How the hell did you do it?"

"Which question do you want me to answer first?" I asked.

"How did you do it?"

"I used a little logic and a little deduction. I knew that Keetley had been riding herd on Dr. Quay's conversations and I surmised that he would have had at least one very interesting conversation after I brought the anchovy paste out to Mrs. Ballwin."

"Of all the brainstorms you ever had," Bertha said, "that was the damnedest. You thought you were going to put psychological handcuffs on her. All you did was play into her hands. Some day you'll wake up to the fact that it takes a woman to know a woman. You've got to learn a lot about feminine psychology."

I said, "I certainly did start off a chain reaction there."

"You're damn right you did. And then you had to go out and fall for another skirt. My God, I don't know why it is that you always go overboard every time I start you working on a case."

"I always come out on top, don't I?"

"You have so far," Bertha admitted grudgingly, "but you've got pretty close to the end of your rope a couple of times. I certainly thought you were headed for a fall this time."

"You blame me for falling for Ruth Otis. It seems to me that most of our troubles came because you were playing ball with Frank Sellers."

"Frank's a nice guy," she said. "And he gives us the breaks."

"Yes," I told her. "I noticed him giving me the breaks."

The telephone rang.

Bertha scooped it up, said, "Oh, hell, it's for you. Some jane," and pushed the phone across to me.

I said, "Hello," and Ruth Otis's voice came over the wire. "Hello, Donald; you okay?"

"Yes."

"Everything all cleared up?"

"Uh huh."

"I've picked up some really good steaks," she said. "I find your broiler still works although you haven't used it for quite a while. They say I make really good French-fried potatoes and I have a nice salad and some cream of mushroom soup. I'm a whiz on biscuits. Are you going to be home for dinner?"

"Home?" I asked.

"You heard me."

"I'll be there," I said.

"How soon?"

"Half an hour. Start things going."

I hung up.

Bertha was glaring at me. "We didn't make so much money out of this case," she said, greedily.

"I did all right," I told her. "I put a hundred dollars on the nose of Fair Lady and won five hundred. You'd have done all right if you'd had nerve enough to back your judgment."

Bertha's eyes glittered greedily. "Donald, what did you find out about that system? Tell me. What about that system Keetley worked out? Did you get it?"

I said, "Keetley left to get married. He told me about his system before he left."

"What did he tell you?"

"He'd been working on it while he was waiting there listening to Dr. Quay's conversations. He insists that theoretically it's a damn fine system. Of course it all depends on the fidelity with which one plots the curve of consistent performance of a horse. Everything depends on the accuracy with which performance records are evaluated."

"I don't give a damn about the theory of the thing," Bertha said. "What I want are the concrete results."

"Well," I told her, "in that case, Keetley admitted to me that Fair Lady was only the second winner his system had ever picked. He thinks the best thing to do is to just buy a dope sheet and save all that trouble."

The KNIFE SLIPPED

by ERLE STANLEY GARDNER

Lost for more than 75 years, *The Knife Slipped* was meant to
be the second book in the Cool & Lam series but got shelved
when Gardner's publisher objected to (among other things)
Bertha Cool's tendency to "talk tough, swear, smoke cigarettes,
and try to gyp people." But this tale of adultery and corruption,
of double-crosses and triple identities—however shocking for
1939—shines today as a glorious present from the past, a return
to the heyday of private eyes and shady dames, of powerful
criminals, crooked cops, blazing dialogue and wild plot twists.

RAVES FOR THE KNIFE SLIPPED:

*"A remarkable discovery…fans will rejoice at another dose
of Gardner's unexcelled mastery of pace and an unexpected
new taste of his duo's cyanide chemistry."*
— Kirkus Reviews

"A treasure that's not to be missed."
— Book Reporter

"A gift to aficionados of the Cool and Lam series."
— New York Journal of Books

*"A time machine back to an exuberant era of
snappy patter, stakeouts and double-crosses."*
— Publishers Weekly

The Cocktail Waitress

by JAMES M. CAIN

AUTHOR OF 'THE POSTMAN ALWAYS RINGS TWICE'

The day Joan Medford buried her first husband, she met two men: the older man whose touch repelled her but whose money was an irresistible temptation, and the young schemer she'd come to crave like life itself…

Top of the Heap

by ERLE STANLEY GARDNER

CREATOR OF PERRY MASON

The client had a perfect alibi for the night Maureen Auburn disappeared—but nothing made P.I. Donald Lam suspicious like a perfect alibi.

The Twenty-Year Death

by ARIEL S. WINTER

"EXTRAORDINARY"—NEW YORK TIMES

A masterful first novel made up of three complete novels, written in the styles of three giants of the mystery genre. Stephen King says it's "bold, innovative, and thrilling…crackles with suspense and will keep you up late."

**Available now from your favorite bookseller.
For more information, visit
www.HardCaseCrime.com**